Pirates,
SCOUNDRELS
AND SAINTS

Published by Advantage Publishing Group

ISBN: 978-1-954024-07-6   Hardcover
ISBN: 978-1-954024-08-3   Paperback
ISBN: 978-1-954024-08-3   E-book

To contact, please e-mail: media@advantage-publishing.com

Pirates, SCOUNDRELS AND SAINTS

PARAISO

TIMOTHY GRANT ACKER

Pirates are still out there, flintlock pistols and schooners traded for assault rifles and black-painted Zodiacs.

Based on his experience as an international lawyer and pilot, Timothy Grant Acker tells a riveting tale of modern-day pirates in the unpredictable waters of the Caribbean.

The statute of limitations has run, so the story can be told.

SOUTH HAITI 1985

J uan's woman, Silvia, was waiting. She knew adventure excited him, and he would stay awake a long time making love to her. She was young, petite, and beautiful. Her heritage was of mixed blood, mostly Black, but some white, Portuguese, and Spanish. Her mother cared for her two children from a previous man.

She greeted the pirate with genuine affection and desire, wearing skin-tight, low-cut jeans and a large tank top that exposed her breasts when she moved. Juan responded by taking her into his arms. Although he didn't love her any more than any other woman with whom he had lived, he liked her looks and enjoyed the way she made love. After eating the breakfast she'd prepared, Juan stood up. He was tall for a Hispanic man — about five foot nine inches — and well built, with a face that was commanding, framed by full dark hair. They stared at each other for a moment. Juan held out his hand. Silently she took it, and with a smile she led him into the bedroom.

Juan's house was located a short distance upland from where he beached his boat. The seven-room home was built solidly of high-quality concrete and roughly finished — rustic and semi-painted. It was comfortable, with high ceilings and fans that increased the sea breeze entering through the shutters of the glassless windows. A covered veranda bordered three sides of the house. For Silvia, and virtually everyone else in Haiti, the rustic house was a palace amid desolation and desperation.

Juan's crew of outcasts and thieves from various countries lived at the edge of the dusty community located in Southern Haiti, not far from the Dominican Republic border. In Haiti they were safe – a country where pirates and thieves, as well as injustice and abuse found refuge.

The village consisted of fewer than a hundred hovels made from sticks, paper, and earth, or poorly constructed of cheap brick. The poor dwellings were clustered together. Most of their inhabitants made their living from fishing and hard farming. Their bodies were thin, their souls depressed. It was typical Haiti.

The community, though, prospered a little from the thieves' spending. A few of the residents dedicated a portion of their homes to selling groceries, supplies, and light hardware, or provided their skills—a couple of seamstresses, a mechanic, and a *panga* boat repairman. Opportunities to buy alcohol and drugs were abundant, as were women who offered the usual services. A "policeman" was paid by Juan to guard his belongings, keep problems from being created, and to report on all activities. He wore the mock badge Juan once pinned on him.

The village had a tiny school, consisting of two rooms, for the children who wanted to attend. It was funded by the few people in the village who had a little money. Maria, one of Juan's crewmembers, contributed heavily to its support.

The only doctor in the village was the witch doctor who taught Voodoo customs to appease the spirits. Those few who could afford real medical care traveled to a border town in the Dominican Republic. A small Catholic church with a lay priest served the parishioners. There was no building, just a plastic tarp to give shade. The lay priest was a righteous man who feared God, but he feared Juan more. He had once seen Juan shoot a regional army captain who demanded too much money to "look the other way." No sermons were preached against Juan's activities.

Stephen was the only true American among Juan's crew, although Juan's mother was from Florida. The other pirates were from the Bahamas, the Dominican Republic, Antigua, and Colombia. Stephen was the oldest and strongest of the pirates. He was also the tallest and most muscular. He had always lived a life of petty, and not so petty, crime until he fled from the United States to escape a lengthy jail sentence. Stephen escaped to Haiti where he met Juan. His wife, Isabela, was Maria's best—and only—true friend. Isabela was thirty years old, more brown than black, and attractive, as a South Haitian woman. She was faithful to her husband — a rare phenomenon in a country rife with sexual immorality. She gave thanks to the Voodoo spirits for her escape from malnutrition and the hardship of living in a one-room shack with her six siblings. She bore Stephen two children. With his money and help her kids were well, and they prospered modestly.

Ivan, the product of Juan's first and only real wife, Elizabeth, prepared the list of the things stolen on the previous night's boarding of a yacht they encountered off the Southern coast of Haiti. He oversaw the bundling and packaging of them. He sold the Boston Whaler, that they managed to get off the yacht's davits, to a fisherman who illegally transported items and people to and from the Dominican Republic. The electronic equipment he planned to sell to drug runners, of which there were many in Haiti. The ship's silverware and the passenger's jewelry he would send to Colombia to be sold.

A few days later, after the costs of transportation to market and the high sales commissions on the stolen merchandise was deducted, the share of each crewmember came to $2,500.

Juan's pirates were jubilant. Twenty-five hundred dollars was a wild sum of money to earn in Haiti. As they made plans to go to the capital city, they talked about drinking and finding the best women, chanting, "We are rich! Praise to the great god, Ogun!"

Ivan used some of his share of the money to hire two workers to paint the schoolhouse. When one of the men asked how much they would be paid, Ivan responded with "Ten dollars a day."

The men glanced at each other. "Your work must be very good."

Ivan shrugged his shoulders and smiled.

Ivan had studied in the little concrete block schoolhouse. He became an avid reader: learned about nations, types of government, studied limited business concepts, math, and algebra. He spoke proper Creole. From his father and the Hispanic crew members he learned Spanish, which the pirates mostly spoke among themselves. From Stephen he had acquired English.

When the teacher found out that Ivan was having the school painted, he went to thank him. "Ivan, you were my best student—very smart, steady in personality, and with imagination. Tell me, what do you plan to do with your life?"

Ivan paused. "I like business."

The teacher looked hard at the young man. He was lean and tall, almost six feet. His face was rectangular, his teeth perfect, his hair dark and thick.

"Find a different business," the teacher advised.

Ivan gave him a candid look. "What kind of business?"

"I don't know. But of all my students, you have the most potential, Ivan. If you are to do well, you must learn how to become legally successful. You are too much the son of a pirate."

EL CLUB DE LOS INDUSTRIALES

Juan learned that *el Club de los Industriales de Argentina* had chartered a former expedition ship, which had been converted into a small but exclusive passenger cruise ship. The Club was to board the ship in Maracaibo within a few days. It would host thirty couples in very deluxe accommodations. It had two restaurants, a small theater and bar, a casino, a swimming pool, and a water center with scuba gear and jet skis. The cruise plans called for three nights in Caracas, two nights in Tobago, and three nights in Saint George's, Grenada. From there they would proceed directly to Havana, before returning to Maracaibo.

Juan sat on his veranda drinking coffee with his brother, David. He told him about the small ship and the wealth that would most likely be on board.

David cocked his head, "How many crew members does it have?"

"I don't know. Sixty? Perhaps more," Juan said as he turned his head to look into the eyes of his brother.

"The owners of the yachts and small ships are thankful to still be alive and do not seek us afterwards. The people on that ship are wealthy — they may search for us," David continued.

Juan's face became serious. He nodded, "*Posiblemente.*"

After a long pause, David eased out a sigh, "Pirating that ship is too dangerous."

There was a silence that gradually slid into the shadows. Both men let it go . . .

Dressed in ragged cutoffs, a t-shirt, and barefoot, Juan took a long walk through the arid land of the southeast coast. The strong coffee and heavy thoughts quickened his pace. He knew that his brother was right, taking the ship would be dangerous for many reasons. Just to take control of the ship he would have to divide his crew into groups. Each group of his crew – poor men and women with little discipline — would have to work with flawless coordination. If they were successful at seizing control, it would require a lot of time to strip the passengers of their possessions and then force the ship's crew to open the safes and the vacationer's safe deposit boxes. Loading the stolen property and money into his boat would take some of his crew away from controlling the passengers and ship's crew. That would make protecting the pirates more difficult. Without a doubt, some of the travelers and crew would be armed or have weapons in their cabins.

Stomach tight, his face filled with anxiety; Juan continued his walk for some time as he evaluated the personalities and skills of his crew. He chewed nervously on the inside of his mouth. There was a good chance the boarding could fail — that he and his crew could be captured by the US Coast Guard or Navy or be killed.

Returning to his house, Juan took out his charts of the Caribbean. The best place to intercept the cruise ship would be at high sea, well south of Haiti, as the ship traveled on its course from Grenada to Cuba. The nearest Coast Guard ship would most likely be in the passage between Haiti and Cuba, at least 300 miles away. Another Coast Guard ship could be on the east side of the Dominican Republic, also about 300 miles away. He would have less than two hours to board, subdue everyone, open the safes, steal everything desired, and escape before a helicopter could arrive. A potentially nearer ship could be a patrol boat from one of the island nations. But that possibility did not concern him greatly. He could fight them off.

The risk of failure was considerable, but the promise of two or three million dollars in cash and a pirate's dream of expensive jewelry drove him forward. The thrill and challenge motivated him. The excitement also drew him and vanquished his worries. He knew he would need two boats. He had a second boat stored on the north coast of Colombia. He used it for smuggling consumer goods into Colombia and Venezuela. That boat, of similar design to his Haitian one, was open decked with high freeboard and powered by four large outboards. It was fast and well equipped, with immense gasoline tanks built into the hull. If necessary, due to weather during the crossing, the boat could be covered with canvas over steel battens. They extended across the vessel leaving only a small space for the helmsman.

Jose, his Colombia skipper, possessed the skill to transport the boat and its crew of smugglers and part-time fishermen to Haiti, but he knew that Jose was not a good choice to captain it to board the cruise ship. In violent situations, Jose was limited, at times becoming befuddled, lacking decisiveness.

Juan considered his possibilities. Maria came first to his mind. Maria could handle the boat and any situation. The boarding of the small ship would go well with her in the lead, but he knew that Maria was struggling with something inside that kept her from giving herself one hundred percent to piracy. Juan saw the struggle and thought that, unlike his friend Samuel, who had one foot in each world, Maria would eventually give her heart entirely to piracy. Or she would become someone else, leaving her present life behind. She could be tender . . . but he had also seen her shoot two men. She didn't kill them, but she shot them . . .

After the recent pirating, Maria returned to the one-room concrete house she called home. The walls were dingy white. The furnishings were sparse, though comfortable. A cheap metal bed frame, painted blue, held a good mattress. A wooden nightstand also painted blue stood beside it. A wooden chair and table separated the bed from the small kitchen area. Two kerosene hurricane lamps provided light.

Maria had arrived tired but pleased with the things stolen from the yacht they had boarded. More importantly, she had enjoyed being at sea. She had been on shore for a month and was bored. The days had begun to loom before her—empty days, and emerging enemies without form or substance, in which to sink into depression. Except for Isabela, she had no friends among the natives who lived in the area, and few who could even be considered candidates. Those few had come to fear her as a pirate and remained polite, but distant. It was common knowledge that she carried a gun in the waistline of her skirt or strapped to her leg. There were rumors that she had killed a man, but they weren't true. Ironically, although feared, Maria was also known for being a soft touch in hard times. Many had come to her asking for money for medical expenses or other needs. More often than not, she had given to them all.

Maria was of medium height and build, with a pretty face and long dark hair. Her very dark brown – almost black – eyes commanded attention. By almost everyone's opinion she was an attractive woman. Men wanted her. She slept with many of the best, usually when drunk or lonely. But Maria had not, however, formed any relationships with men, whether rich or poor, Haitian, Dominican or from some other country. Twice, men had tried to rape her in her house. On each occasion, she might well have killed them if Isabela hadn't heard the blows and cries and convinced her friend to let them go. Each time, Maria later cried in her arms.

In such moments, Maria often remembered her girlhood ambitions to be loved, to marry a good man, and have loving children. But it all seemed so distant . . .

Isabela had no conscience about her husband's profession. She was grateful to not live in the grinding and crippling poverty she had known before becoming Stephen's woman. Her lack of conscience helped calm Maria's very real conscience. Isabela was smart and savvy, qualities that coupled with natural wisdom kept her faithful to her husband, who was old enough to be her grandfather. The marriage allowed her to pull her parents and siblings out of poverty and early death. That same natural wisdom helped her to push her children in school and to become friends with the schoolteacher, to whom she gave money in exchange for home lessons for them.

Juan presented his plan about the cruise ship to Maria. She weighed his words carefully. For her, it was an honor that he considered her capable of handling one of the boats, and of being a leader in the boarding and taking of the small cruise ship. In essence, she would be co-equal in command. The side of her given over to thievery urged her to say yes, to move up the hierarchy, to have the respect of all as a real leader of men and women. But her heart warned that it would be another step deeper into the acceptance and surrender to this life she was living. She sensed taking on the leadership of the second vessel would take another part of her soul. Perhaps, all of it . . .

Juan observed Maria as she considered his proposal. He could see the battle inside her. She was a woman he had held and made love to in prior years, but she was also a pirate — smart, dangerous, sometimes harsh, and capable of violence. He also knew there was another side of her—a person who struggled to be good, and who was at war with herself.

Maria asked, "It is dangerous?"

"Yes."

"Could I die?"

"I think we will be able to do it without any pirate dying."

"Others could die?"

"Perhaps. There will be many on the ship. Some will have guns."

"I don't want to add killing to my sins. No, *jefe*, I must not do it."

Juan was not usually a cruel or mean man. He did not exact obedience to his orders. Men and women followed him of their own will and were free to leave at any time. Maria was the best choice to captain the boat, but with her decision made, he went on to his second choice—his oddly unsettling and rapidly changing son.

As Juan turned to leave, he said, "Maria, it will be interesting to see if, in the end, you are a pirate or a saint."

Maria gave her friend a perplexed look, and he shrugged, humor and truth dancing in his eyes. "You are mostly a good soul, but you are always a good pirate."

As the words "always a good pirate" sunk into the deepest part of her being, she turned away to hide her tears.

Juan's son, Ivan, knew boats and the water, and had learned much about leadership through years of watching his father and crews interact. He was a good leader, and he had garnered the skills of a pirate—how to board the boats, to coax, threaten, and steal. Still, there was no meanness, cruelty, nor even greed in him. At that time in his life, he had yet to define himself. He was a pirate because he had been born into it. Juan saw that deep inside Ivan something was occurring, and he wondered if the instincts and genes of his mother's family, with its hundreds of years of sometimes elusive power, wealth, and social position, were stirring. Roberto had been the name his mother had given him. After she left, Juan renamed him Ivan, after a character in a Russian novel often spoken of by his mother, Elizabeth.

In the late afternoon, Juan found Ivan on the far end of the beach. Dressed in a faded black bathing suit, Ivan swung a long fishing rod

over his head and cast his line past the breaking surf. His deeply
tanned, well-developed body was that of a man, not a child. His thick
hair fell to his shoulders.

Although he saw his father approaching, Ivan remained focused
on fishing.

"Did you catch anything?" asked Juan.

"Nada," said Ivan flashing a smile.

"There have not been many fish lately."

The younger man shrugged. "It is not important. I like to stand by
the water."

"We have bigger fish to catch," said Juan.

There was a pause, then Ivan spoke again, still staring at the ocean.
"Uncle David told me that you want to go after the chartered vessel of
the Argentine Industriales Club."

Juan tilted his head slightly. Staring at his son he asked, "What do
you think?"

"There are not enough of us."

"I am going to use the Colombian boat." The older man added.
"Jose?"

"Yes, but only as a member of the crew. I want you to handle the
boat. You act better under pressure."

There was a pause . . . Ivan nodded and turned to his father. Not
knowing the change it would spark, he said, "I will do it. Fishing for
their money will be good." A slight smile touched his lips. "And I like
fishing . . ."

COLOMBIAN PIRATES

Juan's Colombian skipper, Jose, drove his old truck into the hills above Santa Marta. The armed watchmen knew him and let him pass. Arriving at the governor's plantation, he parked in the shade of the trees. The vegetation was thick. He walked uphill where the large platano plants were arranged in rows. He could see the marijuana growing in between them and along the periphery. He found four men who sometimes worked with him. They were pressing the marijuana into small, tight bricks.

"*Que tal amigos*?" inquired Jose.

"Working hard," said one of the men without stopping.

"Where is your boss?"

"He is in Miami with his young girlfriend."

"Can you leave?"

"For what?"

"For work at sea to board a small ship."

"We can't leave now. Tonight a plane comes for the marijuana," said one of the men.

"We prepare tomorrow," Jose replied, non-plussed.

"Is the money good?"

"Very, very good."

"Someone must stay," said one of the men.

"I need a full crew."

"We cannot all go. The boss would be very angry, and that would be dangerous for us."

"Leave one to work then."

"Is there much danger?"

"Yes, this trip is dangerous."

The men glanced around at each other, words passing in their eyes. Then the largest turned back to Jose. "For very good money, we will take big risks."

A small smile touched Jose's lips. "You will make very good money."

Returning to the more humid coast, Jose searched for a friend and his wife who were fishermen. They eagerly accepted his offer. Needing more crew, Jose sought out two women who worked for him when loading sailboats or small ships with marijuana. He went from strip club to bar looking for them. He refused the bar women who asked him to sit and buy them a drink.

In the fourth strip club, he found them sitting at the bar in bikinis, talking to customers. He took the women aside and asked, "Girls, you want to go to sea and steal a lot of money?"

The two women lifted their heads in unison and shook their long hair from their faces. "How much?" they asked in unison.

"Enough to never work again."

They looked at each other, politely said goodbye to the men they were speaking with, gathered their personal belongings, slipped on large T-shirts— as if they were dresses— and walked out of the club.

The manager cursed them as they left. "You whores. You will never work here again."

Giving the manager the finger, one of the women turned and said, "Yeah, until we come back . . . if we want to come back."

On the beach, Jose found other men he had worked with in the past. Enticed by the promise of a large amount of cash, they agreed to leave their fishing and postpone their other illegal businesses saying, "Why wouldn't we? Of course we want to go with you, friend."

Juan's Colombian boat was kept hidden in a small, mostly dry arroyo on the little bay where the fishermen lived. Juan kept it fully fueled at all times. The family next to the arroyo guarded the covered boat. The large array of high-intensity lights, electronic navigation instruments, radar, and communication devices were stored in a locked concrete building. The dancers and four of the men reinstalled the boat's equipment and electronics.

In the early predawn of the departure morning, the crew assembled at the boat with their gear, guns, and knives. The few who had someone who cared about them hugged and kissed their loved ones before they left the shore.

The trade winds were blowing medium strength. A long and deep sea swell was running. Small whitecaps were breaking on top of the swells.

As soon as they were clear of the bay, Jose thrust the throttles forward, and the boat jumped as though kicked. The waves threw themselves against the hull as the craft surged forward like a warhorse. The boat shuddered.

To clear the coast before dawn, Jose kept to thirty knots. He didn't want the Colombian patrol boats to discover them. The crew of ten braced themselves. They nervously searched the horizon for American ships and Colombian patrol boats. In the first morning light, one of the dancers spotted diesel smoke rising into the eastern sky.

"*Capitán*," she said, "there is a boat coming."

"It may be nothing but a fishing boat," Jose replied cautiously. As the light increased, he got a better look. "It is the patrol boat from Barranquilla. That is better. The American boats are faster, and they carry helicopters."

The entire crew stood up and stared into the distance. The same dancer asked, "What will they do?"

"We are too many to be fishing. With the boat equipped like this and all of us on board, they will demand money. I do not have much money so they will take us and the boat. They will sell the motors, and the officers will keep the money. If it were the Americans, they would mark us and track us by satellite," responded Jose.

"The sailors are as corrupt as the government," muttered one of the fishermen in a flat voice.

Jose increased the speed of the boat; it beat against the breaking whitecaps and rolled deeply in the sea swells. Both dancers came and stood by his side.

"We are much faster than the government boat," Jose added. "The danger is that they will tell the American authorities, and later, ahead of us, they will track us." Motioning to an instrument, he continued. "Look. The radar scanner shows that the patrol boat is tracking us to determine our course."

The members of the crew glanced at each other nervously.

Jose changed course and headed to the east of the Dominican Republic.

"The new course will confuse them," he said in response to questioning looks from his crew.

Approximately 150 miles north of the coast of Colombia and far from the Columbian patrol boat and its radar, Jose reduced their speed. They were 340 nautical miles from Juan's location. His instructions were to arrive that night.

"Why are we going slow?" asked the dancers.

Jose explained that if the Americans were to look for them, they would calculate their location based on their speed.

"We will stay here for a while, so we are far from them at the time they think we will arrive. We will then change course and arrive far to the west of where they think we will be."

"It is a bad omen that we have trouble this early," muttered one of the dancers.

The sea breeze moderated the temperature, and the boat provided some shade from the sun. The comfort, however, was enjoyed by only part of the crew; the rest had not spent enough recent time in a boat rolling up and over swells, and were sick. The most seasick hung onto the sides and vomited, or wished they could.

There is little in sickness equal to that caused by the sea—the whole body revolts. Vomiting turns to dry heaves, the head hurts, and the person desires death to escape from the horrible pain. Jose increased the vessel's speed to reduce movement. The change brought some minimal relief to those stricken.

Later in the day, Jose again increased the boat's speed. They ran fast broadside to the waves. With speed, the boat was more stable, although it still rolled and slammed against the waves. The dancers leaned over the side, their arms around each other for comfort. The ocean extended to the horizon on all sides.

The younger dancer said to her friend, "We could die, and no one would know."

By late afternoon the clouds were thick. They darkened and formed into the anvil shapes of thunderstorms. The wind continued to rise, and tension settled upon the men and women like thick fog on a seaside village. They were conscious that they were inside a speck of fiberglass upon a sea that stretched limitless in all directions. Jose slowed the boat.

Just before dark the threatening clouds moved off to the west. The harsh fog of fear lifted from the men and women. As the sun fell into the ocean, the darkness deepened rapidly. The stars shined clear in the sky. The half-sphere of the heavens appeared pin-pricked with a myriad of holes emitting light of varying intensity. The sight caused the dancers to huddle in awe.

"May God have mercy on our souls," muttered Jose as he prayed to Saint Nicolas, the patron saint of Barranquilla and sailors.

One by one, the crew members spread mats on the floor of the boat, not for warmth, but as cushions. The boat rocked and regularly pounded against the waves. The noise of the sea running beneath the hull and the fuel sloshing in the tanks was a harsh distraction. Most of the crew members fell into a light and fitful sleep. Jose and one other of the crew remained standing—Jose to steer and navigate, the other to keep watch. The light from the stars and moon was sufficient to see other vessels, though not enough to clearly see logs or half sunken cargo containers fallen from some freighter. Almost in vain, the watchman strained to see the sea's surface. At midnight, the beautiful— and older— darker-haired dancer took the position in the bow to watch. For now, they ran without lights or radar.

After midnight the sea settled some, and the boat sped rapidly northward, taking only an occasional heavy blow from a rogue wave. Jose pushed the craft hard. At 4:00 a.m., the Loran indicated they were about twenty miles south of Juan's base. The compass and Loran receiver took him into waters of adequate depth – directly to the beach in front of Juan's house.

HΛITI

Juan, Ivan, Stephen, and Maria sat on the shore listening to the Colombian boat as it approached. Juan and Ivan pushed a skiff off the beach. The rough fiberglass hull made a sharp sound as it rasped against the sand as it slid to the water. At the oars, Juan rowed to where Jose had anchored. Even in the dim light, Juan could see the stress of the small boat crossing on the face of Jose. Jose for his part saw confidence and excitement in Juan's demeanor. He also noticed that although the daring pirate moved like a younger man, there was a lot of gray around his temples and a crease in each side of his masculine face. As the Colombian boat rose and fell with the swells, the crew members lifted themselves off the floor. Flashlights illuminated their belongings. Cigarettes were lit. Men coughed. Holding the skiff next to the portside of the Colombian boat where Jose stood, Juan stretched out his hand to Jose.

"What a pleasure to see you, my friend."

"No, amigo," Jose responded. "The pleasure is mine."

Aware of Juan's presence, slightly in awe of the renowned pirate, some of the weary crew addressed him as *patron*, others as *jefe*, their boss and chief. Sleepily, though with deliberation, the first of two groups climbed into the skiff. Ivan helped them to board.

David led the men and women up the soft sand beach to two small concrete sheds nearby.

David said, "Here there is safety. No one will take anything. The people are afraid to steal from Juan. Don't worry."

The crew did not doubt that the people were afraid of Juan. The men and women dropped their belongings in the sheds and followed David as he escorted them to Juan's house. The pirate's woman, Silvia and Isabela, were preparing breakfast.

There was little talk. The quick juxtaposition from Colombia to Haiti, the long hard ride across the vast expanse of water, the stress, and the seasickness weighed heavy on them. Juan and those who had waited with him on the beach were also tired. Only members of Juan's international crew were fully awake. They had slept while Juan waited for the Colombian boat.

Silvia and Isabela placed eggs, tortillas, beans, bacon, juice, and coffee on the long black-painted table in Juan's house. In front of each person, the two women set chipped, blue-speckled metal plates and cups that showed their black undercoating. The early morning light began to overpower the illumination of the kerosene hurricane lamps. A few geckos clung to the walls. They stared at the human beings, one wide eye at a time. Awakened somewhat by coffee and food, the crew began to talk. A few of the men flirted with Isabela and the women crew members. Sitting together at the head of the table, Juan and Ivan listened to Jose's account of the crossing.

One of the dancers asked Juan, "Tell us, *patron*, what is the work? Jose told us that it was not a boat, but a ship we are to rob." She paused, "I am not afraid, but it is dangerous, no?"

"Daughter," he said to the young unrelated woman, "it will be hard, but we will take the ship, and you will have money. We will have to do it right and with skill so that there will be no deaths."

A glance passed between the dancers and conversation at the table ended at the word *death*.

Breakfast continued for quite some time. The crew ate and drank coffee, then went outside where they smoked and stared out to sea or into the desolate hills behind them. Some went to sleep on mats placed inside the sheds.

In the afternoon, the men and women gathered once again in Juan's house. The leaders sat on wooden chairs painted dark-brown with woven seats. The others sat on cheap metal chairs or termite-eaten benches. Isabela placed *tortas* on the tables. As they finished the hearty sandwiches, Juan taped a basic diagram of the small cruise ship to the wall.

Juan began, "It is a small, older expedition ship converted into a yacht type luxury cruise ship. It is only eighty meters long. There are four levels. The engine and machinery rooms are located on the lowest level. The laundry, workrooms, and crew quarters are there also. The next level is the passenger deck. There are a total of forty deluxe passenger suites, twenty on the port side and twenty on the starboard side. The guests of the Industriales Club occupy thirty-five of the cabins. The restaurants and public areas are located on the third level—a bar, nightclub, library, gym, and a spa with a pool aft. The small bridge deck, aft of the pilothouse, has cabins shared by the officers. Only the captain has a separate cabin."

Continuing with an earnest look in his eyes he said, "*Pongan atención*. This part is the most important. The guests are members of the Club de los Industriales of Argentina. They have lots of money! The other passengers are servants and entertainers."

A few quiet whistles could be heard. One of the dancers asked, "How much money?"

Juan responded, "Enough."

"Enough?"

"If you are smart with it, you will have enough to live on until you die."

The men and women sat up straight in their chairs. Some made excited noises. Others made worrisome comments. Some eyes narrowed. Others lit up. Maria looked out the window.

One man said, "They will have bodyguards."

Another said, "The rich have guns."

Juan answered nonchalantly, but the caution in his eyes betrayed him. "Yes, there will be guns. There will be bodyguards. We will take the guns. The bodyguards will do nothing."

A breeze of fear, mixed with the humidity, blew across the humans. The geckos stared at the pirates — impervious to the humans' emotions.

Juan felt their fear. "The opportunity for you to make a lot of money is because they have a lot of money. The poor and working have little money. Do not be afraid."

A man said, "I am not afraid. The rich are pigs. They keep us, the poor, as slaves. We will take their money. Yes, we will make much money. I will live well with the money of the rich. If they fight, I will kill them."

One of the dancers said, "They buy our bodies for their pleasure. They call us whores, but their words mean nothing. They make us whores for us to have enough money to live. They own the land and factories. They keep all the wealth for themselves. I do not hate them—I *know* them . . . and their sons—but there is no justice. We live by serving them. I want to have what they have, and I will steal it."

"This work is for those who want to make money," said Jose.

The desire for money – to not live in need all the time –overtook the fear.

With her long black hair below her shoulders, dressed in a pretty, belted white sundress that held her automatic pistol, Maria looked uncaring upon the others. Isabela caught her eye and smiled. In the sunshine of the smile, Maria returned the smile. Her dark eyes momentarily lit up.

Juan thought to himself. *A bodyguard or crewmember trying to be a hero could cause a bloodbath of killing and death. Perhaps not even Haiti will shelter us.* He quickly shook off the unwanted thoughts.

Juan signaled his woman and mouthed the word "*Café?*"

She smiled and motioned yes.

Isabela placed cups that had been lightly washed on the table. Silvia put opened cans of evaporated milk and a cracked sugar bowl next to the cups. A rusted spoon protruded over the edge of the bowl. A few lost ants climbed over the damp, lumpy sugar. Isabela set a large plate topped high with homemade *orejas*, a sugary pastry roughly in the shape of a large ear, onto the table.

Juan said, "Grab a coffee and a sweet bread."

The men and women stood up, and took coffee. Ivan drank his coffee black; the others added sugar and/or evaporated milk to the thick liquid. Most of the crew ate the homemade pastries. As the crumbs fell onto the smooth concrete floor, ants appeared to collect them. Returning to their seats, the men and women eagerly turned their attention back to Juan.

"The other cabins are used by the entertainers, casino chiefs, and perhaps personal bodyguards who accompany their bosses. More berths are behind the pilothouse," Juan continued. "The officers use some. They are all occupied." He paused, and with the composure of a trained actor, said, "I know that the ship carries weapons in two hidden lockers. There are pistols and automatic weapons. One such locker is in the engineer's cabin. That cabin is forward of the engine room. The other locker is in the wall of an officer's cabin."

Some of the men and women fidgeted on their chairs. Maria glanced out of the window, her head and body still. Ivan paid close attention to Juan. A few geckos moved cautiously on the walls, indifferent to the mayhem being planned. The lazy overhead ceiling fan barely moved the dusty air.

Even Juan felt uncomfortable as he thought about the ship's weapons. He recognized the real possibility that this could all slide sideways. Counteracting his discomfort, he spoke with a casual and calm emphasis.

"We must take them by surprise. If we do not surprise them, they *will* fight. Also, if they are able to radio the American Coast Guard and other forces, the Americans will come and fight against us. There are military aircraft and helicopters at Guantanamo Bay. Some American Coast Guard ships have helicopters. It is important that we take control of the ship as a complete surprise. The ship must not radio anyone, and the people must not fight."

The members of the crew sat utterly still. A heavy pause filled the time and space.

Changing his tone, Juan said, "but if all goes well the ship's crew will not be able to radio anyone. They will not know we are on board until we are in front of them with our guns."

One of the dancers exclaimed, "*Adelante, jefe.*" The others offered a brief cheer.

Jose agreed, "We will take them."

One of the men said, "They will see us on their radar. They will know we are coming, and they will be ready for us."

"No, *compadre*, there is a plan," Jose replied confidently. "We will not take the boats close to the ship until the pilothouse is under our control."

The man cocked his head, "How is it possible to have the ship under our control, señor, if we do not take our boats to it?"

Juan offered a mischievous smile. "A few will board the ship from the rubber boat— the Zodiac—that we will place in the path of the ship. They will take control of the pilothouse where the radar and the radios are located. No one will sound an alarm or radio for help."

"Bravo!" responded several of the crew. The confidence in the room was growing . . .

But another man said, "Señor, it will be very hard for those in the little inflatable boat to board the big ship . . . and very dangerous."

Maria stood up. She looked like a movie star or fashion model with an attitude. "I will board the ship from the little Zodiac." She answered boldly. "The pilothouse will be mine."

All eyes turned toward her.

"You will only have to take the other parts of the ship. No one will know I am there, except for my prisoners."

Juan added, "Maria is *capitana*. She knows how to drive the ships."

A man said, "The little boat will get caught in the bow wave. She will die."

"I will not die. I have boarded ships before," said Maria in a deadpan voice, with a devil-be-damned expression on her face.

The men whistled softly in appreciation of her courage and certainty.

Juan continued, "However, *amigos*, we must be careful and work well. We must enter and take the ship according to the plan, and not get into a gunfight and kill. That will cause many problems later. The *Federales* will look for us. If no one is, or only a few are hurt, there will be a lot of talk, but little action. You must all know what you are to do and do it just as we teach you. We have a plan, and it will work."

The truth was, Juan had no viable backup strategy to save them if anything went wrong. They could be killed or end up in prison if things didn't go according to the plan. The tough Latin pirate forced himself to refocus. "Once Maria has control, she will call us on the radio. We will go to the ship. The ship's engines make noise so no one will hear us. There will be no moon, and no one will see us, either. We will come alongside the ship near the pilothouse. Those in my boat will board on the starboard side. Those in Ivan's boat will board on the port side. We will dress in black. Maria's crew will turn out the foredeck lights so it will be dark. No one will see us. We will take control of the ship."

Ivan looked at his father's evenly built rectangular face. It was calm, but there was a nervous movement of his eyes. He knew his father was not completely convinced of his statement. He, too, wondered if they would all be killed or jailed.

In truth, Juan wished he had more crewmembers. After discounting the people already assigned tasks—Maria in the wheelhouse, a crew member to guard her and the wheelhouse captives, a person left on each pirate vessel and on the Zodiac—he had only fifteen pirates to take over a ship with perhaps two hundred persons on board.

Juan appointed Ivan and three others to take control of the machinery deck.

He named his brother David as the lead of the group of four assigned to secure the passenger deck. Although David had lost interest in "the business" and desired a straight, domestic life, he was smart, and a good leader. He would be able to take control of the passenger deck.

"The rest of you will be with me," Juan continued. "We will take the main level of the ship."

Juan assigned two of his men to secure the pool and outside lounging area. The other four, under his direct leadership, would take control of the restaurant, bar, and casino. He drilled the boarding plan into his crew. He answered questions. After a while, the men and women yawned; eyes wandered slightly . . . Isabela, and Juan's woman, served more coffee. Juan continued until after nightfall. The men and women, not used to long planning sessions and training, forced themselves to pay attention. The promise of the big payoff, the danger, the timing, the boldness, and finally the fear, held them. After the meeting ran its course, there was a tired excitement in the air. The emotion and fear which had squelched hunger relaxed. Their appetite came back.

The weak electric lights brightened and dimmed, then extinguished as the aging generator ran out of fuel. A man rose to refuel it, but Juan waved him off. Ivan, Maria, and David lit rusted, hurricane kerosene lamps. Some of the men brought in small poorly painted, black wooden tables and placed more lamps on them. The crew members moved their chairs closer to the tables as Juan served cold beer and cheap wine. Silvia and Isabela served food. The pirates ate like there would be no tomorrow, conscious that it might be the case. After eating, the weary pirates retreated to their sleeping quarters, leaving only those few so touched with excitement, or imagination to talk of boarding of the ship. Juan didn't serve any more alcohol. He wanted sober and clear-thinking men and women. There would be a time for celebration later.

The next morning, a merciless sun pulled itself from the blue-green waters surrounding them. Dust hung heavily in the air. The women wore loose-fitting dresses or shorts and t-shirts, the men dressed in tank tops, t-shirts, and jeans or shorts. They gathered in Juan's house for breakfast. Silvia served eggs, beans, bread, and coffee as Maria threw forks onto the tables. The pirates spread butter and jam with their sharp personal knives. Stimulated by coffee, the group grew noisier. The men flirted with the dancers and the dancers with the men. The geckos still stared in silence.

Ivan, with his youth and limited life experience, cast aside all worry and thoughts of personal danger. One of the Colombian dancers sat next to him, eyeing him carefully. She examined his body and face. His thoughts were lost to a collage of adventure, fear, and excitement, and he took little notice of her.

Maria was not greatly concerned about treasure, or life, or death, but she was concerned about the future of the only true treasure she had—the daughter she left behind in Barranquilla. A Colombian fisherman with thick, wavy black hair streaked with grey, sat down next to her. He was muscular, dressed in a tank top and shorts, clean-shaven except for a thick black mustache. He spoke to her through perfect white teeth. "Pretty woman, why do you look so serious?"

She responded with a half-smile. "What?"

Looking at him closer, she decided he was worth speaking with and entered into flirtatious banter. Together, they drank a second cup of coffee and told each other stories, as the sun rose, and the shadows narrowed.

David seemed disinterested. He sat by himself and contemplated his life.

Jose was relieved that Ivan had the first line of responsibility. He knew he sometimes acted too slowly under pressure. Ivan quietly began examining each item in his sea bag.

Juan sat apart from the others; his mind occupied with the upcoming boarding of the ship. He suffered from rare peripheral anxiety, uncharacteristically, worrying for the safety of his son Ivan, his brother David, as well as Maria, Stephen, and the others. For himself, he was not concerned. He always survived.

After breakfast, the crew prepared for the boarding. They selected dark clothing, washing what needed to be cleaned. They tested their face masks and fitted themselves with thin gloves. Everyone cleaned and tested the pistols, all of which were of the same caliber, with hollow point bullets. Some wore side holsters, others shoulder holsters. Others stuck their guns in their belt or leg holsters. Knives were sharpened. Excitement and anticipation focused their thoughts on the upcoming piracy. Adrenaline slipped up quietly and slid into their veins, whispering its tremulous greeting.

Juan inspected the interior of the Colombian boat. He found a stress crack where one of the cross supports joined the hull. Studying the hull, he found some barnacles that would slow the boat and increase fuel consumption. Juan ordered two of the young Haitians to reinforce the cracked support joint. A couple of Colombians scraped the marine growth off the hulls of the two boats.

After the inspection, Juan and Maria worked on the inflatable boat and engine, which had not been used for a while. Maria pumped air into the compartments using a manual foot pump.

Juan turned to Maria, "*No te preocupas, hija*, everything will be fine. You will board the ship from this boat. It is small. If they notice it on the radar, they will not pay attention to it. You will board the ship and take control of the pilothouse without problems."

Maria stopped pumping and looked at Juan – really studying him — for the first time in a long time. She noticed the creases in his dark, tanned face and saw in his eyes a brief, yet genuine care for her.

The look in his eyes made her feel better, and with a half-smile, she replied, "I believe what you say, chief. But I do not care what happens to me."

Maria found no leaks in the boat's inflated chambers. Juan and Maria assembled the steering station and mounted the engine, controls, and fuel tanks. The engine, even after prolonged storage, started without argument. At the end of the day, Juan overloaded the little boat with six crew members. He tested it, running fast and hard through the waves. The dancer who attached herself to Ivan helped him mount the machine gun on the Haitian boat. They stocked the boat with grenades, assault rifles, tear gas, and plastic explosives with detonators.

At dinner, everyone talked at once. The Haitians spoke Creole. Colombian-accented Spanish stormed out of the South Americans' mouths. The men and women gestured to each other, laughed, and flirted.

One of the dark-skinned Haitian men said, "If they shoot at me, I will kill them all."

Overhearing the comment, Ivan said, "No, *compadre*, we will not kill them all. We do not want to kill anyone; only steal their riches."

Everyone stopped talking.

The man glared at Ivan with sheer contempt. "They are rich. They are pigs. They will die."

"No," said Ivan.

"I will kill them," growled the fellow.

Ivan stood, stepped over, and held out his hand. "Give me your gun, now."

The Haitian stared at his antagonist, his face tightening. Ivan calmly repeated, "Give me your gun, now."

The man shook his head. In anger, he stood up and squared off, face to face with the younger man. Suddenly, the Haitian threw a vicious right hook. But Ivan anticipated him and dodged the punch with a fluid move of his shoulders, then hammered the Haitian in the face. As the man's hands went up to his battered nose, Ivan followed with a solid blow to the solar plexus. As the Haitian dropped to his knees, gasping, Ivan stepped in and wrenched the gun from his hand.

He removed the ammunition, and returning the weapon, said, "You will have no bullets."

The pirates looked at Ivan, then at Juan, who remained seated.

Ivan said to them all, "We will work according to the plan and instructions. No more argument!"

Ivan calmly sat down and continued eating, conversing freely and lightly with the younger Colombian dancer.

Normal conversation returned, with no more talk of violence. Instead, the men and women spoke of the riches they would steal.

They united as a team, letting their personal hostilities, competitions, and independence fade. No one wanted to die, be excluded, or miss a share of the profits.

Ivan hardly noticed that Juan, sitting at the end of one table, spent some time contemplating him. At the end of dinner, the aging pirate rose and said, "When we are one, the team wins!" The pirates responded with a cheer.

As the gathering wound down and darkness crept in, the younger Colombian dancer that held Ivan's hand leaned in and whispered throatily, "Make love to me."

Ivan shrugged his shoulders, then offered a smile. He led her to his father's house and took her into his bedroom. As the moonlight pushed its way past the weary drapes and into the small room bathing them in soft chartreuse, they made passionate, almost desperate love, because tomorrow offered no guarantees . . .

AT SEA

The following morning Juan assembled the crew after breakfast. Ivan and David provisioned the boat with water and food. Maria unpacked boxes of bullets. A handful of rounds in one hand, Maria pulled the pistol out of her belt-mounted holster. Placing the bullets on the seat of the Haitian boat, she removed the magazine, filled it, then professionally snapped it into the butt of the weapon. Nonchalantly, she loaded her two spare magazines.

As Juan ordered, David circulated among the pirates distributing more ammunition, dark clothing, gloves, and knit watch caps to those who still needed them. Ivan fueled the gas tanks and inspected the engines. The men and women checked their weapons one final time while talking of riches.

Sweating, the pirates boarded the two boats and left their hideaway — the desperate island of Haiti. Distant from land, they fired at buoys Juan set adrift. With time, their aim improved. The pistols' bullets tore into the buoys rather than the ocean. The pirates in Juan's boat challenged those in Ivan's. Juan's team out-shot his son's. His crew taunted the other boat's crew. "You need to learn how to shoot. We are real pirates. You are children."

Maria picked up one of the automatic rifles, she fired it, tearing up the water with bullets, then destroyed the distant buoy. No one out-shot her.

The wind was light. Except for the almost ever-present sea swell, the water was relatively calm, ruffled only by the light trade winds. The day was hot and humid, but the breeze created by the vessel's movement as they headed south mildly refreshed the pirates. Juan piloted one craft, Ivan the other. Juan ran his boat smoothly, and Ivan followed in its wake, the two boats rolled with the swells.

The pirates sat or stood, their bodies loose and comfortable with the boat's motion. They talked, listened to music, they told stories. Some played cards for money. Just before dark, Maria served Juan's crew shredded chicken, bread, tortillas, beans, and rice. Ivan's dancer served his crew. As darkness fell, the men and women sprawled on the floor of their respective boats. Some slept fitfully. Sleep escaped others. The pilots relied on their Loran navigational systems for their course, but still occasionally studied their compasses, just to be sure . . . David monitored the radio scanner in hopes of picking up useful communications.

The intensity and brightness of the stars, uncontaminated by human-generated light or by pollution, was only slightly reduced by the sea mist and humidity. The inverted bowl of stars marked the line between sea and heaven, and faintly lighted the waves. There was no moon. Even though every pirate knew that danger lay ahead, and perhaps death, there was a peace at being at sea. . . being so closely connected to nature, and there was that sense of being part of a "mission" and belonging to a team. Nothing binds men and women more than challenge and danger. It makes the strongest, most enduring of friendships, and sometimes it defines who a person really is – good or bad – and it can leave an indelible mark on the soul.

Juan smiled broadly as he ran the boat through the night. He rejoiced in his pirate life, thinking that in no other way could he be on the sea and experience this type of awe—his soul aware of the almost surreal magic of the night.

David looked silently into the inky darkness. He wished he had become a chief officer or legitimate sea captain, so he could have experienced being a member of society while still having the privilege of marveling at the sea and sky from his ship.

In the other boat, Ivan, practical, but not insensitive, was moved by the immensity of the sky and felt a stirring in his soul. Without identifying its nature, he felt the foreshadowing of change.

Other pirates remembered their families or thought of old lovers. Some wondered if God, could ever forgive them for what they were about to do. For a few, the fear of Hell overshadowed the fear of being killed or put in prison. Perspiration slowly dripped from their arm pits. Ivan's dancer, a part-time prostitute, drug runner, and pirate, lost herself in her past girlhood. She remembered such nights at sea, fishing with her father. Aware of the danger and hidden in the darkness, she was momentarily able to forget what she had become. The lies she wrote in letters home about working in an artesian factory passed from her mind – giving her temporary relief from the guilt she felt.

When Juan and Ivan slowed the boats, everyone refocused on the present: night at sea to rob a cruise ship. Arriving at the place near which Juan calculated the ship must pass, Ivan's boat stood off to the port side of Juan's boat. Juan's crew pulled the inflated Zodiac alongside the larger boat, the waves and its rolling made it difficult to position the smaller craft for boarding.

With effort, Maria climbed over the gunnels and jumped into the inflatable. She struggled to maintain herself in a standing position as Ivan passed her the sea bags containing water, boarding equipment, and weapons. Lastly, Maria's crew of three men and one woman climbed over the side of the larger boat to join her in the inflatable. Their fingers were pinched, and legs chaffed.

Juan and Ivan motored away from the Zodiac at moderate speed to begin the hunt for the Argentine ship, steering easterly courses at ten-degree angles to the north and south from each other. They set their radar on high power.

The two boats were invisible almost instantly. Their radar showed their positions to each other. The tiny blimp of the Zodiac on the radar screen soon disappeared. Near 11:00 p.m. both boats picked up a large ship on their radar screens. The ship – hopefully the cruise ship they hunted — was almost directly between them. It was certain that the ship had them on their radar, but because of their distance from it, Juan doubted they would take much note of his boats. They would be considered to be yachts or fishermen.

Juan radioed Maria and said, "Little Tiger, we have a big ship on our radar. It is headed for you. It should be there in an hour."

To avoid alarming the ship's captain, at the time planned for Maria and her crew to board the ship, Juan and Ivan would be almost forty-five minutes away. Juan would have preferred to be closer.

The Zodiac rolled up and over the waves, presenting itself broadside to them, it's outboard motor still. Seawater occasionally lightly splashed its occupants. Floating so very close to the surface of the water magnified the sense of beauty and awe experienced by Maria and her crew of four. The impact of intense, personal feelings and memories flooded each of them. Even those tormented by painful memories and sad lives lived, found a peace brought on by the beauty of the sea and sky, the comfort of the warm, wet air. Maria was the most seduced. Her thoughts wandered.

Maria was thirty years old, light tanned in color, strong but not heavy, well developed with full breasts. Her face carried an attractive grace, with compelling dark eyes, and a pretty, seductive mouth. Even though she received the special treatment enjoyed by attractive women, she had no conscious awareness of her beauty.

Maria thought about her education as a young girl in the convent after her mother died. She could come up with no personal memory of her mother; only the locket she wore around her neck bore recollection in the form of a faded photograph.

Her father was a freighter captain with no family. By force of circumstance, after his wife died, he boarded her in a convent for most of her childhood. He maintained a small house in Barranquilla, which they shared on the occasions he was in port. In the summers, she travelled on the ship her father captained. There she learned of the sea, navigation, and how to operate ships. These were her happiest memories. His death in a hurricane at sea was devastating to her. He had been the only one who loved her, and she knew that he had done his best for her.

At the present moment, upon a relatively calm sea, Maria reflected on the loss of her father—the loss of the security in her life—and remembered, or rather felt, the brokenness in her heart that never mended and left her feeling alone and abandoned in the world. Her loneliness drove her into the arms of Juan whom she met in a café in Barranquilla. Juan, the man who could make meaning out of no meaning; Juan, who created excitement and adventure out of thievery, took her to Haiti. For a while, she had meaning—the meaning of the excitement and adventure that Juan lived. Like a master magician, he turned the pirate base and the despair of Haiti into an intriguing life, and she gave herself to him entirely. When Juan had finished with her, he left her with an even more broken heart. She sought others to reform or to hide in, going from man to man, some worse than others, some decent. Maria became the whore with a big heart. Her heart and beauty had attracted many, and she became anyone's woman, faithful to no man, ready for virtually any.

After a while, she returned to Juan and joined him as a pirate. In the beginning, she occasionally gave him intimate pleasure, although no love existed between them. Theirs was a working relationship. Yet in all this, she had one treasure—her little daughter born out of wedlock, guarded against the truth, who was attending the same convent she had attended. She had presented herself to the nuns with falsified papers as the widowed Señora de Chavez, and her daughter, as the daughter of her deceased husband. The nuns had shown her pity and love, believing her story.

Maria's thoughts were suddenly interrupted by the distant light of the gaily-lit cruise ship. They had succeeded in finding it and it was almost on a collision course with the small boat. The time of reflection abruptly ended.

SCOUNDRELS, RICH AND POOR

E l Club de los Industriales de Argentina consisted of business and industry leaders. Many of its members belonged to the relatively small group who controlled much of the wealth of the country. A number of the families inter-married and had formed strong alliances through this bond; others were contentious. There were some old friends on board—men and women who had remained close even in their struggle for wealth and power. There were also many who, in their fight for wealth and power, had challenged their own integrity, and lost . . .

Others were members of different political parties in fierce competition with each other for power and money. Through their practices they shut out the members of other parties, passing lucrative contracts or business concessions to their cronies in exchange for kickbacks deposited to secret bank accounts in tax-haven countries with bank secrecy laws. In some cases, the men on the boat had assassinated key personnel of other parties on the ship to stop or intimidate their rivals. Some had kidnapped and killed relatives of those on board. The affected families were reasonably sure who had masterminded the acts, yet had no proof. In some cases, bodyguards were onboard to protect their master from old scores not yet settled.

Although some of the elite felt the need to have their guard up, no one wanted to miss the biggest social event of the year and the first Club cruise on the elegant and exclusive ship. In spite of the competition and vengeance, the cruise had been pleasant. Old scores were temporarily set aside in order to enjoy, as fully as possible, the pleasures at hand. The deep-rooted social etiquette of the Hispanic culture helped keep the peace. Nonetheless, in the depths of their hearts the unsettled scores remained like poison.

Short-sighted, many of the rich did not treat their bodyguards well. Pay was not high enough for many of the bodyguards to consider taking a bullet for their employers or even to defend their bosses seriously. Others were well paid, faithful, and aggressively protective of their masters. Some had murdered for them. Suspicions and distrust of their bodyguards and each other was high. A number of the club members personally carried weapons.

The ship was a lovely sight as it steamed toward the little Zodiac. Its privileged guests were oblivious to the events which awaited them and powerless to prevent them.

In the small inflatable boat, the Colombian dancer steered an intercept course toward the ship's bow. Dressed in black, her face covered with a mask, her tight clothing revealing her shapely body, Maria positioned herself in the forward part of the Zodiac. With a pistol holstered next to her breast and equipped with a knife, tear gas, and hand grenades, she readied the grappling hook attached to a rope ladder. The convent girl disappeared and the other Maria—the pirate—fully emerged.

Unnoticed, the little boat approached the ship. Positioned just aft of the bow wave and behind the stairway leading to the bridge deck, Maria swung the grappling hook high against the side of the ship. It caught and held. The ladder was loose in her hand, and after a moment's hesitation, she pulled it tight handing the end of it to a fellow crew member. Maria took hold of the highest rung within reach. Pushing off from the Zodiac, she swung the distance to the ship, hitting its side hard. Her grip partially slipped. For a moment she dangled above the bow wave, struggling to get her feet into the ladder. But she somehow managed what appeared like a death-defying Vegas act. Her feet finally secure, she ascended the ladder like a black cat—graceful, and slinky— but cautious. At the top, she climbed up and over the ship's railing, placing herself firmly on the deck.

Maria looked aft, and then upwards towards the wheelhouse. No one yelled at her. No one was near. She motioned to the others in the Zodiac. One by one, the pirates ascended until the four members of the boarding crew were on board. The Zodiac moved away from the ship where it remained hidden in the darkness; the dancer piloting the inflatable sat motionless behind the steering station, an automatic rifle at her right hand.

On the aft part of the ship, along the side of the pool, the lights shone clearly, but not intensely. The air was warm and humid. Some of the guests were in the pool, drinks in their hands. Others were seated at the pool's edge with their feet in the water or resting on chairs. A waiter, dressed in white trousers and a starched short-sleeved shirt with a red carnation pinned to the front, exited from the restaurant located forward of the pool. He carried a polished silver tray containing fresh drinks and beer.

Neither the passengers nor crew had seen the black-colored Zodiac approach the ship, nor did they hear its engine over the sound of the ship's machinery and the four-piece band playing in the casino lounge. They were like guests on the Titanic—unaware of the iceberg . . .

There were stairs on both sides of the upper deck which contained the pilothouse, aft of which, there was an open continuation of the structure where the ship's communication equipment, security cameras, and older backup navigation equipment were located. In front of the helm were the GPS, VHF radio, depth finder, and radar screens, along with the engine and other instruments. Behind the pilothouse and connected to it, was a long superstructure containing various staterooms, opening onto a single, rather narrow hallway.

Maria left part of her small crew on the starboard side of the ship and circled to the port side with her remaining crew man. At the same time, from the starboard and port sides of the ship, the two pairs of pirates entered the pilothouse — their masks covering their faces, pistols in hand. The wide-eyed occupants sucked in breaths, surprise and fear the big winners. The ship had been boarded.

The captain, a proud man nearing sixty, who was good both at sea and in company politics, turned red with anger and indignance. He yelled at the intruders with the full pride of a man born and bred in the upper-class.

"You scum! Get off of my ship or I'll —"

Maria's dark eyes blazed. In a single breath she covered the distance between them, grabbing the man and shoving her pistol against his cheek — hard enough to make him wince. "Shut up, bastard," she hissed.

He opened his mouth to reply. It was shut almost instantly by the fist of one of the pirates next to him. "You no longer rule here, fool."

The captain glared at the pirates with hate. He did not tolerate classless criminals in any situation – least of all in his pilothouse. His attitude ignited his captor's pent-up anger toward those who kept wealth and social position for themselves. Anger and violence were thick and filled the room, the mood dangerous. The man who hit the captain looked for someone else to hit. Maria put her hand on his back to calm him down. The ship's crew members dipped their shoulders in submission to avoid the temper of the pirates.

Maria was no enemy of the sailors or ship's officers. Her respect for them caused her to stop the pirates from further violence. Nonetheless, she was angered by the captain. She forcefully ordered him to sit with his hands around a pipe behind his back. He moved slowly. A young pirate pushed him to the floor. Out of condition, and armed only with pride and anger, he was no match for the younger, stronger man.

Subdued and silent, the pirates handcuffed the hands of the ship's crew behind their backs and around an electrical pipe. Maria cuffed the captain's hand tightly. He squirmed and hissed, "You will never get away with this! The Club will hunt you down. There will be no place to hide!"

Maria shrugged, and offered a bitter smile. "What is life but a roll of the dice? I have always been a gambler."

Maria taped the captain's and the rest of the crew's mouths with duct tape, wrapping it completely around their heads. She disconnected the antennas and power from the newer communication and navigational equipment. She caught the eyes of the captain, then smashed the older equipment of no commercial value with the butt of her pistol and ripped the wires away from their connections. The captain stared at her in anger and disbelief.

"Be quiet, asshole, or I will kill you," hissed one of the pirates.

Maria took the ship's wheel in one hand and called Juan on her radio with the other. She said simply, "The pilothouse is ours."

Maria remembered well the helms of the ships her father had captained. She recalled the calm nights at sea, the black sky with diamonds scattered across it as though upon a jeweler's cloth. She could feel the warm, humid air wrapped around her like God's arms, holding her. And she remembered the sea upon which the smallish ships her father captained would ride, gently moving and passing over the swells.

Suddenly, the girl inside her rose. She was again, for a small moment, thirteen or fourteen, her father standing not far from her, telling her about a ship's systems, explaining the texture and fabric of life in his distant way, preparing her for life. Looking out the window, the ship's wheel in her hands, tears momentarily welled in her eyes. She blinked them away and disregarded what she had become.

When Maria radioed Juan and Ivan and told them that she was in control of the pilothouse, they ran their boats towards the ship at maximum speed. Their boats careened wildly, as though out of control, as they slid down the inside of the swells. At the bottom, they plowed through the troughs. Hitting the top of the waves at high speed, spray ripped up from the sea tore at the sides of the boats and crashed over the bow. Far from each other, father and son stood behind their respective boat's center console; knees bent, bracing against the jarring lunges, white knuckled hands gripping the steering wheels. Experience having taught them where to lean, how to balance, and how to stand, they were survivors in this bitter contest with Mother Nature. The men and women sat on the floor in the shadow of the hull, trying to keep dry, braced against the waves.

Juan lost himself to the boat and, in a sense, became one with it as they jammed through the frothing sea. His life was piracy and all that came with it. A broad smile lit his face.

Ivan, in the flush of youth, enjoyed the ride; although exhilarated, even at that moment, he was aware that his mind was elsewhere. He suddenly found himself reflecting on a revelation — that this was not the life he wanted.

Hidden by the darkness, the two boats raced past the cruise ship. Well ahead of it, they stopped and waited. With Maria in control of the pilothouse, there was no concern of them being recognized as a "bogie" on the ship's radar. They only had to slip by the passengers on the aft deck. Wrapped in the night, fear and excitement fell upon the pirates as the ship approached dead on. They had to let it pass between them without being run over, then come alongside the pilothouse.

The cruise liner closed in, looming menacingly above them as Juan and Ivan carefully nestled their boats against the sides, just aft of the bow wave. Juan used the ladder Maria had left dangling. Ivan threw his grappling hook onto the ship's railing. The hook caught and his rope ladder hung securely. All the pirates, except the helmsmen, climbed up the sides of the hull. Their small backpacks bounced against their bodies as they pulled themselves over the railing to stand upon the darkened forward deck.

Ivan and his companions entered the forward port side door of the superstructure. Inside, they descended two floors to the engine room. David, came in through the starboard door, descended to the passenger cabins. Juan walked into the pilothouse.

"What's happening, chiquita?" asked Juan with a grin.

"Nothing," answered Maria offering a smile of her own. "Only passing time."

Juan glanced around. "Who are your companions?"

"They are more . . . *amigos*." She replied pleasantly. "Only the captain is an ass."

Juan laughed at her.

"Shut up," she replied with mock indignity.

The ship's crewmembers were silent and avoided looking at the pirates, except for the captain; his face was white with pride and rage as he glared at the intruders.

David found no one moving on the cabin deck. Pistols in hand, his men stationed themselves at each end of the corridor—one man at each end facing the cabins' hallway.

As Ivan descended to the engine room, the roar of the machinery increased. He slipped wads of paper into his ears, not to protect them, but to be able to think clearly. Opening the door to the engine room, he encountered two men. One with an oil can was bent to lubricate the exposed parts of one of the engines. The other was studying the numerous gauges.

Ivan's face was half covered. Perhaps the two men thought he was protecting it. Unalarmed, they acknowledged him with a nod and a pleasant expression. When the other pirates came into the room behind Ivan, the men's expressions changed – first, to a questioning look, then quickly to disbelief. Focusing on the guns held in the pirates' hands, a wave of fear darkened their faces. They raised their hands and allowed themselves to be handcuffed to a structural support. The engine room secured, the pirates opened a sound-deadening door leading into the laundry, another service area, and the crew cabins.

Two men were at work in the laundry room. Upon seeing the black-dressed, hooded men enter, one of the men readied a knife to throw it as he moved toward the protection of a bulkhead. Ivan shot him in his exposed right arm. The impact caused the man to drop his weapon and tumble to the floor. One of Ivan's men picked up the knife and handcuffed the hands and feet of both men to the ship's bulkheads.

Through clenched teeth, the wounded man cried, "I am bleeding. Help me!"

The pirate ripped the shirt off the man and bound the wound, staunching the flow of blood.

Ivan and another pirate entered through the door to the crew's quarters. There was one man in the crew's small dining area. He was on his feet, his food on the table before him, a startled look on his face. He saw the guns in the intruders' hands, and quickly raised his arms. The pirate with Ivan took handcuffs out of his backpack and fastened the man to a pipe.

The two pirates entered the crew's dayroom, found it empty and opened the door to the crew dormitory. The noise from the ship's machinery had covered the sound of the shot from Ivan's gun. Some of the men in the room were lying awake in their beds, others asleep.

Holding a pistol in his right hand, Ivan repeatedly banged a pair of handcuffs against an empty locker with the other.

In a loud and commanding voice, he cried out, "*Compadres, pongan atención!*"

Those awake immediately gave him their attention. Those asleep slowly roused themselves, puzzled.

"We come to steal from the rich," Ivan announced. We will not steal from you. If you do nothing, we will only handcuff you."

The ship's men *stared* at the pirates and their weapons, eyes wide with shock. There was an electric moment of encounter, then indecision, as a few of them glanced toward their own weapons by their bunks.

"*Amigos*, do not be afraid," said the other pirate. "You only have to be afraid if you fight or do not take the handcuffs. Why die to protect the rich? They only exploit you."

After a moment, another pirate entered the room. "The other crew members are all handcuffed to the ship," he said. "All is good."

The crewmembers in the room realized then the two pirates were not alone, and that the ship was evidently under their control. This pretty much closed the deal. The few men who considered fighting had serious second thoughts now. They were not well paid. The owners were rich and only the senior officers made enough money to live on. Why die or be hurt? With dropped shoulders and downward gazes, they allowed themselves to be handcuffed, and their bunks searched. The two pirates who handcuffed the men returned with three knives and a pistol.

Holding the weapons high, Ivan said to everyone, "You are very smart and very alive now. Continue being smart. Do not aggravate this situation, amigos. If you do not make problems, things will go well with you."

The men were at least thirty years old, and some of the immortality of youth had left them. They were not heroes, only poorly paid men who wanted to return home to their families and were guaranteed to do so, if they kept still and stayed quiet.

Leaving an armed man in the engine room and another in the crew's quarters, Ivan took the remaining woman pirate, and opened the door of the cabin shared by the second and the third engineers. The two men were standing by the weapons locker located at the far end of the small, green-painted, metal-walled room. The locker, hidden behind a false wall, was built to prevent easy access. The men had just removed the false wall and unlocked the double locks. The younger engineer held a pistol in hand and turned it toward the pirates. Teresa fired. Her opponent was thrown against the locker behind him from the impact. The man, struck high in the shoulder, dropped his gun and collapsed. The other engineer put his hands into the air. His eyes-were full of rage and fear — but the fear outweighed the rage.

Ivan addressed him as a friend. "Amigo, why do you want to die? We are many. We are going to rob this ship. You will not stop us."

The man's eyes continued to blaze, his face fierce. Incomprehensible words came out of his mouth. Ivan put his gun in his belt and struck the man hard in the stomach with his fist, then smashed the man's face against his knee. Bleeding profusely from the nose and gasping for breath, the rebellion and hate in the man's eyes was replaced by pain. The man's thoughts turned to his four children in Argentina. He was one of the Argentine crew members which the Club had insisted crew the ship along with the Venezuelans. It occurred to him that his physical beating would show both the club members and the company that he had done more than his part to save the ship . . .

Now that the man was subdued, Teresa turned her attention to the engineer she had shot. By chance the bullet barely hit his shoulder. She handcuffed the man's hands and feet to the ship. Proceeding to the weapons locker, she removed the guns, slung the rifles over her shoulders, put the pistols in her belt, and placed the additional items in her backpack.

Ivan helped the wounded man. After bandaging his arm, he looked at Teresa. Only her eyes were visible, her hair hidden under her mask and hood except for escaping black strands which revealed its dark color. Tall for a Hispanic woman, solidly built with full curves, she was almost fully dressed with weapons. The confiscated pistols hung from her like ornaments.

Ivan said, laughing, "You look like the sister of Fidel Castro or Che Guevara."

Her eyes dancing, she slapped him lightly on the side of the head and said, "I am comrade Teresa the Terrible. Don't forget it!"

Inside the pilothouse, the air conditioning blew refreshingly cool air. Seated before the video monitors showing the casino, bar, restaurant, and pool area, Juan watched the unsuspecting passengers as they continued swimming, drinking, eating, and playing roulette. The waiters, red carnations bright against their white uniforms, came and went with silver trays. The hostesses and waitresses moved about, speaking in an animated fashion, mostly with the older guests. The hostesses were demure with the women and gave frank, open, and inviting looks to the men.

The casino staff members were attentive to their duties. Juan particularly noted the location and placement of the persons who might be bodyguards or casino security staff. Only a relatively few of the passengers were not accounted for.

Ivan entered the pilothouse with Teresa, still dressed with the weapons. He said to his father, "Everything went well, the lower deck is ours. Manuel is in the engine room to care for the machinery. *El Negro* is with the crew."

Juan nodded and then, looking at Teresa, laughed in a relieved fashion. All was going remarkably well . . . Leaving her to protect Maria, he took the others through the back door. The passageway was empty.

Juan entered the captain's cabin. He found the weapons compartment in the back of the hanging locker. With a pry bar, he removed the crosspiece that sealed it, forcing open the door. One of the pirates removed the weapons.

The thieves then began opening the doors of the cabins. The first ones were vacant. Musical instrument cases indicated they were used by entertainers. There were no weapons. Further down the hallway, near the end, the pirates found two locked doors. Juan knocked hard on one door, Ivan on the other. The doors opened almost simultaneously, but not entirely. At each door, a man's face appeared. Sleep was still in their eyes, but as awareness entered, their faces paled. The group in the hallway, black-masked and with pistols drawn, presented a clear message.

Responding to a motion to move to the back of their cabins, the men raised their hands and took steps backward.

Speaking to the men from the hallway in a loud voice, Juan said, "*Amigos*, your suits are cheap. You are not paid much. We are not here to kill your bosses, only to steal their money. Do not choose to die."

The first man accepted the handcuffs peaceably and was secured to a support beam.

The second man's face reddened. Veins bulged from his temples. His eyes narrowed. His body tensed.

Juan saw it coming, "You should take my advice . . ." he growled.

Before the man could act, Juan struck him in the stomach. As the fellow bent forward, Juan hit him twice in the face. He crumpled to the ground.

Juan knelt over him. *"Comprendes?"*

Traces of vomit were on the man's mouth, and blood spilled from his lip. He gasped for breath. Juan looked into his eyes. He still saw fight.

"I will kill you if you make problems." Juan handcuffed him to a post.

They found the chief engineer in the last cabin. He was asleep when Juan entered.

"Old man, wake up!" demanded Juan.

The fellow struggled awake, looked at Juan and the other pirate in his room, and lifted his hands. He said, "Señor, we are only working men. Not even the officers are rich. We are not paid very much."

"We do not want your money. We want the money of the members of the Club."

"Soon I retire. I want to be home and enjoy my little pension," continued the frightened engineer.

Juan responded, "You will not die, *viejo*. We want only money, not your life. Put your hands here."

The pirates bound his hands around the base of a table that was fastened to the floor.

The keys taken from the captain and chief engineer opened the locked cabin doors. In four of the cabins, the pirates found older couples. They reacted with disbelief, shock, and anger when their doors were flung open. Scum had violated their sanctuary! These were rich men and women, who, although now older, had used every trick and scheme to climb their way to the economic top of their country. They had employed violence and occasionally murder to achieve their ends. They considered themselves above everyone and everything—including the law. Regardless of their age, David and Ivan knew these rich men to be dangerous.

Breaking into the weak safe deposit boxes and ransacking every corner for cash and jewelry, the pirates stripped the cabins of anything valuable.

To the club members in the cabins, Juan said, "We are pirates. The ship is in our control. We want and will take your money and everything that is valuable. Remember, what you have here is only a little. You have much more in Argentina. If you let us steal and do not cause problems, you will live. If not, I will kill you and feed your bodies to the sharks."

The women remained mute. Observing Juan's manner, his tone, and the look in his eyes, the old men believed him. Usually resourceful and aggressive, they uttered few, well-considered words.

Down the corridor from the cabins of club members, Ivan found a sleeping bodyguard in a small room. The man snapped to consciousness as Ivan entered. He looked at Ivan and reached under his pillow. Ivan brought his pistol down hard on the man's temple, and the contest was over.

From under the man's pillow, Ivan carefully removed a pistol and a knife. "Stupid bastard," he muttered angrily.

The woman pirate with Ivan pulled the dazed man onto the floor. She placed his hands and legs in handcuffs, then searched the cabin and found another pistol and boxes of bullets. The man remained quiet as he coped with the pain of his injured hand.

After ransacking the upper cabins, Juan took his crew down to the forward part of the busy entertainment deck. He divided them between Ivan and himself, placing Ivan on the port side of the ship. He took the starboard side.

Juan and Ivan's entrance into the main salon was perfect. Dressed in black and masked, they suddenly seemed to appear everywhere at the same moment.

Memories of old scores, long waiting to be settled, arose in the minds of several of the passengers. They had long awaited an opportunity to avenge the schemes, murders, and kidnappings. Now the chance presented itself. They did not worry about protecting their aged wives, long since supplanted in their hearts by young lovers and younger families. Nor, at that moment, did they care about their money. It was revenge they desired. They saw an opportunity to kill business adversaries and blame it on the pirates, and they were armed for the task.

Ivan examined the opulent interior of the ship's salon. The paneling was walnut, the curtains velvet, and carpet thick. Heavy silverware was on the tables. The men and women lived and dressed in casual elegance. He stared at the authority and power he saw sculpted into their faces. At that moment, he realized his father had spent his life on a small playing field. Here, in the absolute splendor of the ship's interior occupied by well-dressed men who were accompanied by beautiful women, young and old, was real wealth and power. These men ruled Argentina and much of the economies of the nations around it.

The veils of dissatisfaction within him suddenly parted and it became clear – he wanted to walk among them as one of them – not as a thief. He wanted to experience their influence and lifestyle, with the freedom of living without fear of the US Coast Guard and other government authorities. *These were the men who took the bribe. They did not pay it.*

Standing at the front of the room at the ship's microphone, Juan commanded, "*Damas y caballeros*, we are pirates. We have control of the ship. If you cause no problems, you will not be hurt. It is money and jewelry we want. You are lucky—we do not want your women nor do we want hostages to ransom."

At Juan's order, the helmsmen in the pirate boats turned on the high-intensity lights mounted on the radar arches. Suddenly, the ship was bathed in a harsh, surrealistic flood of light. The intense barrage which intruded into their privileged world blinded the passengers and crew.

Through the microphone Juan continued, "The ship is ours; it is foolish to resist."

Seized by the nightmare fear of being kidnapped or being killed in front of their friends and adversaries, a woman collapsed to the floor and two men stumbled to chairs, suffering chest pains.

Maria stopped the ship's engines. The salon became quiet. The silent ship slowly swung sideways to the waves and rolled in the troughs. The faces of the passengers blanched at the reality of the moment. Terror rested on the faces of many of the women and some of the men. Women pleaded with their men. "What will they do? Do something. Save us."

Pirates spread among the passengers. Rather politely, they said, "Please sit down." Going from passenger to passenger, less politely, they demanded money, jewelry, and all else they found of value.

Guns in hand, Juan and Ivan supervised the pirates from opposite sides of the ship. Standing in groups, the passengers were not individually visible. Suddenly, gunshots rang out. Ivan and some of the younger, less-experienced pirates prepared to shoot at the passengers.

Juan held up his hand and said in a commanding voice, *"Wait!"*

Women were screaming. Two men lay on the floor, their life's blood pooling around them. Juan knew what had happened and in a passive tone said to the pirates, "This is not our matter. They are killing each other."

The wives of the dying men knelt next to them, hunched over their husbands, screamed for help. But the effect of the shots to the chest and heart could not be reversed. Death was already on the men. Their years of dirty tricks had caught up with them; their power and wealth would pass to others.

Juan cautiously studied the scene. "Make as few enemies as possible, for there comes a time of revenge," he muttered.

Ivan stared at his father and nodded.

Oblivious to the pain of the wives and friends of the dead, the pirate crew continued to demand valuables from the passengers. They emptied wallets and purses and took jewelry, occasionally responding to tears by leaving a passenger with a sentimental item of low value.

Ivan and Jose persuaded the effeminate, neatly uniformed purser to unlock the ship's safes. The casino safe was large and full of cash and gold – much beyond what Juan had hoped. Ivan's Colombian dancer emptied the contents into canvas bags.

Two of the young bodyguards, known to kill for their masters, subtly reached for their hidden pistols. With a gesture, their masters pointed at Juan and Ivan, who were the obvious leaders, and made a motion to kill them. Guns in hand, the bodyguards cautiously moved from the back to the forefront of the passengers, into a position of advantage. Communicating with a nod, they lifted their guns and fired.

The first two shots missed their targets, but the third hit Ivan's Columbian dancer in the chest, near her shoulder, passing through her body. Two other bullets just missed Juan. But one lodged in the neck of one of his men; the second passed through the man's spinal column, killing him instantly. The bodyguards were still trying to get a clear shot at Juan while hidden behind passengers.

Knowing the bullets were meant for him, and in a moment of uncanny heightened awareness, Juan quickly calculated the position of the shooters in the crowd. Ducking and jagging, partially shielded by the passengers, he managed to get to the perfect vantage point. In its panic, the crowd fell open for a moment, exposing his assailants. Juan aimed at the two men and pulled off four rounds. Both men jerked from the impact of the bullets and fell. As the crowd folded back in panic, Juan moved in slowly, gun ready, searching for additional antagonists. He kicked the guns from the hands of his assassins – one was dead, the other dying miserably, blood spilling from a belly wound and seeping out the corners of his mouth. Taking the dead man by the hair, he dragged him over to his companion (who was holding his stomach — his weapon tossed aside). Without thought, adrenaline pumping in anger and retribution, Juan grabbed the second assailant by the collar and dragged them both out of the salon. The passengers mechanically, quietly opened a path for him.

Red blood trailed on the floor behind the men. The one man still alive cried in pain as the movement tortured his torn entrails.

Reaching the starboard railing of the boat, Juan lifted the live assassin up and over the railing. The man screamed at him, begging to be spared. Juan threw him into the black sea below. Without hesitation he grabbed the other, already lifeless, assassin and tossed his body into the water.

The pirates continued to work the ship and passengers, but now with anger and rudeness, saying to the men, "You sons of bitches, where is your money?" To the women, they demanded, "Tell us where your jewelry is—all of it." They threatened to throw the women who hesitated into the sea. The men who hesitated were backhanded. Expensive watches and personal items were stripped forcefully from the passengers. The pirates took the wedding rings they had previously left with their owners. A third safe, filled with expensive jewelry, gold, and more cash was disclosed and emptied quickly.

As the other pirates loaded the boats, Maria destroyed more of the radio equipment. The bound, red-faced captain muttered through the duct tape across his mouth.

Maria responded, "We robbed your boat old man. What you thought was yours is now ours. We command the ship, not you, and what we want, we take; what we want to destroy, we destroy."

Looking the captain in the eyes, she took a large wrench and smashed the navigation equipment. The bound captain thrashed against the cuffs on his hands and feet. Holding the wrench high above her head she said, "Captain, the ship belongs to the company. Why are you so angry? We are in control. Do we hurt your pride?"

The violence of the explosion from the captain's mouth at the word *pride* partially loosened the duct tape. Looking at the captain,

Maria unnecessarily smashed the compass and the old-style electrical gauges. She proceeded to break everything in sight. Dropping the wrench on the floor not far from the captain, she turned and left the pilothouse.

Juan shook his head incredulously. "Do not anger the tigress," he muttered to the captain with a small smile, then he followed.

When there was nothing left that the pirates chose to steal, Juan assembled his crew next to the treasure-laden boats. For the sake of the ship's crew members, Juan threw the handcuff keys onto the deck. After everyone was aboard their boats, he and Ivan climbed into their boats. No one made a sound or effort to stop them.

The two pirate boats left the wallowing cruise ship and headed south, as though for the coast of Colombia. Out of hearing range of the ship, they changed course, passed far behind it, and went north, towards Haiti. Juan and his son ran at almost full throttle; the fiberglass pirate vessels rolled with the waves. Heavy in the water, they didn't bang against the waves that ran on top of the swells.

After the pirates' departure, the passengers stood in silence and shock for a considerable time. Men were dead. Money and riches were stolen. Old scores settled. They had counted on their wealth, selfish privilege, and power to protect them, and it had failed. The owners of the dead bodyguards yelled into the sea. "We will hunt you and kill you bastards. You will not be able to hide from us!"

RETURN TO HAITI

The wounded Colombian dancer lay on the floor next to the helm of Ivan's boat. The other dancer pressed the bandage against her wound. The injured woman wept. In her pain, she said, "The rich said they loved me, but they never did. They just used me for their pleasure. I gave them sexual services. Now they shot me."

Ivan looked at the thin, pretty woman, stained with blood. "You will get well, and you will have their money."

The body of the dead crewman lay on the floor of Juan's boat. Standing at the helm, Juan glanced at the body from time to time. He was a Haitian; an unmarried black man of middle age who had been a faithful worker. While Juan had no feeling of closeness to the dead man, he had respect.

Juan said aloud to Maria, "Sons of bitches, they killed him."

Maria responded, "How would you feel if I were shot, *mi capitán*?"

Juan thought for a moment and looked at her. "I would miss you. You are the best."

Maria responded, "I would like to die."

Juan knew she spoke the truth.

Juan's thoughts turned to his killing of the two bodyguards. They paid for the death of his crewmember. He ran the mental tape of the evil acts performed by bodyguards for their masters, but not to justify himself. They died because they shot members of his crew. He had killed them, and they deserved it. He felt no remorse for his acts. The words "sons of bitches" escaped from his mouth again. The only unpleasant emotions he felt were for his dead crewman and the wounded Colombian woman. Those emotions momentarily muted the pleasure he felt in that his plan had succeeded – they had robbed the rich and escaped with their money and expensive jewelry.

Ivan, lost in thought about what he had seen and heard, steered the boat mechanically. He had seen wealth, luxury, privilege, comfort, and men of power beyond anything he had before experienced. He had seen revenge against old men. He had seen his father, in explosive anger, kill two bodyguards, aware that his father would hardly think of it again.

Ivan thought about his life growing up. He had robbed many boats with his father and the other pirates. There had been little violence, no destruction, just the taking of money and equipment. But in his heart there was no liking the life to which he had been born, nor any real disgust, but as he steered the fast boat across the sea he encountered something deep within himself—a desire for a new life. He did not want to steal, small or large, and considering the violence and deaths that night, he did not want to be a pirate. At that moment he decided that the cost his father paid to "freely" steal from boats and ships was too high. He had no desire for the "freedom" his father claimed was his.

Perhaps due to the lineage from his mother's family, who had at times controlled portions of the government of the Dominican Republic and parts of Spain, came a desire for a life he could not picture. That and much more stirred from the deepest part of his being. Ivan wanted a different life.

He had occasionally experienced nice hotels in Haiti and Colombia and other places. He had seen the move toward building small yacht facilities. In the hours of the trip to Haiti, he decided to learn the business of hotels and marinas, to join the life of society. Haiti was not an option; it was a wreck. The tourist world had abandoned it due to its evil decline, violence, and filth; but the Dominican Republic was open to major tourist development and was well situated. He spoke fluent Spanish, and because his mother took him into the Dominican Republic to be born, he was also a citizen of that country. He was trained to act and was young, good looking, and smart. The world was to belong to him.

David, riding quietly in his brother's boat, also considered his life. He wanted a wife and family. He knew some women in Colombia and the Dominican Republic—good women—and decided that not far in the future he would look for a wife and seek a new, safer life.

The boats, riding almost side by side, sped across the sea. In spite of the deaths of the bodyguards, the corpse riding next to Juan, and the wounded dancer crying in Ivan's boat, the warm sea air was comforting. The pirates began to relax, and rejoiced in their hearts at the wealth that filled the boats. Only a few of the men were touched by the death of the one pirate. They had been his friend. The second dancer comforted her friend with alcohol and her nearness. The sobbing wounded woman asked, "Will anyone ever love me?" The other woman said, "Yes, and you will not love them for their money. You will have your own."

As time passed, the men and women felt the death of the pirate, danger, and tension fall further and further behind them. Their thoughts quieted as they continued running across the water, underneath the moon and stars through the warm, damp night air, with the land still distant. The sea swells lifted the fast laden boats and caused them to roll as they passed underneath. The warm spray from surface waves drifted over the speeding vessels. The powerful sound of the large outboards was steady and comforting. With each passing moment, the enchantment of the Caribbean and adventure settled into the men and women. For most, even for Juan, time was momentarily lost in a bubble of peace and beauty. The men and women who had lived by and through the sea were now upon it and forgot themselves in their dash across it.

The boats seemed alive, rolling and occasionally jumping a wave. In the cocoon of darkness, warmth and humidity, the pirates melded with the sea and became part of it in united motion. Identities were lost to the moment. There were no pirates, no whores, no desperate people—just men and women who momentarily returned to being simple human beings. The myriad of circumstances and forces in existence before their birth, that had led them to a life of crime and violence, disappeared. God, who knew their hearts, some good and some bad, seemed not to condemn them. After all, born at the bottom of society, most of them were just trying to survive.

The depth meter indicated the shoaling of the water. Ivan's mind filled with thoughts of a new future. He pondered how to learn what he needed to prepare for a new life. His thoughts turned to his father. He would need his help.

South Haiti was a disappointment. As the sky reflected the first sign of light, dry hills appeared. The faces of the pirates were lined and off-color in their exhaustion. Yawns distorted their appearance. No one was pleased to step ashore. On the beach, life became business. The jewels, merchandise and money remained under Ivan's and David's watchful eyes. Stephen cleansed the boats of blood. Maria and the Colombian dancer took care of the wounded woman. Ivan drove to the Dominican Republic border for the doctor. No one joked. There was no laughter.

The corpse was wrapped in a canvas bag and weighted with old iron for burial at sea. Mid-day, two men carried the stiff body to the water's edge. They placed the body in Juan's boat, then pushed away from the beach.

No one talked as they motored away from the coast. Distant from shore, the body was lowered into the sea. Before it was let go, Maria muttered a prayer to God and committed the man's spirit, soul, and body as she recalled some of the Catholic funeral service and duplicated it in essence, if not in accuracy. The men and women listened; their heads bent.

As the body sank, Maria wept. In a soft, but audible voice, she cried, "Father, forgive me my sins and save me." Ivan looked at the torment of her face and watched the tears flow from her eyes. An embrace from the uninjured Colombian dancer stopped Maria's shaking.

Ivan felt the sadness of the moment. There was a final awareness that life as a pirate was something other than what lived in his father's mind. Struggling against all that he had been told and lived, Ivan concluded that piracy was wrong.

THE SMUGGLER

The sixty-five-foot vessel used to smuggle marijuana, and other 'merchandise' arrived that night. Skippered by Samuel, an aging white American fluent in the multiple languages of the Caribbean, the small ship dropped anchor after dark. As though it were nothing, the American pirate Stephen half pulled and half carried a small shore boat into the water. Maria, dressed in baggy cutoffs and a loose bikini top, comfortable in her young body, gracefully climbed aboard. She lifted the little outboard motor off its bracket and lowered it into the small waves.

Samuel listened as the boat approached, its two-stroke engine marking its progress. It was not until Maria motored alongside that he was able to see her in the light that fell from his ship. His eyes examined her body and with a slow appraisal rested on her partially exposed breasts and exposed stomach.

"Come up here, daughter," he said to her, using the Spanish meaning.

Maria laughed in response. "No, you old goat, you would try to take me into your arms, and I would have to kill you. You come down into the boat."

"You are always a difficult woman," said Samuel with a laugh.

The trip to the beach was momentary. Stepping into the water from the bow of the boat, Samuel pulled it onto the sand where Juan was waiting.

The two men embraced and patted each other on the back. Juan led his friend up the beach toward his house. Speaking in Spanish, he said, "*Amigo*, cómo te va?"

"Everything goes well."

"Thank you for coming as agreed," said Juan.

"Why is the timing so important?" asked Samuel with interest.

"As I planned, we found the treasure ship full with the wealth of rich bastards. I wanted you to take the 'merchandise' to sell. Now it is even more important, because some people were shot. The ship has certainly arrived in Cuba. Perhaps someone will look for us. The merchandise must not stay here. You will find a good market in South America for many of the items. The rest you can send to Europe."

"Of course, I will transport whatever you want," responded Samuel.

"I want you to take everything. There must be no evidence here in case the Americans become involved."

On the beach, under Ivan's direction, the pirates loaded small boats with the stolen items and took the treasures to Samuel's ship. The ship's crew stored the booty.

Juan led Samuel to the porch of his house. They sat where they could supervise the work of loading the ship. Juan asked, "Did you have any troubles on your trip?"

For a brief moment, Samuel thought about the series of typical misadventures that they experienced at sea and hesitated. In the faint light emanating from Juan's house, Samuel looked directly at Juan and smiled broadly as he mentally recounted the problems.

Finally, thinking of the ruptured fuel line that caused him to shut down an engine for a while, Samuel replied with a shrug, "There are always problems."

"Yes, problems. I had to kill two bodyguards. One of my crew died. And two of the rich shot each other."

"That is not good. The news people will make a big story of it. Even in Haiti, you may be in danger."

"I will go to Cuba and fix it."

"Do you need help? I have friends in Cuba."

"No, I have a man who works high in government propaganda," answered Juan.

After a pause, Samuel said, "Tomorrow night, I will unload the merchandise near Barranquilla. In two days, everything will be sold, moved to another market or hidden. Do not worry. No one will find the merchandise."

"You are the great smuggler."

After a pause, Juan asked, "How are you?"

"My wives are never content."

Juan laughed hard at his friend, "That is because you are stupid enough to marry two women. You should just keep one as a girlfriend."

"I am a fool for women."

"No, you are a fool to marry them."

Hearing an argument on Samuel's ship, the men stood up.

"They are quick to fight over nothing," said Samuel, speaking of his few crew members.

"It is the same with some of my pirates," Juan replied.

Samuel yelled, "Shut up and get to work!"

The ruckus stopped, and the two men sat down again on the porch of Juan's house and poured another drink of *aguardiente*.

Samuel asked, "Adventure, sex, or money—which is first, my friend?"

"The theft from the ship was a great adventure, but I worried that we could be overwhelmed. We were few. The passengers, crew, and bodyguards outnumbered us. Some were armed."

"You took the risk because of the money?" Samuel asked.

"Yes, but I must be getting old. I was worried," answered Juan.

"There is always some fear, boarding a ship is risky and fearful. So which is first: sex, adventure, or money?"

"They are *all* my life."

"Every time I see you, you are more a pirate."

"As they say, 'A pirate's life for me.'" said Juan with a laugh in accented English.

Drinking more *aguardiente*, Samuel said in a slightly slurred voice, "I feel alive when there is risk. Also, I like to be at sea on my ship. Then I am far from my women." After a moment's reflection, he added, "And the sea is beautiful."

"Danger and adventure are the only ways you can escape."

"Says you," observed Samuel.

"Yes, brother, I like adventure and risk. We share them, *amigo*," answered Juan.

Samuel sighed, "Yes, but in adventure my life seems to float on top of some true reality that other people live, but in which I do not participate."

"You have your pretend life of a businessman, but you are a smuggler. You do not fully participate in either. You cannot fully enjoy life."

"I make good money," responded Samuel.

Both men had money in banks in the Cayman Islands. The talk turned to the US Coast Guard, the Colombian patrol boats, the plane patrols, and satellite tracking, and the difficulty they present, given the men's line of work.

"Yes, we have money and it makes life good. Life is meaningless, an absurd joke, but I am not the butt of the joke—I am rich and free and laughing at it. I screw my woman and fill the holes of life with adventure and pleasure. There is nothing better. Never worry my friend."

After Maria and the other pirates finished loading the ship, some girls from the village ventured to the beach in search of a client or two.

In a brash, taunting voice, one of the girls yelled to Samuel's smuggler crewmen, "Hey, honey, you want to make love to us?"

In the dark, the men could not see the girls on shore. A smuggler replied, "Come here. Someone on the beach will bring you."

Maria took the prostitutes to the small skiff which she and Ivan used to transport the plunder to Samuel's ship from the shore. Talking in loud, crass voices, the girls awkwardly climbed aboard. Maria expertly pushed the boat off the sand. When the water reached her thighs, she climbed aboard with the grace of a feline. In one sensual motion, she lowered the outboard into the water and pull-started it. Her head was straight, her long black hair behind her.

At the ship, the few men took the women's outstretched hands and hoisted them aboard. The little light coming from the ship's superstructure reached the aft deck. It gave them a chance to see the service providers. They were very dark, too thin, and not very pretty.

The smugglers offered the women rum with Coke, which they eagerly accepted. The sailors and whores drank on the aft deck. After a few drinks, the girls looked more attractive.

One of the smuggler crewmen asked, "How much do you want?"

A loud girl answered, "Twenty dollars."

"I will give you five."

The girls hissed and swore at the men. Finally, a small compromise price was negotiated, and the men took the women into their shared dormitory. The women quickly pulled off their loose-fitting dresses. The dim light exposed their small dark breasts and thin, malnourished bodies. The smugglers stared at the women, fumbled with their breasts, and put them onto their berths. The men enjoyed the quick hot service, fueled by the Coca-Cola and cheap Calypso rum. A short time later, the men and women returned to the aft deck, drank more, and became louder. Juan's policeman showed up and yelled at the women to go home.

Unmoved by the events occurring on Samuel's boat, Juan and Samuel kept talking, enjoying the pleasure of each other's company. As Samuel was recounting a recent adventure, Juan thought about his friend's story. He knew it well. Samuel repeated it to him on the occasions when he was very drunk or when it welled up inside him and overflowed out of his mouth.

Samuel had begun life with ambition, with a college degree from Florida State, diving credentials, and finally a small diving school in the Florida Keys. A life of crime had not been on his radar. In his late twenties, he was persuaded by drinking buddies to help unload marijuana from a boat. The police arrived, and he was imprisoned. When Samuel was released, his wife, two children, and the business had disappeared. He began using drugs and became a beach bum. After almost dying from an overdose, he knew that he would soon be dead if he continued. He stopped using drugs, tried diving again and worked hard at it. He had a steady flow of clients until the school he worked for went out of business.

Samuel was soon broke, but he lived on a small boat which gave him the possibility to transport marijuana to make some money. He went to the Bahamas and brought some bales of marijuana back at night. Making regular trips he accumulated enough money to buy a bigger and faster boat. He then smuggled marijuana from the Gulf Coast of Mexico to Texas and Alabama. In the midst of his success, he was busted in Mexico and spent eleven months in a Mexican jail. The experience served him well—he paid the imprisoned ex-mayor of the town to teach him Spanish. The man also taught him much about the Latin culture, the drug cartels, and other illegal businesses. Samuel was a quick learner.

After his early release arranged by friends of the ex-mayor, Samuel purchased a boat big enough to go to Colombia. The marijuana was cheaper there and the profits much higher. In Colombia, he perfected his Spanish. As his success continued, there was a succession of boats, including his current custom, diesel-powered turbo vessel. Its specially designed hull could be pushed to high speed but was safe in bad weather at slow speed. Over the years, he became relatively wealthy.

When Samuel finished his adventure story, Juan was brought back to the moment and asked, "Tell me. Are your wives and families well?"

"In the Bahamas, my oldest starts university soon. They grow up so fast! But I don't think his mother in Nassau loves me very much. She just wants me for the life I give her. Samuel shrugged, "It's okay, my wife in Colombia does love me and she's prettier anyway. My children with her are also well. You know that both my wives know of my smuggling business, but my wife in the Bahamas pretends that everything is legal and that she doesn't know anything about it."

Juan knew that Samuel was thought to be a legitimate businessman, especially in the Bahamas. He had resurrected the old college man to play the part. Juan had often seen the smoothness and sophistication with which his friend played his respectable role in the drama of his life. When advantageous, Juan copied Sam's manners. It gave the pirate a veneer of sophistication when he needed it.

"You should have given yourself over to be the smuggler you are and found women to join you. You are trapped between your legitimate businessman front and the truth. You worry too much about being exposed, shamed, and losing your pretend life. You suffer in your heart because of all the lies and fear. I tried, mi amigo, to teach you to live as a true outlaw, and you couldn't learn because you are a trapped man. Your double life makes you unhappy. And you worry that your wives will find out about each other. Your old life is dead. Your first wife left you, and you still love her. That life is gone, let it go. You are not the college businessman anymore. You are a smuggler trapped in a lie. Because of it you cannot enjoy your life or family in Nassau, and you have only limited enjoyment with your wife in Colombia."

Samuel looked thoughtful, then said, "My trips and stays in Colombia and the Bahamas give me time to fulfill my duties with both. I like being married, but I do prefer Colombia and that wife, and my business of smuggling commercial products onto the docks of Barranquilla is good. I also take a decent amount of merchandise into Venezuela. My business there is also good and low risk. My marijuana business isn't what it used to be. Many people in the United States grow their own and I do not like to deal in cocaine or amphetamines. Although that market is large, those drugs and the people in that business are often unscrupulous and many of them end up dead."

Mildly boasting, the pirate said with a grin, "I do not hide from anyone. I live as I am—a pirate. I have nothing to hide."

Samuel sighed, "Yes but at a horrible cost. You and your thieves from many countries have to hide in Haiti, while I live well; you live poorly. But better than either is my sea life. I don't like the land. In my boat, I have Carmen, who cooks and satisfies me. There I am one with the salt water, the hot sun, and the storms, while piloting my boat day or night, and sleeping in the pilothouse. I love the ship life with its adventure and electronic toys: radar, satellite read-outs, and radios. And finally, the occasional chase by the patrol boats that are too slow to catch me is always fun and an adventure!" said Samuel, laughing. His eyes sparkled, even in the darkness.

Samuel was completely Latin, American, and Bahamian—all at the same time, and separately. When required, he appeared to be a white-skinned Latino, moving with the nuances and expressions of Colombia. Sometimes he appeared as an American Jimmy Buffet. Other times, just a good citizen of the Bahamas.

Although Juan had always lived in Colombia or the Caribbean, his American mother had imparted some of the US culture to him, as well as the language which together with Stephen, he imparted to Ivan. Without speaking of it, he and Samuel shared the confusion of mixed cultural and linguistic heritage. It was an undercurrent in their lives, hard to detect, that made life both easier and confusing. They usually spoke in Spanish to each other.

Juan said, "You are a lucky man. You have two wives, your lover Carmen, children who are well, money, adventure, a large boat, and you have good health to enjoy them all. All that men say about good and evil is a lie. There is no good and evil, only life. And if God exists, he or she is both good and bad. Religion is used to justify men's lives and to control others. Pay no attention to such things. You're a man who is truly rich, let nothing control you. Especially, not your wife in the Bahamas —if she does you are not free."

Samuel looked at his friend. In his heart, he was happy to have someone who knew him well and helped him carry a small part of the burden of the lies. He was also happy to have someone to share what he considered to be the best part of his life— his life of escape.

Neither of them wanted Samuel's vessel to be near the shore at daybreak. An hour before dawn, the men embraced.

Samuel said, "I must not get caught with this merchandise. They would say I was the pirate. I would never leave prison."

"Go fast and be safe, my friend" Juan replied.

The little ship left quietly under the power of a single engine. A short distance from the island, Samuel started and advanced the throttles of all the engines. The boat noisily careened forward. The big diesels shoved the boat across, then through, and over the sea. The course heading was to a small inlet near Santa Marta, Colombia, over 450 nautical miles to the south.

CUBA AND THE AMERICAN

The day of Samuel's departure, Juan put out to sea with his brother David. He steered to the west. The sea swells, driven by the trade winds behind them were moderate. There was a light, wind-generated wave on top of the swells. His boat rode easily.

The sky was mostly clear, the temperature perfect. Seagulls followed the boat. Fish jumped. Sitting under the shadow of a small canopy over the pilot's seat, Juan drank coffee from a large thermos. His brother handed him a sweet oreja pastry.

"There is no day more perfect than this," said Juan between bites.

David looked around, felt the sun on his skin, and speaking only of the weather he said in English, "You're right, it gets no better than this."

Juan laughed deep and powerful— a real pirate's laugh. "For *this*, I am a pirate."

David looked at his brother's sun-and sea-darkened complexion and his full hair, kept perfectly black with dye, as it flew loose in the wind. Wearing a black sleeveless shirt, jean shorts, sandals, with a broad smile spread across his face, he looked truly happy. After a moment David said, "My brother, one day I hope to love my life as much as you love yours."

"Life is hell for the poor. We have money, freedom, and security. No police bother us in Haiti. Enjoy life and enjoy this being at sea!"

"Yes brother, I do enjoy it, but not like you. You love your life. I don't want to live in Haiti and I want a good woman," David replied.

"If you take some other life, you will find that it is just a trap. You will work all your life and die with nothing."

Juan passed the thermos to David who poured them both another cup. David opened a can of evaporated milk and added one-fourth cup of the thick, white liquid to his brother's coffee.

"There is no better coffee than this with *leche evaporada.*"

After a while, David stretched out on a mat in the forward part of the boat and lay half-naked in the sun. It was not long before he slept. Almost without a thought in his being, Juan steered the boat across the open sea, enjoying every moment as though it would last forever. A cruise ship passed in front of him on its way to Miami. Some passengers waved from a distance. In the afternoon, he saw two motor yachts and one sailboat. David awoke just before darkness fell.

It was night when they neared Cuba. Fishing boats using gas lanterns to attract the fish bobbed on the sea. As they neared the boats, coastal lights became visible. Then, the glow of a small city on the Cuban coast lit a portion of the sky to the north of their position. To the north, the phosphorescent spray of an approaching boat flashed. Juan presumed it was a Cuban patrol boat due to its speed.

Juan turned to the south, pushed the engine controls forward. After a while, the patrol boat's lights fell behind the horizon. Juan then turned west and ran fast, paralleling the Cuban coastline. A half hour later, he turned toward the southern coast of Cuba.

"Do you think the crew of the patrol boat know where we are going?" asked David with an edge to his voice.

"They know nothing about us."

"Because of the pirated ship, they may be looking for us."

Juan nodded agreement, "Because of the piracy we must take care of business before it gets worse. Set the Loran for the beach near Sergio. Do not mention our piracy of the Argentine bastards. The true pirates are the rich who rule nations for their own pleasure and wealth."

Juan turned the boat onto the new course. He slowed to conserve fuel and called Sergio on his VHF radio.

"I am here waiting for you. You are late," Sergio answered.

"We had a problem with a patrol boat. Is it safe?"

"I have some soldiers from the army to protect you. Bring the boat onto the land where I am holding the lantern."

Using his depth finder, Juan steered the boat towards the shore. A hook of land partially protected the little beach.

"I see your lantern," said Juan into the radio.

"Come . . . put the boat onto the sand. We will cover it with old cloth and netting. It will look like a fishing boat. No one must see it because it is new and with good motors. There are no motors like that in Cuba."

David asked his brother, "Will he double-cross us?"

Juan made no response as he edged the boat close to shore. Still in deep water, he gunned the motors, then turned them off and lifted them out of the water with the hydraulic engine lifts. The bow of the boat slid six feet onto the beach.

Sergio stood with the soldiers. At his signal, they came and pulled the heavy boat further onto the beach.

"It is a great pleasure to see you, Juan," said the Cuban as he shook the pirate's hand.

"No, Sergio, the pleasure is mine."

Sergio led them to a nearby fisherman's shack. Inside, Sergio poured drinks and handed Juan and David a cigar. "It is only the best."

The men smoked and took a drink of rum. After small talk, Sergio asked, "What is so important that you come from Haiti to see me?"

"The cruise ship," replied Juan.

"Yes, the information is in my office. Soon, I will have more. Tomorrow, we will make it a big story."

"You must make it a very small story."

Sergio stared at Juan for a moment, smiled, and then laughed. "I should have known that you were the pirate."

"I did not say that I was the pirate. But I do want the news in Cuba and around the world to say that only a little was stolen, no one was hurt, and the ship got away safely. You may even say that the pirates were killed or maybe that the ship ran them over."

"*Si, compadre*, I can help. But it will be expensive. I will have to pay many who work for me in the news department. Officers in the navy and people on the docks all will demand money. Also, I must tip these soldiers. It will be very expensive."

"How much?" asked Juan.

"Three hundred thousand dollars, in cash," replied Sergio.

"You are a thief."

"Do not insult me. You are in my country."

"I will not pay what you charge. It is too high. I will do nothing. I was not the pirate. I am just trying to protect myself from those who give pirates a bad name."

Sergio looked at him. "Maybe you are not the pirate, but there will be news, and the Americans might look everywhere for the pirates. It will be very bad for your business, Juan."

"Give me a fair price. There is no money in Cuba; there is nothing. With dollars, you will do well. You can invest."

"The money must pay many."

"Give me another price."

"Two hundred thousand dollars for all and the news will not be bad—only a little damage, nothing that will alarm the Americans or any other government."

"I will pay $60,000 and give you $30,000 now. I will send you the second $30,000—if you do as you say, the news is very clean, and there is no problem. There is no money in Cuba. What I offer is very generous."

"You know that when the ship returns to Argentina, there will be reports."

"Yes," answered Juan. "But by then, the news will be old, and you will dispute the news reports saying they are lies."

Sergio studied Juan for a moment before answering. "Give me the money."

Juan counted out $30,000 from his sea bag.

"The news will be good," Sergio said as he reached for the cash.

"I believe you," replied Juan.

Sergio escorted him back to his boat. It was not yet light, although the distant eastern sky was lightening. They took the covers off and pushed it back into the water.

"This is good business," said Sergio.

"Make sure that the news is good and then I will send the rest of the money."

"The news will be very good."

Sergio entered the water to his waist, shook hands with David, and embraced Juan over the edge of the boat. "Do not worry."

The day Juan left for Cuba, a worrisome rumor reached Maria's ears. People told her there was a tall white man, fluent in Creole and Spanish, walking the villages and countryside. He was talking to the people. Nothing as to his purpose was known, but he was an American and Americans can be good or they can be dangerous. In cases where there are dollars, people respond. If he were some type of police officer, then money would be paid for information. On the other hand, if he were an aid official, food and seed for small farms and businesses may possibly be distributed. If he were with the health department, medicine and medical help could be provided. The good thing was that, in her experience, other than for personal benefit, the people would have little desire to know him—a white man of a foreign nation and culture.

After talking with several individuals, Maria learned the American got up early each day. He would find and pay for breakfast in one of the local houses. He would walk and visit new places, and revisit places he had already been. After a while, he visited Juan's village. Maria tucked her gun into her belt—any US government worker could report the work of the pirates.

That evening, Maria drank with the men on a corner of the main village dirt street. Someone said, "The American is very pleasant. He talks and only asks about the people, their health, and families. He may be mentally simple and he walks alone."

There was speculation that he carried money. But he did not have the look of someone with money and those who were thieves worried that if he were a US agent, reprisals would come if they robbed or killed him. No one had yet attempted to harm the man.

When Maria reported the events to Ivan, he paid attention and carefully considered the matter. He told Maria, "No worry. My father is protected both by the army and police authorities. He has been very generous. The officers of the army and police are his friends and because of Juan, they are not in poverty. Their children go to school. Others have good jobs and are powerful because of him. Only direct action by the United States could threaten my father. One American can do nothing."

After speaking with Maria, Ivan's thoughts turned to the wealth, power, and revenge he had seen on board the Argentine cruise ship. He contemplated the shootings between the old men who used the distraction of the pirates to settle old scores. He concluded that abuse of power, above a certain level, brought deadly revenge.

Ivan thought of his life. Raised on petty crime, piracy, and other illicit activities, he wanted part of the life he saw on board the cruise ship—life in society. And suddenly, seemingly from nowhere, something previously not considered important— he now wanted respectability and honesty. He wondered why such thoughts came to him.

Without realizing it, the genes of his mother's family and an inherited self-assurance were surfacing. The daring, impulsiveness and sharpness of action he learned from his father connected with the attributes of past generations. Surprising himself, Ivan searched his mind for someone who could help him in the transformation—someone to train him in business, manners, speech, and whatever else he needed to succeed. He found no one.

The following day, Juan's boat approached the coast of Haiti just after noon. Juan was still thinking about the prostitute country known as Cuba. Virtually everything was for sale. Corruption did not surprise him—he lived safely in Haiti because of it. What did surprise him was the ease with which the Cubans sold themselves and how completely they rewrote the truth.

Juan shook his head and focused. The low mountains behind the coastal plain were visible from afar. Arriving at his beach, he ran his boat onto the sand. He left David to find crewmen to carry it further ashore. He walked to his house.

Maria was the first to find him. She entered the open door to his house. "Chief, there is a tall American walking throughout the area. Many say he is an agent of the government. Americans come and take people to America to put them in jail."

"How many Americans are there?" asked Juan, looking at Maria.

"One. A tall man," said Maria.

"I am not worried about one American. If you want, go and see where he goes and what he does. Do not be afraid of one American."

After Maria left, Ivan came by. "Juan," he said, "I want to talk to you."

Juan nodded and motioned for him to get a cup of coffee. Ivan poured the coffee and sat down in front of the pirate.

Ivan said, "There is an American . . ."

Juan stopped him. "Maria told me. I don't think it is important, but I told her she could watch and see what he is doing."

Ivan nodded.

Juan looked at his son. There was something different on his face. "Are you worried about the American, Ivan?"

"No."

The two men sat drinking their coffee. The geckos moved up the wall and swayed their necks to look at them. The light in the room was that of early morning, without brilliance. The roosters crowed before the barely rising sun.

Ivan poured another cup of coffee and looked at his father. "I do not want this life."

Juan looked at him. The comment did not surprise him. He had seen his son begin to change. The transformation that can occur in a man in his early twenties was happening with his son. A new person was emerging from the boy turned youth who had grown into a man. He saw in him the ability to lead, to think, to take action, and to learn. He also saw the raw hope and stamina of youth, yet undamaged by life experience.

Being blunt, confident, and without vulnerability, Ivan stated, "I want to go into honest business. I need someone to teach me."

Juan had plunged into smuggling illegal Haitian immigrants into the US, and later drugs, and still later piracy. He had not been prepared in any of those areas other than by observing others and listening to what people said. Juan took sips of his whitened coffee. He reasoned that perhaps Ivan could be fortunate in a straight business.

"What do you want from me?" asked Juan.

"Help," responded his son.

"I will consider it," Juan said in a flat tone.

He got up and poured himself another cup.

Sitting down, Juan said, "The trip to Cuba was a success. Little news of the piracy is known, and that which is coming is not the truth. The news reports will be what I paid the government official to report. They will make up a story; maybe say a ship was boarded, but that the pirates left a short time after. There will be no report of the deaths. The ship will return to Argentina from Cuba. The Argentines will report the truth, but the news will conflict with that out of Cuba, and it will be old news by the time they return. The Americans will do nothing. The news will be old and Argentina far away."

"When the rich find out that no one will do anything, what will happen?" asked Ivan.

Juan looked unconcerned and gave no response, but in his heart he wondered if they would hunt him. They certainly had the money to do so.

Juan shrugged the question off.

After his son left, the pirate sat with his cup of coffee in hand and rubbed his lined forehead. His mind ran down an internal labyrinth. He remembered an old business associate, Fernando. When he worked in Puerto Principe people who had fled their own country, often in poverty or with few resources, came to him for work for favors. Fernando was one such person. Now he was a successful businessman and a citizen of Haiti. Fernando knew the social and business world.

Juan called Fernando by a telephone patch through his radio. Surprised to hear his voice, Fernando said, "You are my old friend, Juan. Yes, come to my house."

Driving an old Ford Bronco, Juan made the trip from the southeast coastal plain to the hills above Puerto Principe, where the prosperous live above the filth of the city.

FERNANDO, THE ARISTOCRAT CUBANO

A thin, very Black servant opened the high metal gate to the estate, then led Juan past a security station, occupied by two armed guards, to the house. Fernando received him at his front door with a warm embrace. In Cuban-accented Spanish, he said, "*Que bueno verte capitán.* I haven't seen you in a long time."

Juan responded, "The pleasure is mine to see you, my friend. You look good, *mi amigo Cubano.* I can see you are doing well and prospering, even more than I am told."

Fernando remembered his arrival from Cuba. Well-educated but with no money, he came from a family that was wealthy before the revolution. They were blacklisted as counter-revolutionaries and his family's goods confiscated. He was forced years after the revolution to flee to Haiti. Juan gave him a job on one of his boats transporting illegal immigrants, some of them Cubans, to the US.

Fernando's house of French Colonial design was constructed of painted, textured concrete. It featured a large covered porch which overlooked the sloping land. The distant ocean was visible. The elevation moderated the worst of the humidity. His property was landscaped and surrounded by a concrete wall with barbed wire on top. Noisy birds perched in the trees.

The two men sat on the porch in large wicker chairs. They appraised each other and smiled. A little amazed at the persona of his friend, Juan said, "I always knew you were very capable. That is why I invested in your idea to make baseballs. But I did not think you would look like you should be the president of Cuba."

Fernando had indeed prospered, and with his educated, aristocratic family background, he easily found a place in Haitian society. He also established himself, in a lesser way, in the Dominican Republic through his business dealings in land speculation and investments in the timeshare industry.

"I will be president, and you will be admiral of my navy. I will put you in charge to stop the pirates," said Fernando in Spanish.

"I will stop the bastards, and then I will take all the business," laughed Juan.

"You think like a Cuban," said Fernando with a genuine smile.

In the years since Juan's last visit, Fernando had become entirely middle-aged. His hair was partially grey, his hairline receded, and he was quieter, more reserved, more like his wealthy Cuban ancestors. He was aristocratic in manner, but it was his air of competence that had caused Juan to believe in him years ago.

The conversation drifted, touching many topics. The hours passed as the two men talked of the intervening years and the successes, failures, gains, and losses they had experienced.

Juan told Fernando, "I no longer transport people. I am a simple, aging pirate."

Fernando looked at his old friend. "You have always been a pirate at heart. It is deep within you."

Juan asked, "Do you still manufacture baseballs?"

"Yes, in Haiti and Mexico, and also I make other sporting equipment," replied Fernando. "But I do more. I manufacture some electronics. Business is good. I am cautious. I am honest. I do everything correctly."

Fernando had become the man Juan had foreseen. He did not doubt that Fernando's businesses were not only profitable, but also reasonably generous to his employees. In a poor country that could be difficult as people with money made their fortunes through manufacturing at a low cost because they paid their workers *una miseria*—very little. That was the way of all of Latin America, and even more, the way of Haiti.

"How are your wife and children?" asked Juan.

"Well. They are in Miami, shopping. There is a big party planned, and they needed new clothes," replied Fernando.

Fernando's family was on everyone's party list. Juan remembered the wife, a beautiful woman of mostly French blood.

Fernando, for his part, was not surprised at what he saw in Juan. Juan had been raised in a survival environment first in Colombia then in Puerto Principe, Haiti where his American mother abandoned her family. He had experienced too much. Life and hard experiences had marked him. He was a pirate, although he did not excessively look the part. He was solidly built, reasonably handsome, in a Latin way. Fernando had seen his charm, easily winning the hearts of women, among them Elizabeth, Ivan's mother. Men respected him and feared him. What most had impressed Fernando was Juan's energy and reckless entry into life. From rejection and hard survival that had been his early years, Juan had created a life—that of a prosperous pirate. From rejection and without money at the beginning, he had built a good business of pirating yachts. Through being generous with poor crew members and others, he had formed a life with friendships and loyalty among those who had worked for and with him.

The two men spoke long and laughed much— Juan with his hardy pirate's laugh, and Fernando with his aristocratic laugh. The years that had intervened seemed nothing to the men. The inflections of their voices, the tone of the words, were as the men remembered. Neither man had become heavy, the form of their faces and bodies familiar.

After a lengthy conversation, Juan said, "*Amigo*, you remember my son Ivan?"

Fernando's life with Juan had coincided with the latter part of Juan's marriage to the Dominican woman Elizabeth. She was in rebellion because of the persecution of her prosperous family in Santo Domingo and had hooked up with Juan. Fernando was then poor and a nobody, Elizabeth had taken no notice of him. He remembered their little boy who Elizabeth and her family abandoned. On her side, the boy had blue blood heritage. In response to the question, Fernando nodded.

Juan continued, "Already, he is in his early twenties. He has grown, and he does not want my life. He wants to learn business."

Fernando wondered if Ivan, after his lifetime with Juan, would be able to leave his past behind. Knowing the success of his mother's family and that of his father, Fernando mused that just possibly there could be an honest future for Ivan.

Out of obligation, Fernando would have accepted the responsibility of recreating and training Ivan, but there was much more to Fernando's consent. There was his friendship with Juan and curiosity about Ivan. He also intuited that there might be a good business opportunity with Ivan.

They agreed that Ivan would go to Fernando and Fernando would train him. "I will take charge of the young man. Do not worry, my friend. If he will learn, I will see that he is taught all that he must know about business and business life."

After a pause, Fernando added, "The timeshare business is a very good business now."

MISFITS

T he American continued to walk throughout southeastern Haiti. Maria reported that people were beginning to accept him and invite him into their houses. After a while, Juan feared that in time the American would learn of his operation. He assigned crew members, in turns, to discreetly follow him.

After a period, the American began speaking about Jesus. The people listened politely; they had heard of the Christian God, but most people practiced and belonged to a religion of Spiritism and Voodoo. Being aware of the spirits and afraid of them, they were careful not to say anything against Jesus for fear that he would punish them, as did the Voodoo spirits when not appeased. One day the situation changed when a child was dying and Peter, the American, was called to pray. The child healed almost instantly. Peter, who had never in his life seen someone healed in response to his prayer, was the most amazed of all.

After learning of Peter's preaching, Juan was no longer concerned about him. But when a small group of Peter's converts planned to have a meeting not far from Juan's base, out of precaution Maria was assigned to attend. The night was lit only by the moon and a few flashlights. The stars were bright. It was the end of hurricane season, and clothing no longer stuck firmly to the skin. There was dust in the air. Maria chose to stand at the very outside of the small circle of people.

Peter felt something oddly strange in his heart that night. He thought to himself that he had never felt something similar.

In a loud, though pleasant voice, Peter began to speak of the love of God. Maria wondered why Juan had even bothered sending her to the meeting. She crossed her arms.

Peter stared at the beautiful young Latin woman who stood apart from the others. It seemed that he had seen her somewhere before, but could not place her.

Maria looked at Peter. She had seen him many times, but until that moment, she had never really seen him — a simple man. Dressed in outdated US clothing, he was handsome in a way, well-built, tall with an evenly proportioned face that appeared kind and without guile. How could she ever have been afraid of him? For a moment, she remembered her dream of a husband and family.

Maria stared at him, turned, and left.

The months passed slowly. Many nights, Ivan lay sleepless for hours. The day's events and teachings were difficult. Even in bed, he tried to wrap his mind around the lessons about polite conversation, social customs and social manners, banking, economics, real estate, accounting, legal concepts, and business practices that the teachers and Fernando drilled into him.

As time went on, Ivan became impatient and angry. Fernando, though, did not decrease the pressure. Instead, he explained to Ivan, "Castro stole my family's money and life in Cuba. I hated him. Then I had the great pressure and hardship of staying alive in Haiti. I had to learn to work hard and release all anger, forgive, and to go on . . . no matter how I felt. You must learn the same because it is the great secret to success in everything."

Lying in bed, frustrated, angry, and not appreciated, Ivan struggled to apply the business lessons that Fernando taught him. He re-thought what he learned at work: business structure and productive tasks — from ordering raw materials to production, to shipping and accounting. He struggled at releasing the resentment he felt and forced himself to forgive his teachers who, with contempt, demanded he quickly learn all aspects of the business, its customs, and rules of personal behavior.

Eight months after entering into training with Fernando, his uncle David called him from a hotel in Puerto Principe. Ivan joined him for dinner. Before ordering, Ivan exploded. "I hate every day. I study. I work. I am continually corrected. I seem to do nothing right, and when I do something right, no one notices. Life was easy as a pirate. I did what I wanted until I had to board a yacht and steal. Afterwards, my life was my own. I enjoyed fishing and the women. I did not know how good I had it."

David looked at his younger nephew, and after some thought and soul searching, responded, "Yes, life as a pirate can be easy at times, but is it really what you want? I am also ready for a change. If I had an opportunity like you, I would take it. I don't want to be a pirate, but rather want other people around me besides pirates and the poor. I also want a good woman. Not the woman of a pirate."

Ivan looked at his uncle and remembered what he saw on the Argentine ship. "Yes, I want much more," he said.

"This may be your only chance Ivan for a life which is not piracy or poverty. If you want to change, pay the price for it now."

"I don't know if I can do it. I hate my life."

David ordered a bottle of aguardiente.

Ivan had known little in the way of imposed discipline, but his hard life on the streets of Puerto Principe and later with the pirates had taught him stamina and self-motivation. That stamina and discipline coupled with his total, even angry, determination to succeed — produced in him a will to make the change no matter the cost. That enabled him to endure the intense, painful, and unrewarding experience he was living. Even so, his self-control and strong-will were barely sufficient to continue on. When most on the edge, he went to a night club and bought the prettiest prostitute for the night. It gave him relief.

Nonetheless, Ivan's stomach and head still hurt every day. His mind was full of information that didn't fit together in a pattern. Every part of him felt like the proverbial square peg being forced into a round hole. He felt pinched everywhere. He concluded that true pleasure was impossible, and success if it existed at all, was distant. He continued on by every day applying the lessons Fernando kept insisting were the most important—perseverance, forgiveness, and release. By doing so, he did not hit anyone or tell anyone off. He did not live in anger and did not even seriously offend anyone.

Many nights, Fernando was also unable to sleep. He used antacid pills for his stomach. Ivan's teachers often came to him and reported, "*Señor, the young man just doesn't get it.* I don't think he will learn." As a result, many times in the first half of the year, Fernando considered telling Juan: "It is not working." It was only Ivan's acceptance of the discipline without causing serious problems that prevented Fernando from making him leave.

Finally though, Ivan connected the pieces he learned. The teachings became relevant to a greater whole as he learned how to think more profoundly. As he grew, Ivan began to envision a new life that was not just a dream, but something concrete. When the vision became more real, he began to become the new person who would live it.

A year after Ivan's arrival, Fernando said to him, "There is a special party in my club next week. I want you to come."

Ivan stared at him. Not knowing what else to say, he responded, "Okay. I will."

An actor playing a role, Ivan, costumed in a tuxedo and patent leather shoes, entered the club at Fernando's side. He held himself and walked as he had been taught; he greeted the people as instructed. He talked about the things he was told to discuss. He ate in the way he had been shown. He smiled and laughed at the appropriate times.

At the end of the evening, Fernando said, "You talk, eat, and behave within the limits of what is acceptable, Ivan, but you do not seem like you were bred to the social class. Still, you did well. You are not the pirate's son—just a cowboy."

Ivan was not sure how to respond to the word 'cowboy' but figured it was more acceptable to be a cowboy than a pirate.

"Working at the baseball plant helped me understand the lessons," Ivan responded.

"More importantly, use the torment from jealous and condescending plant managers as an opportunity to master controlling yourself. Due to your past and the risk of discovery, you will have to be strong in self-control. You are being taught skills for business and life, but I am also molding you into a man who will be successful."

FIREFIGHT

The steel-hulled De Fever motor yacht was on a long shakedown cruise after being repowered and refitted in Caracas. In Martinique, one of the yacht's crew members fell sick, and a man who scouted prey for Juan took his place. He told Juan that the Venezuelan owner, a banker and industrialist, had stopped at ports on both the Leeward and Windward Islands where he and his guests gambled in the casinos and had lost little and won big. He gave Juan the ship's course, exact cruising schedule, interior layout, passenger list, and location of the safe. He also reported that there was at least $300,000 in cash in a compartment located in the owner's stateroom and that the captain and mate each carried a large caliber pistol. Otherwise, the ship was unarmed.

The yacht's crew was made up of three men and a woman: the captain, a mate/engineer, a steward/deckhand, and the cook/maid. Their accommodations were in the forward part of the ship. Aft of the crew's quarters, there was an owner's suite and two guest cabins. The owner and his wife occupied the owner's stateroom; their daughter, son-in-law, and their young child shared a cabin. A fellow manufacturer and his wife shared the third cabin. The women wore expensive jewelry, and the men wore expensive watches.

After making preparations, Juan and his pirate crew departed Haiti to intercept the yacht along its course to the Yucatan Peninsula.

The yacht's captain was an exacting and careful man. He kept to set schedules and courses in an almost neurotic fashion. The yacht departed the island almost to the minute of the scheduled time. Extreme in his ways, the captain preferred to be in the pilothouse when underway. He was rarely found in his small private cabin; he chose instead to rest and take short naps on the pilothouse settee. That night, the captain awoke from his nap about midnight and took the helm. The mate was not yet tired, and the two men talked.

As the large yacht approached the location where the pirates awaited, Juan reasoned that the yacht would almost certainly be piloted by the mate or the seaman, and the yacht's radar, if turned on, would not be watched. It was common that a yacht's captain, oftentimes the untrained owner, did not consult the radar in good weather. From his position to the north of the yacht's course, he planned to wait until the large boat passed him then approach it from behind. He figured that his presence would not be known and that it would be easy to board and rob the yacht.

But Juan was wrong. The yacht's radar was turned on, and the captain consulted it often. He spotted the pirate vessel when it was still thirty miles away. It took him only a short time to decide that the vessel might be unfriendly.

The captain told the mate to inform the owner of the danger. The mate found him reading in the salon. "*Señor*, the captain says there is a boat to the north of us. He says it has altered its course." Speaking more rapidly, the mate added, "Boats disappear. People say they sink in storms, but many believe that Colombian drug smugglers use the boats to transport drugs, and then sink them."

"How near are they?"

"The captain says they are thirty miles out."

"The bastards will not get this boat," said the defiant owner as he stood up. He put his reading glasses on the table.

"What do we do, Capitán?" asked the mate.

"Wake up everyone. Tell the women to go to the inside bathroom and stay there. The steel hull will protect them. Tell the steward to go to the pilothouse."

The steward had been wrong about the ship's armament. The owner kept a secret locker concealed behind the back wall of his closet. In it were four automatic assault rifles, ammunition, and several pistols. Going to his stateroom, the owner opened the secret locker and removed the assault rifles. Within minutes, he appeared in the pilothouse with the weapons.

If the owner had known the approaching vessel was only a pirate boat, he would have hidden his money and let himself be robbed rather than risk a firefight; but he, too, had heard the stories of boats taken by smugglers from which the crew and passengers disappeared.

Juan approached the yacht with little sense of concern. He trailed the vessel, approaching it at good speed. Two pirates and Maria, armed with pistols, were in the bow prepared to board the yacht. Automatic rifles, loaded and ready, were clipped into brackets on the inside of the hull of the pirate boat for ready use in case the yacht defended itself.

The yacht's owner had been an officer in the army. The captain had previously skippered a mega-yacht owned by a very rich man who had sent him to school to learn how to defend his huge yacht. The mate and the male passengers were less experienced with arms but had used weapons for hunting or practice. The owner of the yacht put the steward at the helm.

Now well-armed, the captain and the yacht's owner positioned themselves at the stern, protected by the steel hull. The owner on one side, the captain on the other. The mate and the passenger with the most experience with weapons were on opposite sides of the ship. The other male passenger was positioned near the cabin door. The women were given pistols. Juan's man, the steward, alone in the pilothouse, piloted the yacht.

Aware of the ship's armament and the danger to the approaching pirates, the steward was fearful. He had assumed the pirating of the ship would be a simple affair. Now, he realized the pirates were in danger. They were approaching a ship with a crew fully aware of their presence, armed to defend it, and protected by the ship's steel hull. He wondered if the pirates would kill him after encountering the armed vessel. He frantically searched his mind for a way out.

The men on the yacht trained their weapons aft, aiming into the darkness, crouched behind the ship's steel hull. Juan's boat could not be heard over the sound of the yacht's diesel engines and the noise of its wake.

The yacht's radar showed the approaching boat less than four miles astern. The black hull of the pirate vessel hid it in the night. The owner told the men on board to wait until he shot first, then to rake the darkness with bullets.

Juan could easily see the lights of the yacht. It proceeded on the same course and at the same speed. The matter seemed simple. He was about to give the final order to prepare to take the vessel when he noticed that the yacht was changing course, veering off to the port. The change was slow but steady—ten, twenty, almost thirty degrees.

The course change made Juan wonder. Mexico, the vessel's destination, lay dead ahead. Still distant, the ship should not change course. "There is something wrong," he said to his crew. Everyone looked towards the yacht.

As he got a little closer to the vessel, Juan strained to see through the night. On the unlit aft deck of the yacht, he barely detected small shadows above the combing. The pirate pulled the throttles to idle and let the ship move ahead.

The yachtsmen were too focused to detect the change in their course, and then the shift back to the original course. When the pirate boat did not appear, the captain made his way to the pilothouse to look at the radar: the pursuing boat was far aft.

He returned to his armed men and huffed, "The bastards are not approaching. Perhaps they saw us."

Juan stood at the helm of the pirate vessel and contemplated his course of action. He could now clearly see shadow figures on the stern of the yacht. A short time later, the yacht's defenders shot into the darkness. Juan and the pirates saw the flashes of light from the defenders' rifles. Juan let his boat fall farther aft of the yacht to ensure that they were out of range.

"The bastards are defending," uttered Juan to Maria, who had come to his side. "The sons of bitches, I will teach them a lesson."

To David and Maria, he said, "Prepare the little boat." He pushed the throttles forward and banked his boat into a hard turn to the starboard, and well out of gun range of the defenders.

The pirate boat flashed across the sea. Spray from the boat's sharp entry into the waves poured out from each side of the bow. Inside the careening vessel, David and Maria struggled to inflate the Zodiac from a compressed air tank.

"Brother, slow down," yelled David.

On board the yacht, the owner stood up and said, "They left."

The captain walked forward to the pilothouse. On the radar, he saw the pirates ahead of the yacht, running away at high speed. Returning to the aft deck, he said, "They are ahead of us and going very fast."

The owner said, "I do not trust them. They have a plan." When the boat disappeared from the radar, the owner began to relax. "We have beaten them," he said to the crew and his guests. They opened two bottles of champagne and toasted their victory.

Juan did not give up his plan to board the yacht. He ran the pirate boat fast and hard. After an hour and a half of reckless speed, Juan stopped the pirate vessel more than fifty miles ahead of the yacht.

David tried to persuade his brother to return to shore. "It is very dangerous; they know we are hunting them. They will see even the little Zodiac on their radar. It is better to forget hunting this yacht."

"The little rubber boat is small. If they see it on the radar, they will think that it not a danger to them. Also, I will distract them. The sons of bitches will not escape." Juan motioned to Pilar, an older Cuban woman, and to Stephen to get into the little boat. Stephen looked at Juan and said, "If I die, take care of Isabela."

"It will be well. I have a plan. Get in," ordered Juan. Reluctantly, the older man lunged into the boat, causing it to take on water along one side.

Pilar looked at Juan, her face bitter.

Maria climbed in last. "I don't care if I die," she said as she jumped into the inflatable with her face mask and weapons.

"My plan will protect you," Juan said.

Pilar made the sign of the cross.

Juan turned his vessel around and headed out to sea perpendicular to the yacht. When his radar indicated that the yacht was within 10 kilometers of the Zodiac, he turned and ran his boat towards it at high speed. Out of range, he pulled even with it and switched on the high-powered lights mounted on the radar arch. The pirates with Juan began firing at the yacht even though it was out of range. The yachtsmen occasionally fired back.

As the yacht approached the Zodiac, Maria steered her mini pirate vessel toward the side to a position located just aft of the pilothouse. Pilar, hardened by an awful life full of disappointments and poverty in Cuba, then re-hardened by the devastation of Haiti and her inability to keep a man, had her own plan. As Maria steered the Zodiac toward the yacht, Pilar pulled the pin on a grenade and tossed it onto the yacht's forward deck. It landed just forward of the large windlass where it bounced high off the deck and exploded.

The first Maria knew of the grenade was at its detonation. The windlass lit up and was partially torn from its mountings. The blast was deflected forward, but caused the windows in the pilothouse and forward cabin to shatter.

Bleeding from the shattered glass, the steward pulled the throttles of the two diesel engines to idle. Surprised and stunned by the explosion, the captain and owner ran forward to look at the damage.

Brow compressed, with adrenaline coursing through his veins, an angry and worried Juan shoved the throttles to their stops and ran hard for the stopped yacht guessing she was now unguarded.

Juan's boat ran recklessly against the mounting wave chop, the bow digging into the swells. It veered dangerously into the wave troughs. The crew pulled their masks over their eyes and un-holstered their guns. Emotionally heightened and with heart pounding, Juan thought only of taking the yacht—at any cost.

Forgetting about Juan in their surprise at the explosion, the yachtsmen stood on the foredeck. The captain turned on floodlights to inspect the damage. Out of the corner of his eye, he caught sight of the Zodiac off the port bow. He turned his rifle on it and started shooting.

It took a moment for Maria to realize they were under fire and in range. She turned the Zodiac and ran away into the darkness. The owner continued firing even after the little boat disappeared into the night. Only two bullets hit. One hit Maria in the chest, the second grazed her cheek and then her ear, taking some of the lower lobe with it.

Maria felt the impact, but not the pain. Far from the yacht, she turned off the Zodiac's engine, and with her flashlight looked at her chest. There was much blood, and a small amount came to her mouth. She did not notice the wound on her face or her bloody ear.

Pilar, trained as a nurse before the worst part of the hardness and disappointments of life had overcome her, bandaged Maria with

Maria's clothing and a piece of her own. She quickly realized that Maria's lung had been struck.

Maria said, "God is paying me for the evil I have done." She lay back in a swoon; her face twisted in pain.

As Juan's boat nudged up against the yacht, he rushed forward and leaped off his boat and over the gunnels of the yacht to land on the aft deck. David followed.

Juan was the first to see the yacht's male occupants. They were forward looking at the damage and to sea. Juan saw no sign of the Zodiac—something was wrong.

"*No se mueven,*" ordered Juan to the crew. The surprised men turned, looked at Juan and David, and did not move.

At Juan's gesture, David took their weapons and threw them into the sea.

The owner and captain looked at each other.

"What do you want?" yelled the owner.

"I want the money. I may let you keep your lives if you do not make me more angry," responded Juan.

"I will go and get it," stated the yacht's owner.

"I will accompany you, but if you make me nervous, I will kill you," said Juan, motioning with his gun. Seeing women's belongings, Juan added, "And bring the women."

The owner remembered that he had given pistols to the women. As he approached the center portion of the boat, he yelled, "Love, do not shoot! I am with the pirates. Throw the pistols out the door."

The woman opened the bathroom door and threw them onto the hallway floor.

Juan kicked the pistols to David to pick up and then followed the owner. Returning to the salon with a bag of money, he handed it to

David. Leaving the yacht's owner, friends, and crew with instructions to remain in the salon, they went aft and returned to their boat. Maria was lying unconscious on the floor of his vessel, stained with blood. Stephen was deflating the Zodiac, its equipment on the floor of Juan's boat.

"Is she alive?" he asked.

"For now," stated Pilar without emotion.

Juan raced for the Haitian coast.

MARIA

During the pirate's run back to the coast of Haiti, the boat's movement almost took Maria's life. The vessel's motion did not allow the blood to fully clot. It was only Pilar's decades-old nursing training that kept Maria alive. As he steered for Haiti, Juan slowed the boat to reduce the intensity of the impact of the waves against the hull. Arriving at his house, to avoid the jar of hitting the beach, Juan stopped the boat near the shore. Stephen and another pirate jumped into the water and gently pulled the boat onto the sand.

Juan and David carried Maria to her house. Stephen drove to the Dominican Republic for a doctor. Isabela and Pilar took turns caring for Maria.

The bullet to Maria's chest had hit the edge of her lung and damaged a rib. Although she was mostly unconscious in the beginning, her lung and wounds responded to treatment. Her body started to heal. When she became rational and thought about her life, her condition stopped improving.

She whispered to Isabela. "If I die, make sure to take care of Mariana, my daughter, who lives at the convent school in Colombia. You know where I have buried some money."

Infection set in. The doctor came back and treated Maria with stronger antibiotics. After days of treatment the infection remained, although it did not worsen. The tissue stayed soft. As Maria lay there, she took stock of her life and knew that she had failed in every dream, hope, and promise. She so wanted to be a good girl, but instead she was a pirate rather than a saint. She hated herself, and her wish was to die.

As word spread of Maria's condition, Peter heard she was critically injured. He could not keep her name from his mind. He recalled that she was hard, but was also very pretty. Peter prayed for her day and night. Finally, he went to look for her.

By that time, the pirates all knew that Peter was a preacher. When a man came to Juan and told him that Peter was looking for Maria and wanted to see her, he was surprised, but not bothered. When Isabela told him the infection was worsening, Juan instructed a villager to take Peter to Maria. If nothing else, Peter could see that Maria would be buried with a religious ceremony.

The man led Peter to Maria's little house. There was no hardness in the dying woman's face. Only anguish.

Entering the room, Peter said, "Jesus loves you!"

Upon hearing his words, Maria focused through the haze of the infection. She stared at him as though he were a hallucination of God himself.

Peter sat next to Maria and put her hand in his.

Maria turned to him and thought, *he has come to hear my confession.* At length, she summoned her strength and with a semi-strong voice said, "Father . . ."

Peter stopped her. "I am no longer a priest."

Maria ignored him. "I have slept with more men than I can remember. I have stolen. I have done violence. Everything I dreamed of—everything—I lost. I used to be a good girl. I knew God in the convent and loved him. But I left him to become a pirate. Oh, I so wish that I were that little girl again. I would be good. I promise I would be good. The only good thing I do is to care for Mariana." With those words, she convulsed in weeping.

The defrocked, failed priest listened to her as she rambled through her tortured memories.

Her pain and self-hate rose to the surface. Her face hard, Maria spoke of herself in merciless terms. In an anguished, bitter tone she finished, saying, "I hate myself."

Although no longer ordained to do so, he absolved her of her sins. "Your repentance is acceptable to God, Maria. You are forgiven." Maria laid back, content, no longer tormented and was ready to die.

She responded, "Maybe God will forgive me, but I will never forgive myself." After a while, she sentenced herself to death. "I deserve to die."

Peter sat with her that day, holding her hand. Maria's condition worsened, and Peter prayed. She looked like a beautiful, fragile doll; her face only slightly scarred by the bullet that had grazed her cheek. From time to time, she murmured, "Father . . ."

The last time Maria addressed Peter as Father, he said, "After my mother's death, my father sent me to parochial schools. I was very lonely and missed my mother very much. The school was good for me. Although I had no, or few friends, the priests and nuns took care of me. I decided I wanted to become a priest. There came a moment when I was ordained and became a Jesuit. But I am not longer a priest, and you must not call me Father. I am defrocked."

There was a long silence. Then, through the infection and pain, Maria turned and looked at the simply dressed man sitting next to her. She noted his pained face. "Why are you in Haiti?"

"I was a missionary in Puerto Principe, the capital, and later in Santo Domingo, across the border. I learned Creole and Spanish and served the church and the people everywhere. I did well. But after some years, I got very sick and was sent back to the United States. When I was well again, I was given a church in a rural parish. Life there was very different. I was alone among people with families. At night, I drank the wine from the church. Then I tried to remember my mother, but I could barely remember her. My father died, and I have no brothers or sisters. I drank more."

Maria turned and looked at him. "Then you are a sinner, too?"

"I am a failure. I could not stop drinking. Many, many times, I tried. After many failed attempts to stop, my congregation talked to the bishop, and I was removed. I was sent to a rehabilitation center, but I left. I drank until I was drunk in the street. Eventually, they took away my ordination, and I was alone. I ate and slept in street rescue missions. One day, I had an encounter with Jesus, who, while I had preached about, had never encountered. That began a new life for me. Jesus became my friend.

"I became stronger. I worked in the kitchen of the rescue mission. I entered a program to become a street minister. I ministered to the people in the streets and became part of the mission staff. I tried to become a priest again and was rejected. But I was happy. I told people about Jesus, and some believed and became well. After some years, I wanted to return to Haiti. Some people at the mission and a few from my old parish gave me money, so I came here. Jesus is very kind," concluded Peter.

Maria kept her embrace on death for days. During that time, Peter told her the details of his many failures and losses. In those long hours, the two shared their pasts of failure, loss of self-esteem, and self-hatred. A bond of sympathy and caring formed between the two. Even through the haze of her infection, Maria heard Peter's loneliness and felt sorry for him.

After a few days, tired from little sleep, Peter stood up, stretched, and said, "Father God, I don't know how much more I can take."

Maria heard the despair of his tone. She turned her face toward the wall and stared at the cracks on it for a long time. When she turned back and looked at Peter, she saw thick anguish written across his face.

Still weak, she smiled at him and said, "I will help you." She began to heal.

Peter continued to care for Maria, and Maria began to take care of Peter.

Isabela saw what was happening and left the two alone. Juan visited her at times. After a while, Maria was strong enough to get out of bed, and Peter helped her walk. Her lung self-inflated; the air trapped in her shoulder dissipated. The infection healed, and the flesh became sound.

Peter left to preach again in the nearby towns. Juan sat with Maria in her house. One day, he said to her, "Peter told me that God won the battle for your soul."

Maria smiled her fresh, new smile and said with a curious look on her face, "I *was* a pirate, but now I am a saint."

Juan stared back. "You believe in that crap?"

Peter walked, talked, and preached as before, but something was missing: Maria. When she got stronger, he said, "Come with me."

From that day, Maria walked with him often. She carried his Bible, water, and some clothes. When walking far, they slept where invited. She told Peter, "I like being with you." Although they slept apart, in the darkness, Peter felt less lonely.

After some time, one day while standing outside of a stick and cardboard house in a small village, Maria said, "I was the one who needed to heal, but now it is your turn. I love you, Peter."

Peter turned aside to hide his tears.

THE ARISTOCRAT'S SON

van had been with Fernando for more than a year. It was late fall and the hurricane season had passed. Ivan was no longer the grown-up boy thief, turned pirate. He was the genetic son of his mother's family. He was also the seemingly adopted son of Fernando who had changed him into a fledgling aristocrat and serious businessman without taking away the imagination, willpower, and often reckless courage of Ivan's pirate heritage. In fact, it was that reckless courage that gave him the strength to attempt going into his new life.

Ivan and Fernando hunted property in the Dominican Republic suitable for building a resort. They visited the tourist areas and studied the pattern of development. Fernando contacted his business associate, Luis, the son of a well-connected political family with little money, but with considerable influence. In the recent past, he and Luis had developed a small timeshare project. Fernando's business experience and money, matched with Luis's connections, had made the construction process rapid, economical, and successful. Luis knew of some land in Barahona and took Fernando and Ivan to look at it.

Located in the relatively underdeveloped western part of the country, the property was flat with small islands in front of it. The town was pleasant enough. There was ample fresh water. Electricity, telephone, and other services were available. Although there were no large restaurants or resort services, there were smaller hotels. The highway from Santo Domingo was good, although the distance and absence of other major resort services made investing in the area risky. The price was low.

Ivan immediately envisioned a breakwater which could enclose a yacht harbor. He imagined docks, some mooring buoys, timeshare condominium buildings around the harbor with restaurants and shops, a road behind, and then houses, a small shopping area, and a golf course.

Fernando sent notice to Juan and asked him to meet them in the Dominican Republic. Curious, Juan made the car trip to Santo Domingo.

If Ivan had not been standing next to Fernando, the pirate would have walked by him, never giving a thought that he was his son. As though transplanted from another man, even Ivan's face was different. Instead of a skilled young thief, he looked like a thoughtful but alert young businessman. His casual clothes were those of a scion of a wealthy family, and that persona emanated from his inner self. When he spoke Spanish and Creole, his speech was devoid of slang and well accented. Under Fernando's guidance, with great effort and at times crushing internal turmoil, Ivan had become someone else—the lifelong heir apparent of a wealthy and sophisticated family. So little was left of the street urchin, the boy of the small country school, the pirate, that at length, Juan asked his son, "Who are you?"

"I am the son of a rich man and the son of the aristocracy," he answered with a cocky smile.

Smiling at the irony, and with an edge in his voice, Juan said, "Son, what you say is right. The aristocracy is on your mother's side, but I have the money."

"I have a plan for you to make much more," responded Ivan.

Juan stared at Ivan, and then looked away.

Later in the day, Ivan presented his plan for initial stages of a major resort development. Juan listened to and looked at the proposal which included a cost analysis and income projections, the expected development costs of breakwaters and major construction, and the sales strategies, and growth. The scope was impressive and the cost very high.

Juan laughed, "*Hijo*, I am a pirate, not a businessman. But even if I were interested—and I am not—I do not have the money for your project. It is too large."

"I know, but you and Samuel together have enough to finance the first stages. After that, the project will have the cash flow to finance itself."

Juan grew almost angry, but did not because of the change in Ivan and the laughable scope of the project.

Ivan said, "The investment is like the ship of the industrialists. There is great risk, but great reward."

Juan remembered that Ivan, although so much a new man, had been his second-in-command on the theft from the cruise ship. "Show me the plans again."

Fernando withdrew from the meeting to find coffee. Ivan opened the plans and went through them a second time with his father.

"There is great risk, but great reward," Ivan repeated.

Again, it was Ivan's almost magical metamorphosis that the suggested transformation of the land into a resort seemed possible to Juan. In his mind, the pieces went together much as they did when he planned the raid on the cruise ship of the Club de los Industriales.

Fernando returned with three cups of coffee.

"This development will create its own reality. People will come from around the world."

The more the men talked, the more Juan looked at the drawings, and the more Ivan took him through the stages of the proposed development, the more he began to see that the project could be made real. He was starkly aware, though, that the project would require not only all his money, but that of Samuel also. Even then, he doubted they had enough money to finish the project.

The mature pirate, having lived a lifetime of risks on the sea and land, was not sentimental and would certainly not fund the project out of love for his son.

"I only take big risks if there are money and valuables in large quantity," said the pirate.

"This will make more money than anything you have done. *This* will make the money of the Industriales without the risk of reprisals," replied Ivan.

Leaning back comfortably in a chair, Fernando sat silently – his face was in neutral. Finally, he spoke. "Why did you send him to me if he is not to make the change a complete one? Luis and I will work with him. As in the past, we will make it work. Do you have the money?" asked Fernando.

"Life in Haiti is cheap. Women have always been free. My pleasure has been adventure, piracy, and sex. At Samuel's insistence, I have invested. I have stocks, gold, currency, and properties—but I do not know how much. Samuel manages the investments."

Halfway in jest, Fernando said, "Even if you lose the money, you can steal more."

After a long silence, Juan said, "Samuel has more money than me. I will fly to Barranquilla. I will speak with Samuel about the investment."

Fernando caught Juan's eyes and said, "You asked me to train Ivan."

Juan answered, "I have to be more careful what I ask for."

"Remember, *mi amigo*, that you asked me," restated Fernando in a clear voice with a tone that suggested that it was now Juan's turn.

"You always did your jobs very well. That was why I gave you the money for the baseball plant."

After the pirate's departure, Fernando said, "For the first time, he will steal as a capitalist. Fidel always said that capitalism was a license to steal."

PARAISO

Theodore's plane departed Puerto Principe on a virtually cloudless day. With ease, the old Piper Aztec climbed to the assigned altitude. There were wisps of clouds at the higher elevation. Juan, sitting in the copilot's seat, asked to fly the plane. After some difficulty in maintaining the altitude within 500 of that assigned, he said, "Theodore, the airplane behaves like it is in the hand of God when you fly and like a drunk when I fly."

"That is because you are a pirate and I am a gentleman," replied Theodore, in a deadpan voice.

Juan glanced at the suntanned, distinguished-looking pilot who he often paid to fly him where he wanted to go. The pilot wore his greying hair long. He looked like an aging hippie. "You fly money and marijuana from country to country. You are a smuggler, not a gentleman."

With a half-smile, Theodore replied in English, "As the saying goes, 'I am a gentleman and a scholar.' Those sayings are true in me. But, I have seen the corruption of lobbyists, businessmen, politicians, the legal system, and society—that is, those who claim to be righteous and are not. And I was tired of paying over sixty percent in taxes. I do not want to play with them or let them play with me. It is so much bullshit, although not all bullshit; nonetheless, they pissed me off, so now I smuggle to make money and live. But I remain a gentleman."

"So you think. Really, you are just crazy but very smart and clever. And you let sex interfere too much."

"I may be a little crazy, but I am still a gentleman, and you are a pirate. I should write a story, *The Pirate, and the Crazy Gentleman*," said the pilot.

Juan replied with sincerity and gusto, "You are a scoundrel. Maria is now a saint. And I am a pirate. I don't know what Ivan is, but all of you are bastards. My life is full of bastards. But, that is a pirate's life."

"I will change the name of my book then. I will name it, *Pirates, Scoundrels, and Saints*," responded Theodore, laughing. Juan caught a glimpse of the serious look in his eyes hidden behind rose-colored lenses.

"When you crazy Americano write your book, remember that it is my book. You all are in my life. It is my story."

"*Si, señor,*" answered the pilot in a mocking tone, given with a left-handed salute.

"At least one understands," said Juan with irony.

Theodore landed the plane at the Barranquilla International Airport. The temperature on the ground was mild. The wind blew fairly hard from the east.

After being checked by the narcotics police and clearing customs, Samuel picked up Juan and Theodore in a Land Rover. The traffic was light, and they arrived in time for lunch at two o'clock. Samuel's thin, feisty wife had prepared the food. The maid served.

While eating, Juan and Samuel bantered conversation between them for a couple of hours before Juan got to the point of his visit. Theodore remained silent.

"It is amazing, I can hardly believe it," he began, then paused before continuing with emphasis, "I have seen strange things, but never a transformation so great. Ivan's manner and expressions are different. His dress is that of a rich man. I would have passed my own son on the street and not recognized him."

The two men stared at each other.

Samuel inquired, "You old pirate, are you taking drugs or just losing your mind?"

"You know Fernando?"

"Yes, I know him . . . the aging Cuban from an aristocratic family. He is a good man. I know Ivan has been with him in Puerto Principe. And I have heard Ivan has changed."

At that, Juan told Samuel that Ivan desired to build a large timeshare development in Barahona on the Dominican Republic side of the border.

"I know Barahona. It is a nice *pueblito*. It is the end of civilization, but nice. Distant from Santo Domingo and hard to get to or from in times of traffic. I go there to fish. I stay in an old-style tourist hotel. It is clean, the food is okay, and it is on the beach. A very nice resort could work there—if the development were a destination resort. Otherwise, it would fail. There is too little happening in Barahona," commented Samuel.

The talk about the development, costs, risks, and structure went on into dinner and through a bottle of Scotch that Samuel brought out for Theodore.

Juan said to Theodore, "You are drinking all the whiskey."

"Scotch is my favorite," answered the pilot as he poured himself another big drink.

Samuel opened a bottle of *aguardiente*. Juan continued to explain Ivan's proposal.

Although Samuel spent as much of his life on the sea as possible, he was wearing his businessman's hat, and a risky investment was not on his mind.

After hours of the conversation going in circles, the half-drunk pilot scoffed. "Fuck, Sam, you are being an ass. Do it because it is bizarre. It is worth the ride just to see if Ivan can pull it off."

"You are drunk," responded Samuel.

"And you are a fake," said Theodore.

"*Calmense*," said Juan.

The pilot continued. "When you are a smuggler, you take big risks, and you do things just for the 'trip.' You take risks all the time. This is a risk, a trip, and an opportunity to make huge money. Fernando and Ivan will pull it off. And besides, Juan is maybe your only friend. Do it for him."

"I do not need anyone to do anything for me," said Juan.

"Mr. Macho, it is good to have friends. Be glad to have one," said Theodore.

After a long, thoughtful pause, Samuel said, "I will invest, but it is not for the money, but for my friendship with the pirate."

To which the pilot responded, "The people of crime sometimes are more loyal and better friends than are the people of honest business. I will invest the little I have."

At the end of the conversation, Juan turned to Samuel, "The project will take all our money . . . and maybe more."

Ivan and Fernando formed a Dominican company that they named *Paraiso*, meaning 'paradise' in Spanish. They funded Paraiso through a series of Caribbean and Asian companies, the stock of which was owned by another company or through a trust. Some of the stock was earmarked for the working partners—Ivan and Fernando, as payment for their work. At the end of the trail, the ownership of ninety percent of the stock would belong to Juan and Samuel. Fernando, Ivan, and Theodore together would own ten percent but would have no voting or management rights. The company would always be controlled by Juan and Samuel.

Ivan found suitable office space on the coast not far from the historical part of the city, near the beginning of the high rent district of Santo Domingo. He arranged to meet with the building owner at the leasing office.

Although in the tropics, the aging owner of the building dressed in a dark blue sport coat, collared shirt, and trousers that bore a sharp crease. Ivan arrived in a polo shirt, wrinkled pants, and loafers without socks.

Upon meeting Ivan, with an aggressive tone the man asked, "Young man, do you have any business experience?"

Ivan mentally reviewed his often-rehearsed conversation and etiquette lessons. The question, asked before a proper, initial greeting, did not fall within the models he had been taught. Ivan retracted his extended hand, stared at the man, and stood up straighter.

"There are many that look like you," said the building owner with disgust.

Ivan assumed the posture and facial expression that he had been taught to assume if slighted. The owner looked at Ivan again. From his expression, Ivan concluded that the man was making a second analysis.

After an awkward pause, the owner said, "Forgive me. There are many who make drug money and try to become businessmen, only to fail. Their business is bad, as are their associates. I do not do business with such people."

Ivan remained silent. Inside, he wondered if, after all his work, he could portray the person he was supposed to be and wanted to be. He also wondered if all his work was for nothing – because the Club of the Industriales would one day come after the pirates and find him.

The man interpreted Ivan's silence as being offended.

The owner extended his hand and introduced himself. Ivan met the man's weak handshake with his solid hand. He realized he could squeeze the man's hand so hard he could bring him to his knees. Instead, Ivan said, "I understand."

The man gave him a small smile in appreciation.

"I represent Paraiso, S.A. de CV. Paraiso is a resort and timeshare start-up. I am a junior member, and this is a job the administrators did not want to perform."

Handing the owner promotional information, he continued. "The first resort will be in Barahona, but the head office will be here in Santo Domingo. We, of course, have bank and business references."

The man looked at Ivan, slightly puzzled. It was clear that Ivan had breeding and skills, but he also had the air of something else.

"Tell me . . . have you ever been an actor?" asked the man, searching for an answer.

Ivan laughed. "Not anywhere you would have seen me perform."

"That explains something about you." Interpreting the answer that Ivan had been on stage, his doubt was almost satisfied.

"When I was much younger, I acted in community-theater," stated the man as they waited for the elevator. The office had a partial view of the ocean, was in good condition, and had an adjoining apartment.

After walking through the office, Ivan said, "This will work. We will need the apartment too."

With a slight doubt about Ivan's suitability, the owner handed him an application. Ivan gave him bank references and the business references provided by Fernando. Recognizing Luis' name, the man stood up and looked embarrassed. Luis' family was respected and well-connected.

After leasing the office and apartment, they were tastefully furnished by a decorator, and the new company began the process of purchasing land for the resort.

The property selected for the resort had two owners. The most important piece, the waterfront section, was willingly for sale and at a reasonable price; but the property behind was only begrudgingly on the market due to the financial need of the owners. When they found out that Paraiso wanted to buy the waterfront piece, the owners decided to hold on to the property for appreciation. When Paraiso did not close on the waterfront section, the owners of the back parcel lowered their price to recapture the sale, and Paraiso completed the purchase of the two parcels.

After finalizing the purchase, the architects, construction companies, and lawyers began their work. Under Fernando's experienced hand, through Ivan's likable personality and good manners, plus Luis's contacts, the project proceeded. Plans were formalized, permits issued, and contracts were put out to bid.

There were long meetings with government officials in which the partners sought, and got, concessions and help for the project. Key players seeking economic benefit or power over the project sensed money and opportunity. Fernando, Luis, and Ivan were courted by the high and powerful.

Relying on Luis's established reputation and introductions, the country's political and economic players only lightly analyzed Ivan. Quickly they discovered his connection with Fernando who had impeccable social standing and business experience, although mostly in Haiti. They assumed Ivan was a family member.

As in any large Caribbean business, the question of the capital source, the many millions of dollars required to fund a project, was open to discussion and speculation. There were always rumors that drug money was involved in any significant investment. However, there was no indication that was the case with Paraiso, and no one dared mention it to either Luis or Fernando.

Ivan was guardedly friendly and very observant as the business developed. He had given himself entirely over to his new identity and being sufficiently trained he passed as an educated and reasonably well-bred man; although, evidently, not altogether comfortable in his new business. On many days he took anti-acid tablets. Fernando knew that Ivan's skill level was still thin in places and jumped to his rescue on more than one occasion.

During the days and evenings, Ivan studied every part of the construction, of business, and law related to the project. Social invitations began to arrive. Lunches, dinners, and drinks with government officials, contractors, bankers, and with other businessmen became routine. Ivan and Fernando were invited into the best homes and social clubs. They joined the Santo Domingo Country Club, and during the hours in which the golf course was little used, Fernando began to teach Ivan to play golf. Ivan was active, but not a sportsman – his sports experience was limited to rough street soccer played with few rules. In mild desperation at the slowness with which Ivan picked up the game, Fernando selected a golf pro to teach him. After much practice, his game got better. Under Fernando's hand, step by step Ivan was transformed into a businessman, a learned developer, a man with a fair golf game, and a charming, occasionally offbeat conversationalist increasingly able to contribute insightful comments on many subjects.

As the months passed, no longer was Ivan seen as a much lesser person than Fernando, the mere presumed lesser family member, but rather as a person in his own right and someone worthy to know. When people thought him a bit odd, they presumed he was from one of the "provinces" and, therefore, not more socially skilled. It never entered the mind of anyone that he was the son of a pirate, an ex-pirate himself, educated only in a small, one-room schoolhouse on the southeast coast of Haiti.

THE TREASURE SHIP

W ho knows or fully understands the forces of life that bring change, opportunity, disaster, or good things? Or why a person does one thing and not another?

Although both Samuel and Juan suspected that they would need more money for Paraiso, it was not Samuel's intention to be involved in salvage work. To the contrary, it was very far from his mind. He and Juan had decided that if they needed more money for Paraiso, they would use Samuel's boat to take large amounts of marijuana from Colombia to Florida. However, there was a person pushing Samuel concerning a scuttled drug ship. There are lots of scammers in the Bahamas and Caribbean and Samuel didn't pay any attention to him. Finally, to put an end to the bother, Samuel met with him. He heard him out and rejected his offer, but the man still wouldn't go away. Worn down by his persistence, and thinking that Paraiso might need more money than he and Juan had, Samuel agreed to meet with him once again.

In Nassau, the two men met at the far end of the outside dining area in a somewhat rundown tourist restaurant which specialized in fried conch. They ordered the conch lunch special and drank coffee.

Henry, a tall, very dark man who spoke uncharacteristically good English with only a light Bahamian accent told Samuel, "I was there. The American Coast Guard was after us, so we sunk the ship. We let water into her forward and aft. She just settled in the water and went down bottom first, under us. We escaped to Grand Turk Island in the ship's launches. She is full of the best marijuana from Santa Marta."

"It will be wet and no good," said Samuel.

"No, no, the marijuana is carefully double-wrapped in plastic and sealed with duct tape so there would be no smell. That makes it watertight. It is a true treasure ship. The cargo is as valuable as Spanish bullion."

Samuel gave Henry a look that said, *you are exaggerating.*

The weather in Nassau was warm, but not hot. There was no humidity to drive the men into air-conditioning, so Samuel sat and listened, and studied the man as he told and retold the story. With each telling, the dark man added details in his attempt to close the sale.

At the end of the meeting, Samuel said, "I will think about it."

Not long afterward, Juan came to Nassau to discuss the continued funding of the Paraiso resort. "There is a man I know. His name is Henry. He is from here. He speaks well and does not seem crazy or like one of the scammers who promote some crazy business deal. Henry told me he was on a marijuana ship and that they scuttled it into about a hundred feet of water not too far from Grand Turk Island," mentioned Samuel.

"They did it to avoid the Coast Guard," observed Juan.

Samuel nodded, "What do you think?"

"Can we find it?"

"The man says he has Loran coordinates. I have depth and fish finders. If the coordinates are right, we should be able to find it. Henry says the marijuana is from Santa Marta, Colombia. There is very good marijuana called Santa Marta Gold. If it is that good, then it is a very good product. He also says that it was very carefully double-wrapped in plastic and sealed with duct tape so there would be little odor, and therefore, it should be dry."

Juan laughed. "For years you have claimed that your boat hunts sunken treasure ships. That is how you have explained your income. If you hunt this treasure, you will truly hunt gold."

"It is gold, not only in color. A ship full of Santa Marta Gold is worth many millions of dollars," said Samuel.

Juan looked at him, and after considering the statement, said, "Millions of dollars would help; the investment in Paraiso is a big risk. I think maybe we were crazy to do it."

"I have the navigation equipment, the depth finders, scuba tanks, compressors, the small crane, and many tools. We can go at any time," said Samuel with a smile and heightened interest.

Two weeks later, Juan flew to Grand Turk Island and met with Samuel and Henry on Samuel's vessel.

Minimally pitching forward and aft, Samuel's sixty-five-foot steel ship swung at anchor. From a distance, it looked something like a trawler yacht/exploration vessel with the pedigree of a small working ship. There was an ample aft deck. The hull was a hybrid, semi-displacement design that could go to a full plane with enough power. Her large turbo diesels were capable. At lower speed, she plowed through the sea. At a slow speed, with water ballast, she proved herself capable in heavy weather. Her hull was built to withstand rough use. The aluminum superstructure and decks were lighter to reduce weight.

Accommodations on board were commercial and designed not to shake apart with high speed or in heavy weather. The below deck area aft was set up for multipurpose use—sleeping, diving, and exploration, all to hide its real purpose as a hold to carry contraband.

On board, Henry repeated what he had told Samuel. "We sank the ship because the Americans were after us. We escaped in the ship's fast launches. Months have now gone by, and no one has done anything with the ship. The ship is full of gold-colored marijuana. It is the best quality. And there may be money in the safes."

Juan and Samuel looked at each other and laughed, "I do not know if we are becoming fools or just crazy," commented Juan.

"Maybe both," laughed Samuel. "There is danger from the Americans and from bad weather if we spend a long time looking for the ship."

The morning following the meeting, Samuel woke up early. Going to the galley, he smiled broadly, shoulders back. The air was warm and humid, the sea fairly calm. Seabirds were active, and fish were jumping. The sun, not much above the horizon, was rising slowly. He was soon to lift anchor, and he was enjoying his smuggler persona. Coffee in hand, he went to the foredeck. Life was good and got even better as the coffee energized him. At first, he felt like the American he had been raised to be; but then, in the sea landscape, he felt like the man from the Bahamas. When Juan, with his aging Latin appearance, came on deck, he felt like the Colombian national he also was through marriage.

Because of Henry's presence on board, Samuel spoke to Juan in English. Juan answered him in his good, but little-used English. As he spoke, his accent improved and the men continued to converse, but not with the directness of Americans. Samuel and Juan's conversations wound around subjects and concluded with what they wanted to say at the beginning.

The sky was clear, warm, the sea mostly calm, and the coffee good. The men continued their discussion about the scuttled drug boat. After much conversation, thinking maybe he would like to own the ship, Samuel said, "After we take the cargo, we could raise the ship."

"It would be easier with the cargo still inside. There is so much water displaced by the wrapped marijuana, it would not take much to refloat her," chimed Henry.

"Maybe we could raise the ship, but it is the cargo that is valuable. Why take the risk?" stated Juan, bursting Samuel's momentary bubble.

"The cargo is worth gold, the ship has little value," confirmed Henry.

No one made a move to start the engines, lift anchor, and get under way. To the contrary, when they finished their coffee, Samuel led Juan to the ship's salon.

Carmen, the only crew member accompanying Samuel on the trip, was in the galley. A large, but not too large, strong, brown-skinned woman from Colombia who lived in Nassau, she had worked for Samuel a long time. She made trips with him and, on occasions ran small, fast boats to Florida from the Bahamas. She could also cook and slept with Samuel when he desired her.

Henry came into the salon and sat with them as Carmen served breakfast. The day was still in slow motion. Samuel had recently spent much time on land with his family in Nassau. There, the false life, the lies, and the fear of being caught overwhelmed him, and he felt his life to be worthless and meaningless. On board his boat, Samuel felt free . . . and relaxed.

It was almost noon when they stood up, and Samuel and Juan climbed the stairs to the pilothouse. Carmen, accompanied by an attentive Henry, made her way aft where she lifted the ship's inflatable boat onto the deck using the small crane. The diesel engines were running and warm when she finished.

Juan went forward and activated the electric windlass. With a low grinding noise, the anchor chain rolled onto the deck and into the chain locker. As the anchor cleared the water, the windlass pulled it tight against the stainless steel pad welded onto the hull. The mud clinging to the anchor fell into the sea.

Samuel pushed the throttles forward, the small ship responded to the prop wash and sea against her rudder and its bow turned to the south.

It was early spring and not yet hot, but warm enough that the wind caused by the ship's movement brought a pleasant refreshing breeze. Clear of the sheltered Grand Turk waters, the sea came towards the small ship in long rolling swells that were topped by a wind-generated chop. As the afternoon opened up, the humidity climbed mildly.

The ship arrived at the desired coordinates late at night. Land was far from sight. There was no dock, only more sea swells and the whitecap waves on top of them that were driven by the incessant trade winds. Juan and Henry dropped the anchor. It took hold of the sea floor in about a hundred feet of water. The bow swung to the wind. The ship met the swells head on. Its motion was distinct as her bow dipped into the wave troughs, then rose as the swell swept towards her.

Samuel, Juan, and Henry joined Carmen in the vessel's mid-ship salon for a very late dinner. There the motion of the ship was less. Carmen prepared rice and fish lightly fried in oil until crisp.

Henry said, "Now at last, my ship has come in."

"We all hope that our ship will come in. Tomorrow, we will begin to look for her. We will begin with the coordinates you gave us and explore the seafloor in a grid pattern with the sonar," responded Samuel.

"The ship is there, and the coordinates are the ones that were written down before we scuttled her; although, we were still underway," stated Henry.

"The coordinates are not exact?" queried Samuel, a little surprised.

"They are close," responded Henry.

Samuel gave Henry an annoyed look. "The longer we search, the more danger we will be investigated by the American Coast Guard or Navy."

"Are you ready to eat?" asked Carmen, holding a platter of food.

"I am always hungry," said Juan as he grabbed the platter from her hand with mock force.

"You should marry Carmen. She cooks better than your other women," Juan commented to Samuel as he ate more fish and rice.

"I do not want to marry him," chimed in Carmen. "He is a good boss and a fair lover, but he is an unfaithful husband. He has two wives and is not often with either."

"Only a fair lover?"

"Do not listen to her, Juan. She is insatiable," claimed Samuel. To Carmen, he said, "You will be lucky to be able to walk tomorrow."

"A promise or a threat?"

The following morning, Samuel laid out an east west grid to search for the sunken ship. He took his vessel to the south eastern side of the grid and piloted his vessel to the west for 20 miles before he returned to the east on a parallel course. Late on the third day, the depth finder and fish finder showed a large blimp on the seafloor. It was too late in the day to prepare the diving equipment before sunset, so Samuel anchored the vessel over the area of the sonar blimp. Carmen took steak out of the ship's freezer and Samuel broke out the best Rum. Everyone got drunk.

The next morning, Juan and Samuel entered the water and made their feet first descent into the sea by letting the air out of their buoyance compensators. Halfway to the bottom, they saw a very rusty fishing boat. It was covered with marine growth and obviously had been there for many years.

Feeling very deflated, Juan, Samuel, Henry, and Carmen gathered in the dining area and drank large amounts of coffee in an attempt to lift their disappointment. The following morning, when the four searchers were on deck to lift the anchor, an American Coast Guard helicopter circled the ship five or six times. A crewman sitting by an open door took pictures. They had not only been detected, but were obviously of interest to the American Coast Guard which together with the US Navy controlled the Caribbean waters. After pulling up the anchor, the searchers returned to Grand Turk Island. Juan called Theodore who picked him up and flew him back to Haiti in his Piper Aztec.

CHANGES

In those days, Maria spent most of her time with Peter. She still lived near Juan, even though she was no longer a member of his crew. Ivan lived at the Paraiso office apartment in Santo Domingo. Juan's brother David was distant and quiet, but still lived by the pirate base. Juan pirated only a fishing boat, transferring the cargo of the international vessel to a Dominican fishing boat at night. Time hung on his hands, and Juan spent much of it having sex with his woman. He fueled himself with rum and Coke and cocaine.

For a different diversion, Juan made a trip to Santo Domingo. He took David with him. Although the Paraiso development was only about a five-hour drive from the pirate base and on the road to Santo Domingo, they drove directly to the Paraiso apartment in Santo Domingo without stopping. Finding Juan and David at the office apartment, Luis invited them to dinner at his house. Juan had a meeting planned with a young woman he knew in the city, but David accepted the invitation. When David arrived at his house, Luis greeted him at the front door and led him to his bar where he poured whiskey into a glass over ice and put it in David's hand. Making small talk, he proposed a few informal toasts so that David would finish the first glass of whiskey. Overcoming David's reluctance to accept a second drink, Luis poured him a second glass of whiskey then pointed out Juanita who was changing the music.

"That is my assistant Juanita."

Beginning to feel the alcohol and seeing Juanita as attractive, David let Luis lead him to where Juanita stood. When the music restarted, David took her hand and danced with Juanita. Luis kept distant, only joining them well after they stopped dancing. Luis made sure that David finished his second drink.

"Juanita dances well," said David after a pause. "She is very good."

Juanita blushed.

Neither David nor Juanita fell hard for the other, although they did like each other and talked for several hours. After returning to Haiti, David often thought of her and a few weeks later he returned to Santo Domingo. Luis immediately put them together again.

On his visit to Santo Domingo, at the end of an early dinner, David invited Juanita to the Paraiso apartment. "Come with me. Ivan is not there. He is away on business in Barahona."

She quickly agreed.

In the apartment, as they began to undress, David noticed that Juanita had a little bit of a tummy, but did not care. With her bra off, her breasts sagged a little. She smiled at David with questioning eyes and said, "I am thirty-two, I am not young."

"How is it that a nice woman like you is not married and has no children?"

"I took care of my parents. Their health was not good. It took my time and my money. They both died last year."

That night, their bodies fit together. The next day, Juanita went to work very late. Luis looked at her and asked, "Well?"

Juanita sighed, "He is very nice, but no woman marries when she is my age. The men want younger women."

"This case is different. You and David will marry."

She looked at Luis and said, "I would like to have him."

When Ivan returned to the Santo Domingo office from the resort, Luis spoke to him about David and Juanita. Ivan knew that his uncle wanted to leave Haiti. When Luis offered David a job to work in the marina, he quickly accepted. A short time later, with Juan's consent, David moved to Barahona to help with the marina construction. He traveled to Santo Domingo often to visit Juanita.

When Juan learned of the growing relationship, he said to Ivan, "Maria and David were pirates and lived outside the law. Do they think that they can become normal citizens and have babies so easily?"

Ivan thought of his situation and wondered if he could become a "normal citizen" or whether his past would come to haunt him.

Before Ivan could respond, Juan asked, "Are you going to fall in love also?"

"I have no one to love," replied Ivan.

"That is good. In love, you suddenly have much to lose, and your heart can be broken. Love makes you vulnerable. Love no woman."

The first phase of the Paraiso condominium project was nearing completion. The infrastructure was in place. The marina breakwater was finished, the first set of docks were being constructed, the first section of the hotel was under construction, and one of two planned sixty-unit condominium towers was ready to be plastered. The grounds were landscaped, and the pool and spa completed. The golf course was seeded. Golf cart paths, sand traps, and access roads were roughed in. The first model units, located near a sales office, were ready to furnish. Of good design and brightly painted, the model units impressed even Fernando.

Paraiso formed a marketing and sales company in Santo Domingo and purchased two buses to bring prospective timeshare clients to the resort. Massive marketing of the hotel and resort began with the hotel rooms, condominiums, and timeshare suites offered at a low price. The marina was widely publicized in boating circles. Paraiso made sales, but not enough to provide all the necessary cash to pay for the operation of the resort. There was no cash flow to help with the construction costs. Cost overruns ate up the reserves. Fernando asked Ivan if he could get more money from Juan and Samuel – without more money construction would soon stop for lack of funds.

Ivan knew that both Juan and Samuel had invested most, if not all, of their money. He worried for them, but said nothing. He had trouble sleeping, wondering if his dream would end up impoverishing his father and Samuel. More and more, he wished he had remained a pirate. At night he dreamed of being at sea in his father's fast boat searching for prey. He could feel the wind in his hair and the spray of salt water on his face.

Shortly thereafter, a large timeshare company located in Florida, with facilities in many parts of the eastern and southeastern part of the US, read about the new resort. The company, Havana Dreaming, was actively seeking a new Caribbean resort location. The acquisition team's advance guard visited the property.

They thought that the two seven-story condo towers were well designed. One was completed. They admired the classic Caribbean architecture. The marina was still small but pristine. The service buildings, landscaping, and planning were excellent. The golf course, although not open, was also well designed. Most importantly for Havana Dreaming, there was room to create a destination resort community consisting of multiple first-class resorts that would attract visitors from around the world.

After their visit, Havana's acquisition department contacted Paraiso's Santo Domingo office and began to negotiate the purchase of land with access to the far end of the marina. The Paraiso management team did not expect other companies to be interested in buying into the project at the early development phase and had not even considered it as a possibility. After a time, Havana Dreaming offered a low sum for a portion of the resort property. Paraiso refused. The price was so low it would not help Paraiso. Havana did not make another offer.

One evening, Ivan said, "The resort is beautiful. I am surprised they did not make another offer."

Fernando replied, "Beautiful design and location do not guarantee success. Many beautiful projects fail in the hands of the initial developer, only to become a source of wealth for a later investor. They are probably waiting for Paraiso to go bankrupt."

Ivan's stomach was continually in knots, he began to eat anti-acid tablets at all times of the day. He re-envisioned his life as a pirate.

A month or two after Havana made its offer to buy some of the Paraiso resort property, a company in fierce competition with Havana came to view the property. Upon learning of the second company's interest, in jealous reaction to their competitor, Havana immediately offered Paraiso a better price for a portion of the resort land, conditioned on the use of the marina and golf course, and on the further condition that no property be sold to the other company.

Fernando invited representatives of both companies to a well-publicized, lavish party. Havana only sent two low level representatives, but the other company's acquisitions director attended with his staff. Fernando showed him around the resort. The Havana representatives told their bosses that they thought the competition was making a deal with Paraiso. Immediately, Havana made yet another offer, this one at market price.

Fernando told Ivan, "If we sell to Havana and they develop a big resort next to ours, we will have our destination resort area."

Ivan wanted to tell Fernando that he worried that there was little, if any, money available from Juan and Samuel and that the sale was essential, but said nothing.

At that time, Juan and Samuel were at sea on their second voyage crisscrossing the area of the coordinates given to them by Henry. The wind was extra strong, but their search patterns took them directly into the east wind, and then to west with the wind behind them. It was only when they made the course reversals at the end of each search leg that Samuel had to turn his vessel broadside to the waves and the ship rolled heavily.

Samuel was alone at the ship's wheel in the pilothouse when the call from Ivan came through the radio phone. The ship pitched deeply into the wave troughs as it proceeded on the leg. He had difficulty steering the course, balancing his body and holding the microphone. The Dramamine pills that Carmen took had put her into a deep sleep. Samuel had to yell at her three times to wake her up to tell her to bring Juan to the pilothouse. Carefully holding onto the handrail, she descended to the aft deck where Juan and Henry were double lashing the Zodiac to the ship. The men did not notice her and the wind was too loud for them to hear her. Wind caught spray splashed against her body and drenched her hair which stuck to her face and neckTapping Juan on his back, she indicated that he was to go up into the pilothouse. Juan was content that Carmen relieved him from the work on deck. The spray had filled his eyes with saltwater, and they burned. Inside the boat he found a towel and dried his face before going to the pilothouse. Upon entering, the first thing he said was, "It is rough out there." Samuel gave him the microphone and turned up the volume on the ship's radio. "It is Ivan."

Ivan told his father, "We have an offer from Havana Dreaming to buy one of the buildings and part of the property. We want to present it to you."

Samuel also heard the words, he looked at Juan. Their eyes met. Juan said, "We will go."

Samuel responded, "I'm good that we give up looking for the ship for a while. The wind is fierce."

Once Carmen and Henry finished securing the Zodiac onto the aft deck and were safe inside, Samuel turned his ship to the north to return to Grand Turk.

COUNTEROFFER

After returning to Grand Turk, the pirate and smuggler flew to Santo Domingo in Theodore's old plane. There was some buffeting until they reached cruising altitude. Juan sat next to Theodore in the copilot's seat.

The sun was bright. There were rows of white, wispy clouds in all quadrants—harmless, and pretty. Whitecaps dotted the sea below. At altitude, the cabin was chilly and Theodore turned the heater on low. Before Hispaniola was visible, the clouds marked its location. After a while, the aircraft's navigation radio began to respond and the VOR navigation course needle flickered.

Samuel asked, "You are still flying crazy? And when not flying, are you always with some woman?"

"You got it. Nothing better."

"Where do you fly?" asked Samuel.

"Many places that I can't tell you about," replied Theodore, "but I can tell you that I often fly very good marijuana between Colombia and Mexico. I also fly money and I have other passenger clients besides you and Juan. They don't want anyone or any government to know where they are. I leave them at little airstrips where there is no immigration. Their trips are secret and that business has been very good. Even more than the money I make, I enjoy flying."

"Boats are already on the earth and don't fall out of the sky," commented Juan.

"Yes, but there is adventure in the sky, like the storm over Cuba," said Theodore. "If I had been in a lesser plane, the wings would have been torn off."

"You should go back to your profession before flying kills you," said Samuel.

Theodore turned and looked at Samuel in the eye, "I have seen too much meanness, greed, and corruption in business and . . . too much stupidity. That's why I left San Francisco. Life there was not the way it was supposed to be. I also saw way too much corruption and greed in politics. It's all about power and money. There is no going back – this is a better life. I like to fly. I fly from island to island, from Colombia to Mexico, and to wherever the money is good. I fly in the daytime, at nighttime, at altitude, and at times, I fly across the water or desert at very low altitudes under a full moon. It's amazing! You say I am crazy; I drink too much, bang too many women and take too many drugs and that may all be true, but I truly enjoy my life. It is adventurous and I fly a plane as steady and professionally as any pilot."

"You are a crazy gringo," said Juan.

"And you are a pirate," replied Theodore.

Theodore passed the piloting of the plane to Juan and pretended to sleep. With Juan at the controls the flight was uneven.

Theodore told the pirate, "Keep the altitude and course."

"Your old plane does what it wants."

"It only does what you tell it to."

Theodore took over for the descent into Santo Domingo. The plane bounced up and down in the strong air currents caused by the uneven heating of the ground. Humidity and heat increased. In spite of the buffeting, the pilot flew the plane through the approach and down the Instrument Landing System as if locked onto the beacon, and finally transitioned from air to runway almost without notice.

Ivan, Luis, Fernando, and David were waiting for Juan, Samuel and Theodore at the Paraiso office. It was, in truth, a meeting of smugglers, drug runners, pirates, and partners of the same. Juan, in his dark, aging, and some would say attractive way, most looked the part—the real Latin pirate although he did not have a cutthroat or mean soul. Samuel, comfortable with his partners, looked and acted like the college-educated 'Jimmy Buffet' businessman he sometimes was. Fernando, always the Cuban aristocrat, looked himself— distinguished, skilled, and handsome. Luis was the image of the reasonably successful upper-middle-class Dominican businessman.

Ivan appeared the scion of a rich, society family. His mother's family, with whom he had no contact, and which had no knowledge of his whereabouts, had no real money, but was well placed in society. His father had money through piracy. Physically, he was a mix of his mother's Spanish ancestry, and his father's white-skinned American mother, with only a touch of his dark-skinned Colombian grandfather.

Although they were a group of thieves, drug runners, and associates, they were also just men. Samuel, the crushed college man whose first family had deserted him, became someone else, giving himself over to smuggling and sea adventure. Beyond hope and possibility, deep in his heart he still wished he was an honest businessman and living with his lost family.

Amongst themselves, Paraiso was not funded by Juan, the thief, but by their friend Juan. And Samuel, although a smuggler, was just another person. David was simply the younger man who had followed his bold older brother. He was just now in early middle age, venturing into his own life with his woman Juanita. Ivan, the blossoming businessman, just happened to be Juan's natural son. Of the men, Juan most completely had given in to his illegal lifestyle. Early on, unskilled and rough, he had tried to find another profitable business; but having failed, he found success in crime. Juan had no regrets and did not look back. The little conscience he once had died long ago.

The purchase offer from Havana, well reviewed and annotated by Fernando and Ivan, was straightforward and without tricks. While good, it required Paraiso to finance the balance of the purchase price. Ivan knew that the down payment was not enough to fix Paraiso's need for cash. He figured that his father and Samuel did not have the cash that Paraiso needed. His heart pounding, he fought to control his anxiety. In spite of his deep worry, Ivan ventured, "We should not finance Havana. They want to use our money and pay us from their cash flow. Now is the time to develop our resort and we need liquidity. With money from Havana, we pass the cost of development and risk of Paraiso to Havana."

After some thought, intuiting that Juan and Samuel did not have enough money to refinance Paraiso, Fernando said, "Ivan you're right, also I think Havana is jealous of the competition, and they will pay more, and I think they will pay cash."

Ivan said nothing. They prepared a counteroffer to Havana. During the process Ivan could hardly contain his nervousness that they might lose the deal. In his heart he feared that in spite of all his work, he might lose his father's and Samuel's money as well as his new life.

Havana Dreaming's high-level competition with the other prospective purchaser drove it to accept the counteroffer at the higher price and although it offered a higher down payment, Havana still required Paraiso to finance the purchase. The cash from the sale did not provide enough money to complete the development of Paraiso – although it would help. Ivan pushed hard for more cash, but when the deal was in danger of falling apart, the investors accepted the offer. The subsequent negotiations over the details of the sale, occupancy, joint maintenance expenses, contract terms, and reorganization of Paraiso's business plan absorbed much of Ivan's life. Ivan said nothing, but knew more cash was required. He concluded that he would have to return to piracy. At times he wondered how he had been such a fool to leave the ease and safety of piracy from the South of Haiti.

TREASURE

A short time later, Juan joined Samuel, Carmen, and Henry on board Samuel's small ship moored at Grand Turk. The following day, they departed the island on an east-southeast course. The sea was calm, and the trade winds blew very lightly. The temperature was not excessive. The vessel rose a bit on the sea swells. Passing over the water mound, its bow pitched forward.

Numerous seagulls accompanied them. Small, and occasionally large, fish jumped clear out of the water. The distant horizon was partially obscured by the ever-present tropical humidity.

Henry was in the pilothouse with Juan and Samuel. Carmen walked in carrying a food plate. "Young men, would you like some papaya and mango?"

"You spoil us," said Juan with an easy smile.

"This requires wine and some fish. I want it fried," ordered Samuel.

Carmen smirked good-naturedly, turned to leave, and stuck her butt out toward Samuel.

"You had better be careful, girl," he threatened.

"You may get hurt," said Carmen.

She quickly returned with the wine then went back to the galley to prepare the fish. The men were feeling the wine's effects and were half drunk when she returned with the late lunch. The fish was perfectly grilled, served with fresh sliced limes and mango. The men ate with obvious pleasure.

As they talked of the scuttled drug ship, Carmen said, "After so much time, I think the marijuana will be wet. It will be decayed, and crabs will be living in it."

Henry said, "No. The product is well wrapped in plastic. It will be dry. The pressure of the sea will have pressed the wrapping tight to the product. It will be good. I also believe there is cash in the safe."

Spirits were high. Everyone was happy to be on an adventure and to be out at sea. Juan and Samuel especially so; the slow mounting of the waves, the engine noises, the roll of the small ship, the humidity, and the heat all created a sense of home. Life seemed well, calm and timeless.

The ship arrived at the coordinates after dark. Carmen and Juan lowered two anchors. They held firm, and Samuel turned on the anchor lights. Mildly intoxicated, and happy with the sea and the adventure, Samuel wanted Carmen. He took her to his cabin.

After an hour, she said, "That is enough, I am finished now, go to sleep. For what you pay me, you only get that much sex."

"That is why I have two wives and a sea mistress. One, not even two, are enough."

"I do not care how many you have. I am going to sleep."

At the end of the first day, Samuel marked the area they had searched on a marine chart. He concluded, "We have explored the ocean floor to the south and west of the Loran coordinates. Tomorrow we will start looking to the north."

The following two days, the little ship powered to the north for twenty miles, then turned to the south on a parallel course. The depth sounders and fish finders showed both the ocean floor and fish life. At the end of the second day, the American Coast Guard helicopter that had examined them on their first search made four circle passes above the ship.

"The Americans are looking at us again," observed Samuel with irritation.

"We have done nothing illegal," stated Juan with a casual shrug.

Carmen overheard the comment and looked up from her cooking. "I do not want to go to jail, boss. The Americans do whatever they want, even in international waters."

Henry bit his nails nervously, but said nothing.

"The Americans have nothing on us. Screw them," said Juan as he reached for a slice of the pizza Carmen placed on the counter.

"I'd rather continue being poor than go to an American prison," stated Henry.

Ignoring them, pizza in hand, Juan and Samuel returned to the deck outside.

On the third day, they began searching to the east of Henry's coordinates. The morning of the fifth day, the depth sounders and fish finders indicated a long raised object on the seafloor in a hundred feet of water. Juan and Carmen dropped anchor. It set firm, and the bow of the ship faced the wind and sea.

Samuel, Juan, and Henry, fitted with fins, snorkels, masks, and scuba tanks, rolled off the edge of the ship into the warm water. Although the water was 'Caribbean clear,' it was not clear enough to see the ocean floor. The men descended rather rapidly into the slightly darkening waters. The larger fish looked at them from a distance. The smaller tropical fish swam around them. Their colors flashed.

Fifty feet below the surface, Samuel motioned to the then visible ship. It rested flat on her bottom. Even through the masks, their eyes shared the excitement.

The men swam around and over the ship as the bubbles from their breathing streamed upward. They inspected it with care. Samuel tied an orange marker buoy to its railing, inflated it, and it rocketed straight up. Ascending slowly, the men stopped once to decompress before they surfaced near the boat.

Onboard Samuel's vessel, Henry ripped off his face mask and exclaimed, "Yes!" He offered a high five to Samuel, who was grinning ear to ear.

Juan walked over to them. "Today we are lucky."

"You are always lucky, Juan," stated Samuel, "which is why I like doing business with you."

Carmen interrupted. "I didn't think we would find it."

"You should not doubt your boss," scolded Samuel with a hug and a pinch on her butt.

"I want to see the ship. Are there sharks?" asked Carmen.

"We saw no sharks, but there are sharks in these waters. You may come down with us if you want, but only after you prepare us a *café con leche* and some of the delicious pastries that you baked yesterday," said Samuel with a motion for her to go to the ship's galley.

"Yes sir!" responded Carmen with a salute.

"She is the only one of my crew who salutes me," grinned Samuel. Juan interjected, "She mocks you."

Henry walked in circles. "Man," he said, "we found the ship. It took months and months of waiting and many tries, but we found it! My ship has come in!"

"We will have a closer look," said Samuel, through a big smile.

Carrying the scuba tanks, Samuel and Juan went below deck to the compressor. Juan filled the air tanks while Samuel unpacked a second set. They carried them to the aft deck.

On deck, Carmen served the coffee and pastries, which the men drank as they devoured the pastries that she had set out earlier. When they finished and were still hungry, she brought them freshly baked bread, butter, and mango marmalade. The sun was warm and pleasant. Henry couldn't remain still and began pacing. Juan smoked one of Samuel's Cuban cigars. After a rest, Samuel mounted a full scuba tank into each tank pack and prepared for the dive. He then found a weight belt for Carmen.

The descent was rapid. As before, the light and color decreased as they moved further below the surface. The water, however, remained clear — almost transparent. It seemed as though a liquid atmosphere— surreal and beautiful.

Standing on the platform next to the pilothouse of the sunken ship, the men opened the door leading inside. Ample light streamed through the intact, mostly clear windows. When scuttled, the hull had filled with water slowly as it settled into the ocean and drifted to the bottom.

Inside the pilothouse, two cups were still sitting on a cabin table. Charts were stored in slats in the cabin ceiling. The pilot's chair was still mounted, the compass intact, the gauges of the instruments relatively clear. The closed cabin had little sea life growing inside. It was rather like a storm had overtaken them, and they were looking into the sea washing over a still-floating vessel. The three men and Carmen had the odd sensation of something being very wrong—the ship was too complete and too clear of marine growth to feel like a sunken wreck.

The aft part of the wheelhouse opened into two cabins, both still complete with beds covered by sheets. In the lower part of the superstructure, they found the galley, dining, and lounge. Other spaces looked like perhaps they had initially been laboratories. Inside the ship's hull were the crew and staff quarters and a large cargo hold. The men and Carmen moved aft through the crew and staff living quarters looking unsuccessfully for a smaller interior door to the cargo hold.

Leaving the boat, they made a slow ascent, making two decompression stops. They all arrived at the surface almost out of air. Back on board, Henry dropped his weight belt and slipped out of the air tanks. With his fins still on his feet, he danced a jig to a nautical tune he sang in a loud voice. He took Carmen by the arm to dance with him until she caused him to trip by stepping on his fins. After drinking whiskey from Samuel's stock, Juan and Samuel joined in the merriment.

Henry said, "I still can't believe it. Finally, I will have money!"

Samuel looked at him and answered, "Yes, money is good to have."

"You do not know what it is like, having little money."

"I like the adventure more than the money," said Samuel.

"That is because you have money. To you, the money is a bonus to the sea and the adventure. For me, the ship is a treasure chest. The money will change my life," beamed Henry with a big smile.

With an anxious tone of voice, Carmen said, "The ship was too perfect lying there. It is spooky. Maybe it was cursed and the curse will fall on us, too."

"Don't be a silly woman," stated Juan, irritated.

Carmen said nothing and went to the galley, where Samuel joined her. It was already dark and getting late. Carmen was preparing the predictable fish dinner—pan-fried and lightly spiced. She was steady on her feet, even as the ship pitched at anchor.

"*Carmelita*, sprinkle extra jalapeño on the fish," requested Samuel.

"You be the smuggler. I will be the cook."

"I am teaching you," replied Samuel, with a mocking seriousness.

"You taught me about the sea, and nothing else."

"Nothing?"

"I have your love for the sea, and therefore I put up with you in the kitchen."

Samuel took her into his arms and slid his hand down the back of her baggy shorts. "Let me cook, you old goat," she laughed as she freed herself.

As is the case with many Latin women not chosen for marriage, Carmen had a child, but not with Samuel. Her son was now in his late teens. Latin men wanted younger women; she had little chance of getting married, but had sex when she wanted it. As soon as the meal was finished, Carmen smiled deeply at Samuel and bent over so he could see her breasts. Samuel grabbed Carmen's hand and pulled her towards himself then led her to his cabin.

Samuel cared for each of his two wives. His wife living in Nassau was a mostly white citizen of the Bahamas. She used her husband's money and appearance to move her family into the upper middle class. She loved Samuel only coolly, with a love that Samuel often said would disappear if he ever needed her and was without money. It was a life of mostly form, but not completely devoid of love and his wife, partially from lack of sexual desire, was faithful to him. There was not enough of anything between them to cause him to be faithful to her. That family spoke only English.

His other wife, the Colombian living on the north coast of Colombia, loved him more. She was beautiful, smart, and artistic, with university studies in art and literature. She was also passionate and took better care of Samuel. She and her family entered more substantially into the upper middle class due to their economic ability in a much poorer country. Her kids attended the best school in the area and were fair athletes and scholars. They were closer to their father than his family in Nassau, although neither of his families saw him much because of his preference for work and sea.

During periods of "work," Samuel spent more time with Carmen than with either of his wives.

The next morning, the men and Carmen took their coffee on the deck of the small ship. Henry exclaimed, "Everything will be good. There is no curse. I can feel it. I think the owners looked for the ship, and could not find it. If they had, the cargo hatches would not be closed."

In a flat voice, Juan observed, "It is as though the ship is still afloat."

Changing the conversation, Henry blurted, "I will finally have money!"

Juan and Samuel looked at each other and grinned. "Yes, let's hope!" said Juan in Spanish, then added in English, "If you have money, then we will too."

Carmen clapped her hands and echoed Juan. "Yes, let's hope! I am tired of being poor."

Samuel observed, "Treasure hunting is as much, or even more fun, than smuggling."

"You are finally hunting real treasure with your treasure-hunting ship. Now you are an honest man," responded Juan with a humorous look.

"I have always been a treasure hunter," replied Samuel, as he grabbed Carmen from inside the back of her loose-fit cutoff jean shorts.

Shaking her butt, Carmen smiled and said, "He knows where the real treasure is. But that treasure costs him a share of the marijuana."

"You mean you are not here out of love for me?" asked Samuel with fake sincerity.

"I only tolerate you for the money I make working on the ship. No, I do not love you. But that is OK, you don't want me to love you anyway."

"It is a good thing, *Carmelita*. Otherwise, my Colombian wife would be jealous."

"You are a terrible husband to your wives, but you are a good boss. Our relationship is commercial—with benefits," she winked.

The next morning, the small ship rose and dipped as moderately sized sea swells passed underneath the hull. The treasure hunters put on their buoyancy compensators, scuba tanks, weight belts, fins, and masks. The water was warm. Only Henry wore a wetsuit top.

Descending together feet first, bubbles streaming toward the surface, the divers landed on the sunken ship's upper deck. They entered through the pilothouse door. Samuel and Juan then explored the two decks of the upper part of the ship, while Carmen and Henry went below into the crew area and the machinery rooms. Each team found a safe. The larger and heavier of the two was found in the crew area. It was immovable. They managed to get the smaller safe found in the pilothouse onto the side deck before having to surface to avoid being at depth for too long.

In the afternoon, the three men made a second fast dive to the sunken ship. They wrapped the smaller safe with netting and ropes and secured it to lines that Carmen lowered from the surface. Responding to Samuel's tug on the line, Carmen engaged the winch. The line became tight, pulled the netting firm around the safe, and lifted it off the deck. Juan misjudged the angle of the direction and moved just in time to keep from being pinned between the safe and the ship's railing. The safe grated against the rail then swung free. The three men ascended with the safe until decompression depth. The safe was winched to the surface while the divers decompressed.

Placed on deck, the safe, although heavy, seemed even smaller than it had on the ship. Using a torch, it took less than a half hour to cut it open. Samuel reached inside and pulled out stacks and stacks of $100 bills.

"Oh my God," said Carmen. Juan and Samuel gave each other a high five.

Henry exclaimed, "Hallelujah, my ship did come in." He danced his jig on the deck and Carmen joined in.

"Enough partying. Make us some food," Samuel said to the dancing woman.

"With pleasure, Chief. I like this treasure hunting. Don't forget that you promised me ten percent of any cash found on board—in addition to my wages."

With a big smile on her face, Carmen prepared grilled mahi-mahi, rice, and vegetables for dinner.

Flirting with Carmen, Henry said, "Carmen cooks like a master chef, is pretty, and has money. Maybe I will marry her."

Carmen looked at him. "I would still have to sleep with my boss when at sea."

Henry smiled at her and Carmen gave him an encouraging look.

Samuel broke out the champagne. He lifted his glass in a toast, "To money, to adventure, and to women."

"Especially to women," added Carmen.

Early the following day, as Juan and Samuel prepared for the dives, a black twin-engine plane approached from the west.

"Could be the assholes of the DEA. They are sons of bitches," declared Samuel in anger.

"Do not tell Carmen or Henry," said Juan.

The plane passed off to the north of the ship. When it did not return, Samuel and Juan entered the water and descended as rapidly as possible. They quickly made their way below decks to the storage area near the engine room. The large safe was attached to the steel bulkhead. It took multiple short dives over a period of a day and a half to open the door by using underwater cutting tools. They found no money or valuables inside.

Henry was obviously disappointed that they did not find more cash. He reminded himself that, "The real treasure was the Santa Marta Gold."

Very excitedly Carmen clapped her hands. "This is a real treasure hunt!"

Henry smiled at her.

Just after dawn the next morning, the three men and Carmen descended with hammers and pry bars to open the four aft deck hatches to the cargo hold containing the marijuana. Standing on the aft deck, they worked as fast as possible because of the depth and possible return of the plane or risk of a visit from the US Coast Guard. The levers holding the first cargo hatch did not move. Those on the next two doors were also stuck, but one of the levers that held the fourth cargo hatch moved. When Juan turned that lever, a portion of the cargo door lifted and strained to open. Henry hammered the remaining levers holding that hatch closed as Juan braced himself and pulled hard on the pry bar to move them. They still did not yield. Samuel then placed his pry bar next to Juan's and pulled with all his strength. The first port side lever finally broke free. Henry and Samuel then pulled on the pry bars to open the starboard lever as Juan hit it with a hammer. The lever that held the cargo hatch closed was suddenly freed and slid aside. With explosive force, the door flung open and smashed into Juan's left shoulder, arm and leg. The blow threw him backward and away from the ship. He sunk toward the sea floor, head first. The regulator remained in his mouth, but there were no bubbles to indicate that he was breathing....

ILEANA

Ivan's increasing role in business brought him further into contact with Santo Domingo society — which often worried him. He felt his social and business skills were thin . . . and that at any time, on the basis of some error, he could be excluded from both social and business circles. Nonetheless, he was liked by others. The part of his personality formed through piracy was interpreted as the result being an independent thinker and maverick businessman — rather than an ex-criminal. His boldness in business and growing intellectual capabilities captivated people. He received an increasing number of social invitations. His golf game, much improved through time and with plenty of instruction, won him invitations to play with other young businessmen. He became a member of the golf and country club. Still, the near failure of Paraiso had made him acutely aware of the fragility of his new life. He also struggled with worry that he had caused his father and Samuel to invest in Paraiso and that the company could fail. He felt responsible for their situation and was considering various plans to save them through renewed piracy and perhaps smuggling. He foresaw that he, like Samuel, might have to live the double life of a respected businessman and an outlaw.

One Friday night, after playing a poor game of golf, Ivan sat alone at the bar and drank wine to get comfortable. His game of double and triple bogeys annoyed him. Tired as well from the week's work, he was glad to keep to himself. Thinking he would have to return to piracy and even smuggling brought back some of the hardness that he had lived in Haiti. He was glad to be alone. It was not long though before his golf friends entered the restaurant with their wives and the women friends of their wives.

After greetings, small talk, and laughter, Ivan was compelled to join them for dinner. He politely stood to one side, allowing the couples to sit down. After everyone took their seats, he found himself seated next to a beautiful woman in her mid-twenties. Her appearance, her movements, and her very being were beautiful in Ivan's eyes. He felt an immediate attraction, more profound than he had ever experienced in his life. He dropped his fork on the floor and suddenly felt out of place.

She spoke first. "I have not met you. I am Ileana. Forgive me, but there is something about you. Do you work here in Santo Domingo?"

For the first time since arriving in Santo Domingo, it crossed Ivan's mind in a worrisome way that his past was evident. He looked into her eyes, then at his plate. Ileana sensed his discomfort, took his hand, and gently shook it.

Ivan looked at her again. He felt his heart thumping in his chest when he saw her warm smile. Nervous, he said, "You are beautiful."

Ileana laughed, "You men are all the same. Tell me about yourself."

"I am in the timeshare business. A company named Paraiso."

"But there is something else. Do you fish or sail?" she asked. After a pause, she added, "You have the flavor of a sailor."

"I have spent much time fishing, yes," Ivan responded, without telling her what he had fished, nor even hinting that he was about to go back to "fishing" for yachts from which to pirate. To protect himself, he allowed a hardness to rise up inside him.

"Yes, perhaps that is it. When I saw you talking to señor and señora Rodriquez, I wondered. You move and act a little different from the other men."

Ivan looked at her, "What did you notice?"

"That you are very nice," she said, as her whole body seemed to smile back at him.

Ivan looked at Ileana. He felt tenderness and caring, similar to what he had at one time felt as a young child before his mother left. The conversation grew more intimate. Soon it seemed just the two of them were present; there was no long table full of people around them. They conversed alone, looking into each other's eyes. Except to take only a few bites of the mostly uneaten dinner, their eyes did not leave each other during their long conversation. Ivan's friends noticed, motioned, and commented to each other that they were a perfect match—the successful young businessman, mannered but rough, and the beautiful daughter of a prominent, reasonably successful and well-connected family. They looked good together and appeared to have forgotten the world around them.

Ivan's friend Carlos said in a loud voice to Ivan, "*Mi amigo*, we are seated here, too. Do not forget us."

When Ivan and Ileana looked up, they noticed all the guests were looking at them. Ileana blushed. "Oh, of course. Forgive us."

Carlos said, "*Us?*"

Ivan looked so thoughtful that everyone at the table stared at him, then at Ileana.

With a smile, Carlos's wife said, "Oh . . . us!"

The blush on Ileana's face deepened.

Half drunk, Carlos offered a toast. "May the first child be a male child."

Life was different for Ivan from that day forward. His thoughts regarding business became clearer. His vision for Paraiso sharpened, as did his vision for piracy to finance the company. His business future had definition. Without speaking it, or seeking it, he found that Ileana was included in the plans for his future life, although he knew that she must never discover his past life or know of what he intended to do in order to provide more money for Paraiso.

Capable of multi-tasking at a level that no one understood, he worked Paraiso while processing the growing emotions he found within himself, emotions awakened by his deepening care for Ileana. His inner self visited and revisited the early childhood security he felt when he had a mother to shelter him, and the raw wound of her leaving him. He had never fallen in love and discovered a wall of pain and fear of again being abandoned.

When Ivan met Ileana's parents, they were impressed by the little-known young man who was becoming a success. He was likable, but it was his obvious fondness of Ileana that opened their heart to him. They also found an indefinable quality that made him different. Although they could not put a finger on it, with an American accent, they sometimes called Ivan "Jake" after a character in a Hemingway novel. Ivan did not understand the reference though rather liked the name in English. It suited him. He told Ileana, "I feel more like a 'Jake' than an 'Ivan.'"

One evening, Ivan arrived at the family house at seven o'clock for *cena*. The supper was early because Ivan and Ileana had plans to go dancing at the country club with friends. The house, located in the older colonial residential section of the city, was surrounded by many large palms, plants, and brilliant flowers. The night was humid. Ivan, dressed in lightweight blue slacks, white shirt, and loose-weave, silk sport coat, parked his white Ford pickup inside the front wrought-iron gate. A servant closed it behind him. There was considerable noise in the driveway courtyard from the traffic on the well-transited street. A second servant met him at the door and showed him into the old-style, high-ceiling house without air conditioning. The geckos somewhat noisily scrambled up the walls.

Ileana's parents were seated not far from the large aviary and stood up to receive Ivan as he entered the inside courtyard. Her father embraced him with his right arm and patted his back with the left. Ileana entered from the bedroom hallway and gave him a chaste kiss on his lips.

Seated near the aviary was Ileana's older brother, Eduardo, a budding politician. He smiled at Ivan. "*Que tal?*"

Ivan smiled back and said, "*Bien, y tú?*"

Ileana's friend Elena was there with her husband. They were a couple Ivan knew fairly well and liked. Seated next to them was a couple he did not know, older than Ileana's parents.

The older couple looked like many Latin couples of their age—somewhat overweight, of medium height. The man's sparse hair was mostly grey and combed back. Ileana introduced the older couple as

Elena's parents. Ivan was not good at names. It often took several introductions to memorize them. For a moment he thought he recognized their names, and then they slipped from consciousness for the moment.

Ivan sat on the loveseat with Ileana. He sipped a local brandy which burned his mouth. The birds inside the aviary were quiet. He was at ease with Ileana at his side. He glanced at her from time to time. On each occasion, she smiled at him with her whole being.

The conversation turned to Eduardo's recent entry into politics. Elena's father said, "Be very careful of politics. I stuck myself into politics and learned that it was worse than I even thought. Those who want power will stop at nothing to get it. There is no trick or bad thing they will not do. I had to take my family to Haiti to escape their plans. Only after a time did my friends come back into power and clear my name. Then I returned to Santo Domingo with my wife and daughter."

The old man went on to say that Elena was a surprise baby born late in his life, much after the birth of their older daughter Elizabeth, who was married to a successful politician.

Ivan's attention snapped to the couple, and to the present, much as might the attention of a sea captain brought back from a dream by a shot fired at him from another ship's cannon.

The older couple then spoke of their years in Puerto Principe, Haiti. Ivan focused one hundred percent on them. Feelings rose inside him and began to rush through him like fury. He was puzzled as memories of his early childhood crashed upon him. Feelings of abandonment, those early years on the streets of loveless Puerto Principe, and the violence amongst the street kids. Fear. His father's excesses. Half-images of his lost mother who he could only faintly remember. Memories of the sudden loss of little childhood safety and security he had once had, flooded his soul. He felt afresh the hole that had been left in his heart. Abandonment, sadness, and rejection settled upon him as the eerie calmness before a hurricane.

Ivan looked around and felt for the hand of Ileana. As her hand touched his, he returned to the present and felt better. With all his will, he focused himself on the man he had decided to become. He remembered the unpredicted help that came from his father and Samuel. That help was an anchor—a vote for him. That memory made him feel fulfilled and loved. He was not abandoned.

As the man spoke of his life, Ivan realized without a doubt, as his grandfather's name came to his consciousness, that this man and his wife seated before him were, in fact, his maternal grandfather and grandmother. He also realized that Elena, Ileana's friend, who recently had become his friend too, was the much younger sister of his mother. Elena was his aunt.

After the brief respite, his emotions stirred again, hit as though by a fiercer tempest than the first. Deep resentment and anger came violently to the surface. The pain caused by this man—who took his support and took his mother away to the country in which he now lived—flooded through him like a wild tide. Anger raged and with it came a desire to tell the man to go to hell, to crush him and his family. For a moment, he despised Elena and her husband and the entire room full of guests. He recalled his life as a pirate and remembered his father's killing of the bodyguards on the cruise ship. Piss on them all! Suddenly he was glad that the economic need of Paraiso might force him back into being an outlaw. It was all he could do not to stand up and walk away.

Ileana sensed something was very wrong and held Ivan's hand tightly. Her deep touch calmed him some, even so, his emotions screamed at him. Stand up. Leave these asses. Return to the safety of piracy. Screw everyone. Don't care.

As he shifted his weight to stand up, Ileana pinched his hand to make him look at her. With concern on her face, she stared into his eyes. She saw deep hurt and fear.

She leaned closer to him and whispered, "I love you. Everything is okay."

Ivan settled back into his chair, and suddenly, Fernando came to mind. For the first time, he fully understood what Fernando had suffered from the loss of his family life in Cuba and the importance of what Fernando had taught him.

Ivan felt overwhelmed as he grasped what Fernando had suffered. In an epiphany, he now understood the lesson Fernando had drilled into him—for him to go on in life, he had to release, forgive and grow. He also thought of how Theodore walked away from society and what it supposedly stood for. After a short time, Ivan left the loathing behind, but he was still glad that he might have to be a pirate again.

A short time later, Ileana's mother suggested it was time to eat, and the guests stood up. The older man had difficulty. Ivan gave him his hand and helped him to his feet, feeling nothing for him, positive or negative.

BAHAMAS

Seven weeks had passed since Juan was injured, he sat on the back deck of their safe house located on Long Island of the Bahamas. He was pleased that he had managed to get down the few backstairs with a measure of grace, but more pleased that as soon as Samuel or Carmen woke up they would cut off the leg and arm casts. He had only one week to redevelop the atrophied muscles before taking the marijuana to the buyers.

Juan vaguely remembered that after he had been hit by the ship's cargo doors, Samuel swam to him and forced air into his mouth from the regulator and then half carried him to the surface. He slightly recalled his air regulator being in his mouth and the importance of breathing as he ascended. On the surface, Samuel had inflated his buoyancy compensator and let him float. It was then he began to vomit.

After Carmen lifted him onto the boat's aft deck with the little crane and then half drug, half carried him into the salon, Juan had managed to get onto a settee. When Carmen told Henry and Samuel that Juan was not critically injured, they dove back down to the sunken ship and freed many bales of marijuana from the hold. When it appeared that they had enough bales to fill the cargo hold of Samuel's ship, they closed the sunken vessel's cargo doors and went to the surface. Standing in the inflatable, Carmen was already collecting the bales, all of which floated high in the water. With the help of Henry and Samuel all the bales were retrieved and tossed from the little boat onto the aft deck of the small ship.

Once the marijuana was on board, everyone but Juan worked as fast as possible to get the bales stowed inside. If any surveillance plane saw them, it would not be long before a coast guard or navy armed helicopter would arrive followed by a ship.

Juan's recollections were interrupted when he heard the water turn on in the kitchen. He saw Carmen standing by the sink wearing only a man's long T-shirt. She held an open can of Café Bustelo in one hand, with the other she measured the fine ground coffee into a saucepan filled with water. Juan smiled, he wanted coffee. It was too much effort for him to prepare it for himself with his arm and leg cast, so he didn't drink it unless someone else prepared it. He had been an invalid for almost two months and was completely annoyed at the limitations.

After the saucepan was placed on one of the gas burners, Carmen took a large scissor type pruning tool out of a "junk" drawer of the kitchen and went outside and sat next to Juan. Her nipples pressed against the inside of the T-shirt, which gave Juan a little pleasure.

"Are you ready to be freed, Sr. Juan?" asked Carmen insincerely knowing he was entirely fed up with the casts.

"Can we do this without Samuel?" asked Juan.

Carmen gave him a genuine smile and opened the scissors. With the lower part of the giant scissors inside the leg cast and the top part on the outside of the cast, she began to cut. The large pruning tool easily cut through the plaster. As she worked down Juan's leg, he pulled the plaster apart so she had easy access to the uncut part. It was not long before the cast was cut open. She removed it from Juan's leg. His leg was straight with no deformity from the break, but the muscles were atrophied and the skin was white with some peeling. Juan stood up. He had enough muscle to stand alone and slowly walk.

"Does it hurt?" asked Carmen with concern.

Juan shook his head. "It just feels weak." After Juan further tested his leg, he sat down and held out his left arm. She quickly removed the cast. Juan rubbed his arm, the skin there was also white and the muscles atrophied. After moving his arm, Juan smiled.

"I will exercise and soon they will be strong again."

"Be careful they don't get sunburned, white boy," warned Carmen with a smile. Hearing the coffee boil and spill onto the stove, she jumped up to take the pan off the heat.

Juan walked around the back deck and then took the few steps to the sandy backyard where he walked and stretched his leg and arm. Soon Carmen joined him and enticed him to sit down and drink the fresh coffee with her.

It was not long before Samuel came downstairs. He smiled when Juan stood up and walked to him.

"Good!" exclaimed Samuel, "You look so much better without the casts! You need to get strong my friend. It took me a while to find buyers to whom we could offload the marijuana at sea into their fast boats. In a week we deliver it to them. They wanted us to take it to Florida, but after seeing and smoking some of the marijuana, they decided that it was worth the risk to take it in themselves. Everything Henry said about the marijuana is true. It is the best. There is only one thing, they will not buy it all. We will still have 1,000 pounds to sell."

Juan stood up and started walking around. His leg was stiff. He picked up a medium sized rock from the garden in his left hand and began to exercise his arm.

Six days later, at 10 p.m., Samuel brought his boat from the Stella Maris marina and anchored it near shore. Because of Juan's injury and the delay in finding buyers, the marijuana had been transferred to the deep hidden storage vault located under the house. All except the 1,000 pounds of unsold merchandise now had to be reloaded into the hold of Samuel's vessel.

A little before 11 p.m. they motored northeast at high speed towards the coordinates where they were to meet the buyers. At 1 a.m. Samuel called the buyers on the VHF radio. They immediately answered. They were close, but there was almost no moon and the sea was pitch dark. The two boats of the buyer turned on a red light. Seeing the lights, Samuel drove to them. As he neared the red lights, he turned on the dim perimeter lights of his ship. It took only moments for the two transport boats to tie to Samuel's ship. As quickly as possible the marijuana was transferred to two smaller boats. The buyer handed Samuel a large briefcase filled with hundred-dollar bills. Samuel quickly counted it.

"It is good doing business with you," Samuel said to the buyer who captained one of the small boats. "I wish you a safe trip back to the Florida Keys and protection from the police."

"We have everything arranged, there will be no problems," said the buyer.

The two boats untied from Samuel's vessel. With their lights off they were invisible – hidden in the night. Samuel, Juan and Carmen listened to the boats as they roared towards Florida at very high speed.

MARIA AND PETER

Although no longer part of Juan's crew, Maria still lived close to Juan's house. Standing in her kitchen, she poured hot water over fresh coffee grounds. She held the hot water pot in her right hand, her left hand was on her hip, and her head held upright. Seated on a stool, Peter watched her and thought that she should have been a famous bad-girl actress. Even the way she wore her simple, pretty white dress made it look like something from a New York designer's collection. She broadcasted dual messages—*Love me. Don't tread on me.* Every movement was both beautiful and slightly threatening.

Peter and Maria had painted the interior of the house a pleasant soft yellow and the few furnishings they painted with a white enamel. The windows had bright curtains overflowing with prints of extravagant poppy flowers.

Maria poured the freshly brewed coffee into a white mug and handed it to Peter. He placed it on the little table. Peter then stood up;

his shoulders were pushed back by the confidence of being loved. He put his arms around Maria, and she felt the strength of his arms and his back and smelled the odor of his body through his nondescript clothing. She looked up into his softly lined face. Peter leaned forward, pulled Maria's lithe body against his and kissed her. When the kiss ended, Maria wondered where the defrocked priest had learned to kiss so passionately.

After another long kiss during which he held her tight against his body, he said, "I love you, pirate wench. Marry me."

Without warning, Maria's eyes watered. Her body softened and her knees bent as the remembrances of her girlhood dream of being married and living in her little house in Barranquilla flooded upon her. Peter's grip kept her from collapsing to the floor. He looked at her with great concern and led her to the bed.

"Do you really want me?" she murmured.

"I want you."

For the first time since the death of her father, Maria cried a tropical rain shower. Her body shook, and Peter lay beside her, holding her. Her face looked like that of a porcelain doll, fragile. Her developed and strong body lay weak and soft against his. She cried for a long time. When she fell asleep, Peter left and went to his own lodgings.

Shortly after dawn, Isabela went to Maria's house and found her sitting at her little table with a small bottle of mineral water in her hand. There was a glow on Maria's face, but she also seemed agitated. In Creole Isabela asked, "What's up?"

Maria looked at her and stated, "I am going to marry Peter."

Isabela smiled. "You love him. So what's wrong?"

"I loved my mother, and she died. I loved my father, and he died. What if Peter dies?" Maria's face wore the pain of her broken heart.

"Don't worry. Nothing will happen to Peter. Come. I will help you plan the wedding."

"It will be very small. I will invite you and the few pirates who are left. I will bring my daughter. It will not be a big deal."

Isabela said, "The wedding will not be that way. It will be great. Many people in the little churches love you and Peter. They will come, and the pirates will come—with the Christians!" She laughed. Maria laughed, too, at the idea of the pirates and Christians together.

Peter sent invitations to his few American financial supporters. Maria invited the pirates and would get her daughter in Colombia. She had no other family.

When Juan heard of the marriage, he said, "I can't believe it. She is a pirate." The remaining members of Juan's crew knew that Maria had fallen in love. With great interest, Peter's few supporters in the US read of Maria in his letters. The members of the small local churches talked among themselves of their stories about Peter and Maria. The church people agreed, "What has happened to Maria is proof that God is good." Everyone wanted to help. Isabela coordinated the event.

The small wedding grew in size. Peter's supporters were excited to come and bring their families. All of the ex-pirates also wanted to come, as did their friends. Juan, the metaphoric godfather, blessed the marriage. Samuel also wanted to be there.

Hearing the news, Ivan also made plans to attend the wedding of his one-time shipmate. He remembered the man who tried to force Maria into bed. She had kicked him, and then pulled him out of her house with her pistol stuck in his mouth. He thought that if the American was willing to marry Maria, then she should have a big wedding. He told Isabela to buy anything and everything that was needed and that he would pay for it.

The wedding was to be performed in the center of the district where the churches had been established so Isabela had a wedding pavilion built there and benches constructed. She ordered tarps for shade. The members of the churches decorated the pavilion.

Theodore flew Maria to Colombia to pick up Mariana. She held her head high as she entered her old convent school. When Maria's daughter saw her, the girl rushed into her arms and exclaimed, "Mama, you look so beautiful!" She put her arms around her. The nuns addressed Maria with respect.

The morning of the wedding, the American guests flew into the Puerto Principe airport. Juan had three of his crew members waiting to pick them up. The pirates were bathed, groomed, and dressed in new clothing. Two guarded the three rented Chevrolet Suburbans. The third, who spoke a little English, stood at the airport exit with a sign which read, *Peter's wedding.*

The airport was in poor condition. The terminal was dirty. Outside the building, the sun was harsh, the air humid and dust-laden. The Americans blinked in the glaring sun. After a moment, a tall fit man, a pastor of a church, saw the sign and waved at the man holding it. The pirate asked, "You for Peter?"

The tall American pastor stretched out his hand. "Yes, brother, we are here for Peter."

The pirate shepherded them to the three Chevrolet Suburbans. The Americans greeted the drivers in English; the Haitians responded in Creole. The Americans noticed the drivers had pistols stuck in their belts and they glanced at each other with questioning eyes. The tall pastor again said, "We are here for Peter's wedding."

The pirate who spoke a little English said, "Yes, the wedding. Get in. We drive." He patted his pistol. "All safe for you."

With hesitation, the Americans climbed into the vehicles. The women fidgeted. The Americans spoke little during the lengthy, hot and dusty trip as they traveled through the dilapidated city, and into the poor countryside scattered with small villages before arriving at the wedding site.

The Haitians arrived in cars, motorcycles, old trucks, and on foot. They came dressed in bright colors. Smiles were on their faces and celebration in their hearts. The church people came out of love for Peter and God. Through Peter they had experienced marvelous things in their lives after leaving Voodoo and spirit worship behind. Others came because of Maria. Everyone either knew her or had heard of her. They spoke of how she helped the people, but that she was also a criminal. They came to see Peter marry her. Some of the women said it was like a Cinderella story.

The people sat on the benches underneath the tarps and fanned themselves. When there was no more space on the benches, they sat on rags placed on the dirt or stood in the shade of withered trees or of the flimsy houses made of mud or sticks. Every shady area was crowded. Children played in the hot sun. Sweat ran down their dust-covered faces leaving wet, muddy streaks.

Peter was busy with the final preparations when his American friends arrived. Juan greeted them. In accented English, he said, "My name is Juan. You are Peter's American friends from the States?"

The tall, white man shook his hand hard and said, "Brother, I am Pastor Allen from New York. It is very nice to meet you."

Juan looked at him.

The pastor continued, "We would not have missed the wedding for anything. Peter worked very hard in the rescue mission in New York. We did not want to see him leave New York, but he felt a calling to return to Haiti. We are here to celebrate with him."

"Maria loves him and she helps the people, too," responded Juan blandly.

The American introduced two other pastors, their wives, and members of their congregations to Juan. With the American visitors standing around, the pastor asked Juan, "What do you do here?"

With a smile and a half laugh, knowing what he was doing, he said, "I am the godfather."

Uncertain how to respond, the American visitors remained silent.

"The men who met you at the airport work for me. Maria used to work for me. She is very happy, and I want her to be happy. Come, I will find you a place to sit in the shade."

The visitors looked at the pistol in his shoulder holster, visible inside his loose partially unbuttoned shirt. They then glanced at the men standing guard beside the Suburbans. Juan led the guests to the side of the pavilion. People scrambled out of his way.

"You sit here," instructed Juan.

Isabela watched Juan with the foreigners. She said to Maria, "Look, the devil is taking care of the Christians."

Maria took one look. She and Isabela laughed so hard at the irony that tears came to their eyes.

Peter and Maria were amazed at the crowd. Peter did not know that so many people cared for him. He never considered that the many small, but successful churches he had established in south Haiti, were an accomplishment. He did not know that anyone could see him, the defrocked Roman Catholic priest, as being successful. Maria also thought herself a failure in everything that she once believed important. She felt that no one, except for her few pirate friends, would bother to come to her wedding.

Ivan and David looked upon the gathering. Ivan said almost with a tone of amazement, "There is a God."

His uncle David responded, "Yes, and I think that Peter and Maria represent him."

A Haitian pastor officiated at the ceremony. Peter and Maria stood before the thin, black man who was looking up at his mentor, wondering how he came to be the one to perform the wedding of a person he considered to be a great man. His voice cracked with emotion. Maria wondered if she was now fulfilling her childhood dreams of serving God.

Juan stood in place of family for Maria. His pirate face was not hard. Standing next to him, Ivan said, "I have a new life, but Peter and Maria have more."

Juan shrugged his shoulders.

Completely overwhelmed that so many people came to their wedding, Peter and Maria stood before their many guests. All the congregations had come, to the last member of the families. All of Peter's supporters were present, as well as the pirates and their families. Smiling people filled the wedding area.

A huge party followed the ceremony. Large quantities of meat and fish, paid for by Ivan, were prepared in abundance. People ate and drank Coke until late. Children played in the dirt and dust, then ate some more. For some, it was the first time their hunger for good meat had ever been fully satisfied. Finally, long after dark, people went home.

Theodore said to Juan, "Love is more dangerous than smuggling and piracy. In smuggling and piracy you might lose your life, but love can break your heart. I think Maria is foolish to fall in love."

As planned, after the wedding, Peter and Maria moved to Colombia and into Maria's old house in Barranquilla. Maria's daughter Mariana was able to live with them and attend the convent school as a day student. Her prayers to live at home with a family had been answered.

The house though was in much worse condition than Maria remembered. The corners of the rooms were caked with dirt. The tile floors were stained, windows were cracked, and the appliances which had been her father's were old and in horrible condition. She and Mariana bought a new stove, microwave, and refrigerator, all in a matching maroon color. They painted the walls of Mariana's bedroom, which had been Maria's when she was a girl. They bought a new mattress and colorful sheets for her bed, and new lampshades. Opposite her bed, they hung a large picture of Jesus they bought from the convent store.

Soon after arriving, Peter and Maria met Manuel, a minister in Barranquilla who took them to the most impoverished areas of town. Dust and filth filled the air. The houses were built from brick and tar paper. Peter returned to the area each day to walk the streets and talk to people.

SANTA MARTA GOLD

To sell the rest of the marijuana, Samuel borrowed a Sea Ray boat from a friend who kept his boat at Stella Maris. Just after dark he and Juan drove the boat to their safe house on Long Island. From the beach they loaded the thousand pounds of pot into it. After carefully placing all the bales in the small cabin, Samuel backed it off the beach. Juan commented, "This boat is not good for work. It is all new, shiny fiberglass and luxury upholstery. This is a toy."

Clear of the very shallow waters, Samuel pushed the boat onto a fast plane. He then responded to Juan's earlier comment, "This boat has very powerful motors and long-range fuel. Many people use half-sunken old sailboats that go slow and are not seen, but these are still good because there are so many of them. It looks just like all the other pleasure boats."

Feeling nervous, the ocean pirate said, "I prefer the open sea. These islands are too enclosed."

Samuel responded, "There is some corruption here so you can pay someone off and not get busted."

The air was warm and thick with humidity. The darkness hid them as they headed northwest. Piloting the small craft in the still shallow waters required Samuel's full attention. He carefully reviewed his charts and laid out a course that he marked on a clipboard mounted to one side of the helm. The last thing he wanted to do was run aground with a boat loaded with contraband.

Although loaded with the cargo of marijuana, the Sea Ray was fast. It sped northward. The ride was smooth in the shadow and protection of the islands. Juan went below and poured them both a strong rum and Coke. The rum loosened their tongues; the Coca-Cola sped up their minds and kept them awake. It helped them not think about the Americans who policed the waters between the Bahamas and the US. The Marine Corps' planes flew out of the base in Homestead, Florida to detect boats coming to Florida carrying drugs, illegal immigrants, or other contraband. Once spotted, they informed the Coast Guard and police where to intercept the smugglers. They could not be everywhere though, and none of the salvaged marijuana they sold had been intercepted by the authorities. As the boat sped towards Florida, Juan and Samuel focused on women and sex rather than on the Americans.

Juan stated, "My woman in Haiti satisfies me, and takes care of me. She is hot and good in bed. Only when I'm traveling, do I sometimes have another woman. But it is not like before. The women used to throw themselves at me. Now the young and pretty ones do not look for me to sleep with. They say I am older than their father!"

"You are not very handsome. That is why you do not have more women. I am better looking. And for that reason, I have three, counting Carmen."

"They love you for your money," Juan snapped back.

"*Cabrón!* They only want you because you are the genuine Caribbean pirate. They pick up your nature even though you dress poorly. They want to go on a ride with a real outlaw, but they do not love you."

"If they only want me for sex that is good enough. I do not want them to love me. I like the ride if they are hot and nice. I have gone on the ride with many, probably more than you, smuggler, but I have never fallen in love. They want too much for me to love them, but I like the sex and their care for me. I like to live with them, too."

The boat sped through the darkness. Samuel piloted it to the northwest, and finally directly to the west.

After a while, Samuel said, "My wife in Colombia is a good woman. She loves me. The other is okay, but she is a user. The bitch, my first wife, left me. If she had waited, I would not be a smuggler; my life would be totally different."

"I am tired of hearing about her and tired that she still controls your life. We are on this boat together, and tomorrow, you go home to your wife and family in Nassau."

"All of life is colored by life shared with a woman," observed Samuel correctly.

"Maria loves Peter. They share a life."

"They love each other," Sam stated.

"We will see where that love goes. She has left making money and her previous life and started all over with Peter. I don't know what they will do for money."

"Maria says that God will provide for them."

There was a long silence as the boat sped toward Florida. After a while, Samuel asked, "Was Maria good in bed?"

"She was a tigress."

"Have you ever come close to loving anyone?"

"I thought I loved Ivan's mother. I was young and did not know better. She was a high-class woman who was disillusioned when her parents were unjustly accused of corruption. That was the only reason they were in Haiti. She was great in bed, but she insisted that she be the only woman. She left me because I had other women. She went back to the Dominican Republic with her parents and left Ivan with me. They thought he was going to grow up and just be another street kid."

Leaving the subject of women, they spoke as men of Hispanic culture—long talks that wound around issues and, if not distracted, eventually got to the heart of the matters, at least abstractly. Their conversations were part form, part typical, repeated culture-driven conversations. There were also conversations to remember a person, a place, an event—repeated to relive them. In moments fed by more alcohol, their conversations became deeper and to the heart, touching their most personal selves.

They were still talking when the lights of the Keys came into view. It was shortly after midnight. Samuel turned on the boat's stereo, interior lights, and one of the spotlights.

"You are crazy. You are telling everyone we are here."

"Those who announce their presence have nothing to hide."

Samuel navigated the small craft around the south end of the shoals near Vaca Key. The boat continued northward to the opening of the inlet, where the customer's two private houses faced a small private dock. Samuel could see the dealer and his helper waiting on the little dock as the boat entered the inlet.

"There is always a chance there are police," stated Samuel as they approached the dock. "I don't like this part."

Juan drew his pistol from his belt.

Samuel took a night vision helmet and put it on. "There is no one but the dealer. There is no other vehicle."

"The DEA or police would not be seen. They hide themselves."

Pulling up to the dock, Samuel shook hands with the two men. Samuel and Juan unloaded the bales and passed them to the men. After agreeing on the weight, the buyer/dealer handed Samuel a small suitcase filled with $100 bills. Before Samuel pulled the boat away from the dock, the van full of marijuana was already out of the driveway.

The Sea Ray slowly cruised southward along the east side of the island. The entertainment system played loud music, the boat was well lit, and Samuel and Juan talked freely and loudly like two aging men drinking and partying. As they turned to the East they saw a sheriff's boat.

"Fuck," said Samuel. "The boat is registered in the Bahamas and is not legally here. And you have no immigration papers."

"We are going out to sea, not coming in. They won't stop us."

"Jerks. They are in everyone's business."

"Can we outrun them?"

"Probably.

Juan turned the music up. Samuel sang loudly with his unmistakably American voice. The sheriff paid no attention.

Once in open and relatively deep water, Samuel pushed the throttles forward and brought the boat up onto a fast plane on course for the Bahamas.

The sea swell ran perpendicular to the Florida coast. The swell made the boat rise and fall, then rise again. The boat rocked and rolled as the mound of water slid underneath it. The boat's motion gave a sense of adventure to the otherwise relatively tame crossing and eventless unloading of the merchandise. Juan brought out more rum and Cokes from the cabin. He put his feet on the bulkhead and half reclined on the luxuriously upholstered bench. Samuel sat sideways at the helm. They toasted each other. The unspoken tension and fear faded away.

"We found the scuttled ship, salvaged half its cargo, sold most of it, and got paid," said Samuel.

"Very good business," toasted Juan.

"It is still not enough, but when we salvage the rest we will have enough money both for Paraiso and for us."

"As long as the coast guard doesn't seize us when we return to recover the rest of the marijuana."

ENGAGEMENTS

The Paraiso resort gained a small amount of notoriety through Havana Dreaming. The marina became recognized among boating circles as a superb facility. A few cruising groups began to rendezvous there. A new chef created a good menu and better atmosphere in the main restaurant and also in the marina restaurant. Timeshare sales increased some. The hotel had a small to moderate number of guests. To oversee the operations, Morales, a general manager, was hired. Ivan thought that the company could survive and eventually prosper with a capital infusion to complete the resort. Juan and Samuel, through the chain of companies that hid the ownership of Paraiso, funneled enough money into Paraiso that development could continue, but at a limited pace. Ivan didn't know of the marijuana sale, he just thought that his father and Samuel had more money. He figured they must now be out of money, and he made contacts to buy a fast boat to return to being an outlaw in order to save Paraiso.

As a result of the additional capital, Ivan, Fernando, and Luis met with the resort architects. The previously vague plans for necessary on-site development were made concrete. Morales pushed hard to complete the gardens and plantings located on the far end of the property as a precursor to the construction of small villas. To everyone's amazement, the cash flow from the timeshare sales and the operation were sufficient – although just barely — to pay costs of the operation. The resort was succeeding.

David and Juanita, now his fiancée, bought a boat and lived on it in the marina. David was port captain.

Ileana took over management of the head office in Santo Domingo. Her university training in international business, her command of English, excellent organizational skills, physical beauty, upper-class upbringing, and personal sweetness took the business to a higher level and added prestige to the company already identified as "stylish."

Although visible and highly respected, Fernando's personal business interests and family life often kept him in Haiti, so that he was present only a couple of weeks each month. In his absence, Ivan distinguished himself. He was the man with the original vision, and although without experience at the beginning, his plan for the company, and seemingly rightness for the job went before him. In his presence, it seemed only natural that the business would grow and flourish.

In the process, Ivan continued to work on perfecting his new self. He studied everything. He attended meetings with executives from resorts in the Dominican Republic and throughout the Caribbean. He listened to the plans of other companies and visited many of their resort properties. His understanding and vision for the resort and timeshare business grew. It became clear that to become a big player, Paraiso would have to become a multiple location resort company, both on the timeshare and hotel sides of the business.

As his vision developed, Ivan traveled and studied how other resorts were promoted. After such a trip, he said to Ileana, "I have some very important business in Saint Georges, Grenada. I need you to come with me. Also, I have been looking at Aruba and want to see some property there."

Ileana looked at him and smiled. "Of course, I will go with you, but there must be two bedrooms. I will only sleep with my husband."

Theodore piloted the Aztec out of Las Americas International Airport. The air was damp and hot as they departed. The bumps hidden in the air rocked and jarred the plane. As it climbed through 5,000 feet on the way to its assigned altitude, the humidity diminished considerably and the turbulence lessened.

Puffy clouds lay in all quadrants. It was still morning; thunderstorms had not yet begun to build. Ivan sat in the copilot's seat and watched the water receding underneath the climbing aircraft. Little diamonds of light reflected off the whitecaps that were poised on the wave crest of the swells as they marched through the sea. Alone in his thoughts, he remembered the trips to sea in his father's boat, the overtaking of yachts, and the thievery . . . and the thought that he would have to do it again.

Leaning slightly to speak into Theodore's ear, Ivan said, "It seems so long ago since I was a pirate, but in reality only a few years have passed." He paused and stared out the window at the ocean below. Half to Theodore and half to himself, he said, "I remember the feeling of being at sea at night—the warm humidity and darkness that wrapped around me . . ."

"You had a great life as a pirate," observed Theodore.

"I am no longer a pirate in my heart, but I miss the freedom of being an outlaw. I never knew that this life would require so much work. I miss being at sea." Ivan made no reference to his tentative plan of returning to piracy to save Paraiso.

After a pause, Theodore asked, "Do you ever worry about the police, taxes, or that the Argentines might seek vengeance?"

Meditating on his life, after a long pause, he said, "To be discovered would ruin me, but without piracy, I would not be here. I would be poor in Haiti and a slave to others just to stay alive. I think we are safe; Juan and Samuel have hidden the source of money well. But there are other risks. I still make many mistakes. In business, Fernando protects me as Luis does at times. At each juncture, I have only two choices: either I move forward into my new life – and do what is necessary to make it prosper — or return to being an outlaw. When I make mistakes, or see the future as very difficult, I want to go back—but only for a while. Then I see how to succeed, and I decide to do what is necessary to go on into my new life."

"Your new life is built upon the winnings from piracy and smuggling."

"Yes, but I was a pirate only because I was born one. The Paraiso money is from piracy and smuggling because that is my family, but

Paraiso is new and good. And besides, I learned very useful skills as a pirate. I know how to make quick money."

Theodore turned his head and looked at Ivan, wondering what he meant.

Ileana could not hear the conversation over the engine noise, but noted the earnestness between the two men. She reached her hand forward and placed it on Ivan's shoulder. He turned and looked at her. She was beautiful, smart, well educated, accessible, open, and nice. Ivan figured she was his as long as she did not know his past or his plans. He smiled reassuringly at her and took her hand. Happiness and security, something he had experienced little of in his life, were finding a growing place in his heart. He didn't want to lose her. He found that his love for her was a block in his heart that kept him from moving quickly back into piracy.

On Ileana's part, she loved Ivan, almost in spite of her better judgment. She often thought there was something in Ivan that she did not understand. He was different from the other men she knew. He had a drive to action, with somewhat of a hardness, but there was also forgiveness and generosity. He was kind and capable, but driven – and recently more so — that sometimes she worried that he was fighting some unseen battle from his past. It made her afraid at times. Although he seemed to be a well-bred young man from a family with money — there were crosscurrents in him.

Ileana had pondered long and hard whether Ivan funded Paraiso through drug money, but concluded that no, he didn't take drugs or talk about them. She thought that perhaps his family business included cattle and fishing boats. He seemed to be part cowboy and fisherman ... and maybe something not lawful? She thought hard how to explain the contradictions that existed within Ivan.

Just before dark, the plane descended toward the big airport the Cubans had constructed in Grenada. The airport area, enmeshed in a tropical rainstorm of torrential force, was barely visible—most of the runway hidden by dark clouds and dense rain. As the plane made its final approach, the rain, as though it were hail, pounded the windshield and aluminum fuselage. The noise was alarming, and the inside of the airplane became oppressively warm and humid. Seeing no nervousness or fear in Ivan, Ileana accepted the rough ride. The runway materialized out of the growing darkness at the last minute, just enough for Theodore to make a smooth transition from air to ground.

Very slowly, Theodore steered the plane next to the barely visible taxiway lights to the terminal. The three dashed to immigration and customs.

The torrential rain softened as a taxi carried the young couple the short distance from the airport to St. George's. As the driver pulled into the circular driveway, they could see the outline of a medium sized house and the lights of the harbor. The door to the tropical pink colonial style home opened as the driver came to a stop. A maid greeted Ileana and Ivan, then showed them their rooms.

Ivan and Ileana awoke early the next morning and joined each other on the balcony. The maid prepared bread, pastries, fresh juice and coffee. The air was clear and the harbor quaint. Ivan looked at Ileana and she turned her eyes to him. They reached across the table and kissed long and deep, then looked into each other's eyes—a frank stare that came from deep within their souls and expressed love.

Ivan was no saint and had known many women. He had enjoyed the sex and had taken women in lust, satisfying them and himself. He wanted Ileana in a different way, for love, not just sex. He wanted her in his arms to the exclusion of all other women. In fact, since he first met Ileana, he barely noticed other women, or rather, barely noticed their sexual charms. He wanted only her. He was captivated by her. He loved her.

The view from the house was beautiful and the town below, pleasant. Ivan and Ileana passed several hours quietly enjoying each other's presence and shared life.

Holding Ileana, desiring her to share his life in every way, Ivan said, "I invited you on this special mission. It is the most important."

"I know that it is important for Paraiso to grow," Ileana responded.

"Yes, to maintain our position, we will need to grow. I think Aruba is a wonderful place for another resort when our current resort takes off."

"Why are we in Grenada, then?" inquired Ileana.

"Grenada may be the place for a resort also, but I did not ask you here for Paraiso," stated Ivan with a smile.

He stepped inside and retrieved a package from his suitcase. Handing it to Ileana, he said, "I brought you here to give you this."

"Is it a new dress?" asked Ileana as she took the big package.

"Open it and see."

She shook it. Nothing seemed to move inside.

"Open it," he repeated.

She opened the taped seam on one end and slid the paper off. She then lifted the top off the box.

"There is only paper inside!"

"Look in the middle."

She found a ball of wrapping paper. Unrolling it, she found the gift—a gold ring with a large, single diamond.

As she looked at it, tears came into her eyes. Trembling, she watched Ivan as he placed it on her finger.

"Will you marry me?"

Unable to speak, she nodded.

Without guile, she had taken him. Ivan felt as if he had been boarded and taken captive by a woman – it was the first time in his life. He belonged to her, and at that moment, she belonged to him.

The rest of the day was a parenthesis to that event. Ivan prepared cappuccinos with melted chocolate. Well caffeinated, he led her the short distance to the shore, where they sat and looked at the boat-filled harbor.

She rested her head on his shoulder. That evening, they went to a café for a scallop dinner. On the way, he told her, "The house belongs to Samuel, one of the Paraiso investors. He says we can decorate it, paint it, and do whatever we want with it. It is ours whenever we want. A reward for our success."

Ileana took his hand and said, "I love you. It will be our retreat."

A few days later, they met Theodore at the airport. He flew them to Aruba, a small island belonging to Holland. Aruba was well positioned geographically. Air traffic was heavy and access easy. The island was better known as a tourist location, although not as pretty as Grenada. Oranjestad, the capital city of Dutch flavor, enchanted Ileana. The two nights they spent at a five-star tourist resort gave them an opportunity to explore the island and to view properties for sale.

On the second day, the resort manager learned that they represented Paraiso Resorts. He sent Ivan and Ileana an invitation to dine aboard a cruise ship. The cruise line was hosting a gathering of resort people to promote cruises, and to gain resort access for their passengers.

Having no specific plans for the evening, and always looking for an opportunity to network within the tourist business, the couple presented themselves at the dock at 4:30 p.m. A reception tent was set up away from the passenger boarding area. A representative of the cruise line, together with the ship's captain and other officers, greeted the resort and hotel people as they arrived.

All heads turned as Ivan and Ileana walked down the dock. Ivan was dressed in blue slacks and a polo shirt with the Paraiso logo that clung to his well-developed body. Ileana, always elegant, was dressed in a simple, long, white, thin dress that she made look like an evening gown. She wore her large, new diamond ring on her finger. There was a white orchid in her hair, and a silver crucifix dangled from a silver chain around her neck.

She and Ivan held hands and took matching steps. They caught the eyes of the ship's captain and the company representative. Impressed by their appearance and learning that they were affiliated with Paraiso, the company representative welcomed them graciously.

After a relatively brief gathering on the dock, the guests were escorted to the ship for a tour of the staterooms, restaurants, public areas, and recreational centers. They congregated in a roped-off section of the promenade deck.

Ivan held Ileana close to him as they looked out from the seaward side of the moored vessel. He smiled as he held her perfect well-proportioned body next to his. She, in turn, tightly held his young and strong body. They looked the part that they were living—the apparently successful business couple very much in love.

As they stared out to sea, people stared at them. Their physical appearance and dress made them both look like scions of wealthy aristocratic families. The uniting of piracy and social position was the basis of the aristocracy, but only Ivan knew that they were of that tradition.

To Ivan, neither image nor wealth mattered much. Wealth and power were something that he had seen and desired and was of interest to him, but they were no longer important to him out of the context of taking care of himself and other people, including the investors. Ileana carried some of the burdens of the importance of the wealth, image, and power that was common to her class and heritage; but when compared to others of her class, she cared relatively little about them. She loved Ivan and wanted to be his wife.

The two were oblivious to the comments and gazes of those around them. They were united in the moment as only true lovers can be, and thoughts of their image, future, and position were not in mind. The ship and the world was theirs. They were like Adam and Eve, on their own planet.

With the approach of the captain, the moment evaporated, and they were once again on a ship full of people in the harbor.

"Hello, I am Captain Derk. We met briefly when you boarded, but there were so many others. I want to welcome you aboard again, personally."

Ileana smiled, "Thank you, Captain." Ivan shook his hand.

"Would you like a tour of the ship's bridge?"

The bridge, the ship's control and command center, brought many thoughts and memories rushing to Ivan's mind, especially the Argentine boat they had pirated. It had a bridge, smaller and of an older style, but it was laid out like that of this cruise ship. The memory gates open, remembrances flooded his mind and into his soul. Ivan looked out of the ship's window to the water and remembered the boats, the sea, the adventure, the fear, and the boarding of yachts and small ships.

Seeing something stirring in Ivan, the cruise ship captain said, "Have you been to sea often?"

Ileana turned and awaited the response.

Ivan returned slowly to the present. He turned towards the captain and smiled. "Captain, yes, I have been at sea. My father had a fishing boat and his friend owned a small freighter." He did not tell the captain that they had fished for treasure to steal or that the freighter was used for smuggling.

For a couple of minutes, both men looked toward the ocean, remembering former times. The captain said, "My father also was a fisherman. I spent much of my youth, every summer, fishing with him and his crew."

"Was it good?" Ivan asked.

"Yes, but there were dangers. We fished in northern Europe, and sometimes there was very bad weather. Two times, I thought we would die in storms. But now, I remember the excitement. The memories are good. Are yours good?"

"Not all of them. There are still dangers," said Ivan, thinking of the roots of Paraiso and the need for more money.

"In this 1000-foot ship, fully stabilized, fast, equipped with every navigational aid and radar, and operated by a good crew, there is little danger." After a pause, he added, laughing, "I want to correct that—there is danger, but it is political. It is a big company, so there are always politics on board the ship and in the corporate office."

Within their partially shared world of recollection, they spoke of the sea itself—its smell and feel. They had been much closer to her in smaller boats. But there was something else. For a moment, they disconnected from the present reality and were somewhere else—living for a moment in a different sea at a different time.

Ileana stared at Ivan with questioning eyes. He came back to the present and smiled at her. He held her and left the past behind. The ship's captain also left the past behind, and the three talked about the ship, navigation, systems, and then the nature of tourists—a subject that Ivan, Ileana, and the captain knew well. Tourism was now the source of revenue that kept them all economically afloat, and the discussion went on long until they felt the obligation to return to the reception.

As they rejoined the other guests, Ileana asked Ivan, "What happened on the ship's bridge?"

"I remembered my past," replied Ivan.

"You never tell me about your life."

The cruise company's representative reappeared with several of her friends, influential people in the company. The group knew a little of Paraiso. As the conversation progressed, they were surprised to learn that Ivan apparently had control of the company.

The captain, who joined the group, said, "We are already thinking we would like to stop in Barahona."

"Your boats can unload passengers in the marina," Ivan said. "We have plenty of beach space for your passengers, and we can put up tents to serve food. We own a lot of land."

"You have authority to do that?" asked the captain.

"I do," responded Ivan.

A day later, Theodore returned for them in the Aztec. It was afternoon and thunderclouds were beginning to build over some of the islands and the sea. Theodore flew around the larger dark anvil-shaped clouds that pushed high into the sky. Occasional lightning flashes could be seen within them. Ileana reached out her hand and held on to Ivan. With a smile, he said, "The clouds grow and take direction. We will not fly through the big thunderclouds, but around them. There is little danger; only a rough ride."

Ivan looked deep into the dark clouds. He would have to plot their course with great care. Ileana was not weak or delicate, but she was a woman who was ripe to start a family. It was he who would have to shield her, look into the dark clouds in their life together, and steer a course to avoid them and protect her. The darkest cloud he saw was the current need for money and the source of the past Paraiso investment. Many Caribbean businesses and businessmen were investigated for money laundering . . . and some were prosecuted. He didn't want Paraiso or himself to be among them.

Theodore was untouched by the turbulence. It was just another trip, although an impressive one electrified by the emotions created by the danger of the tropical storm. He looked into the dark clouds of his life and didn't care. There was no one and nothing to protect, not even himself. He was along to make money and hide in adventure and women's bodies. Juan often told him that he was crazy in some logical and sane sense. He had nothing to lose.

Santo Domingo approach control sequenced the Aztec between other air traffic and a thunderstorm passing over that part of the island. The ride down the ILS to the runway was turbulent. It was raining hard when the airplane stopped at the terminal. A man appeared with a large umbrella to escort them into the immigration and customs area. Ivan and Ileana returned to their homes.

Theodore went to see his Dominican lover. That night he took her out to dinner and then dancing. He would stay with her until he had another flying job. He bought some marijuana cookies from someone he knew in the bar. He intended to stay high until it was no longer fun.

HURRICANE

Pressed by the need of cash to further the Paraiso constructions, in spite of the danger from late fall tropical storms, Samuel and Juan met on Samuel's small ship at Grand Turk. Carmen and Henry joined them. After Juan lifted the anchor, Samuel turned the boat and steered a course to the south. The early morning weather was fine, although there was a prediction of a mild tropical storm for the late afternoon. Clear of sheltered waters, there was a running sea swell and surface chop. Juan took the helm, while Samuel selected Cuban cigars. Henry was in the galley helping Carmen organize their supplies.

Much more time than anticipated had passed since the first marijuana salvage. The transportation of the marijuana to Florida had taken longer than planned, other business dealings, and the slow pace of life for people who have no fixed schedules had intervened. Fueled by alcohol and drugs, Juan had spent much of the previous months with his Haitian woman, passing the days idly, making love morning and night.

Samuel and Juan smoked the cigars with pleasure. The heavy smoke hung in the humid air. In Spanish, the men spoke of boats, the events of life, and of course, women. Their women were considerably younger than themselves, and they spoke of how they enjoyed them. Soon, Henry and Carmen joined them in the pilothouse. Carmen was dressed in her typical cutoff shorts with a small bathing suit top out of which her breasts overflowed. Henry stayed near her.

The morning was bright, but hazy due to the humidity. The air was heavy, the wind constant. As the day progressed, clouds formed in the southeast. By early afternoon, the clouds grew in size, turned dark and formed into anvil shapes that extended into the heavens.

Later in the afternoon, the wind direction changed and the velocity increased. The sky further darkened. Distant rumbling could be heard. A storm line marched toward the vessel out of the south. The swells deepened. The wind increased and the sea became rough. The waves broke across the bow of the small ship. Spray pelted the windows of the pilothouse. The seawater flooded the foredeck and ran along the sides of the cabin to exit from the aft deck.

Juan and Carmen waded their way to the foredeck to winch the dual anchors tight against the ship's bow. The warm ocean flood tried to wash them overboard. Carmen and Juan activated the port and starboard winches that pulled the anchors firm against the vessel. Carmen's wet hair flew in the wind, occasionally sticking to her flesh. The anchors secure, holding on for life, they managed to return to the safety of the pilothouse.

As the swells grew, the small ship labored through them. The thunder increased, and the rain lashed the vessel. The severe sky, already dark with ominous clouds, grew blacker in the deepening afternoon. Sheets of lightning illuminated the inside of the clouds.

The vessel buried its bow in the sea, picking up a ton or two of water that churned as it flowed over the decks. Samuel decreased speed so that it rode over, rather than through, the march of waves and swells. The spray became as wet as the ocean itself.

Samuel said, "This is rougher than I thought it would be, but it does not matter. It is only a tropical storm. It is good to enjoy the storms while they put on a show."

Samuel lit up a joint and took a mouth full of whiskey. Juan joined him with the whiskey, but didn't smoke. Carmen smoked much and drank heavily to help her cope with her increasing nervousness. She thrust her chest forward and put her hands deep in the pockets of her shorts, pulling the front down. Samuel reached over and brought her to his side. He placed his hand inside her cutoffs and held her by the hip. Shortly thereafter, he gave the wheel to Juan and took Carmen below to his cabin.

The thunder decreased, and an hour later, the rain was much less. The winds continued. It was night, and the high mounds of the sea swells and the accompanying waves were only seen when the clouds flashed across the sky. Finally, the lightning ceased, and there was only darkness. The racket of the wind continued.

The Loran marked the position of the vessel. The depth finder indicated deep water. The ship's radar protected the boat from colliding with another. Their course was still for the scuttled drug ship. Samuel and Carmen continued to drink whiskey. Carmen found refuge from fear as Samuel made hard love to her in his cabin.

The large swells and waves continued to wash over the ship, and after a time, the wind increased. The lightning returned and the sky lit up in sections. In short time, the celestial show increased in intensity. Once again, claps of thunder crashed all around them.

Eventually, Samuel and Carmen returned to the pilothouse. The waves, seen in flashes, resembled hills. The rain spray and wash from the waves ripped the vessel. Samuel took the helm. Carmen appeared with snacks, sandwiches, and coffee. Henry, sitting in the pilothouse – even though dark skinned — was ashen in color. Instead of food, Carmen handed him a plastic bag.

A half-hour later, the boat was under another advancing squall line. The sea was almost constantly visible in the lightning. Waves crashed over the vessel. The pitching motion increased, and Samuel and Juan looked at each other with a mutually questioning look.

"Not good," said Samuel. Juan shrugged and held up his middle finger to the storm.

The squall line passed, but the wind did not diminish. It occasionally changed directions, adding cross-waves and agitation to the marching army of already angry waves. The ship's bow pitched into the waves, and the vessel rolled dangerously in the cross swell. Waves occasionally struck the vessel from the side.

The steel and aluminum mini-ship could weather virtually any storm head on, but a rogue wave from the side could roll her over. She was built to face the storm, not to encounter her from behind or the side. If a large wave hit her from the stern, it could break open the aft doors and flood her.

Carmen stood near Samuel and held onto a post. She bit her lower lip so hard that it bled.

The storm held steady but did not further increase during the night. At dawn, the wind increased once again. It tore even more loudly at the vessel. The sea waves grew. The smaller cross-waves dangerously buffeted the ship from the sides. The weather service reported that the tropical storm had grown to a category 1 hurricane.

The waves, advancing like moving hills, made it impossible to turn the ship and run for port. The only choice was to continue into the storm. The wind deafened.

Juan and Samuel faced danger often: guns, law enforcement, equipment failure, shoal water, and problems with their crews. In all these, they knew no fear. The problems usually arose unexpectedly and disaster came, if at all, quickly. There was no time to worry. The prolonged storm, however, allowed them plenty of time to consider the danger.

On occasion when the boat rolled hard to the side, the pirate and smuggler would look at each other with the blank stare of possible impending death. Carmen moved closer to Samuel and held on to him as though for dear life. He held on to the wheel and tried to remain steady. Henry braced himself behind the settee grasping the plastic bag to his mouth. He vomited until blood was on his lips.

Juan did not believe in God. He believed that life ended as it apparently began, suddenly and without purpose or meaning. Having decided on his view of existence and not believing in true good or evil, he did not much care what happened to him. He was Juan, the thief and pirate. He had no regrets or second thoughts. He had completely given himself into his life and identity. There was no one else. This view gave him the strength to look at the storm and not give a damn. He braced himself against the port side bulkhead of the pilothouse and drank a moderate amount of whiskey. He looked at Carmen and wished he could take her back to his bed.

Samuel, unlike Juan, was not convinced that this life was all there was. Something in his soul bothered him and told him that his life was not right, but the pain in his heart blocked him from change. He lived for escape and his multi-fold masquerade, but in spite of all the cover-up and his work, his two families, Carmen, and his wealth, he felt disconnected. In the fear and stress of the moment, he felt unfulfilled and mildly fearful. Unspoken, but deep in his heart, he wished that Maria's God existed and would save him, not from death in the storm, but from his life of masquerade and past loss. His forehead furrowed.

The day passed slowly. The pilothouse filled with unease from the extreme noise and the continual roll and pitch of the vessel. Muscles strained. Mildly drunk on whiskey, Samuel occasionally swore at the waves and God. Carmen's face was pale with fear. She asked, "Are we going to die?"

"I don't think so," replied Samuel.

"You don't *think* so?" Tears ran down her face in rivulets.

Henry's dark skin was pale and green. There was nothing left in his stomach. He vomited liquid mixed with blood. "Oh, God, money does me no good if I am dead," he moaned. "I was better off with little. I wish we had just left the rest of the marijuana."

Carmen and Henry looked at Juan. He looked back and shrugged. His actions were not reassuring. Carmen cried harder.

By evening, however, the storm had moved a distance to the north where it was dissipating, never having grown above a Category 1 hurricane. The wind abated in degrees. The sea began to calm. After midnight, the waves had significantly lessened, and the wind was at only forty knots. The inside of the pilothouse was comparatively quiet. Carmen broke herself free from Samuel and managed an unconvincing insolent smile as she went below to prepare food for Samuel and Juan. Henry raised himself from the settee and went below to wash.

Samuel said, "Impossible to salvage the marijuana in these waves."

Juan responded, "Go to Santo Domingo."

Samuel set course for the east side of the Dominican Republic in order to get to Santo Domingo, which was on the south side.

The waters settled much by the time the ship arrived at Santo Domingo. Samuel anchored in front of the city between the big hotels and the colonial zone. He set both anchors and flew the country's courtesy flag. Leaving Carmen and Henry on board to sleep, Juan and Samuel, shaved and dressed in city clothes, boarded the ship's tender—the Zodiac inflatable that had amazingly survived the storm lashed to the aft deck. They motored into the small harbor. They did not bother with customs or immigration. They simply moored the dingy at the dock on the east side of the little harbor.

Juan walked up the dock ramp like it was his marina. He didn't look poor, but neither did he carry himself like the often self-important rich. He was of more than average height and still in good physical condition. No one provoked him. There was nothing in him that projected sleaziness.

In truth, Juan had morals. He simply rejected that with which he disagreed. The thing that most bothered him was when he failed to live up to his standards, which he did with regularity. Few people took him for a fool.

Samuel was a well-built man and taller than Juan. He had the air of a man of money, which he was, and of a man who knew how to handle himself.

The dock policeman looked at them and politely greeted them. Other, less imposing persons, and especially the poor, he questioned. Samuel and Juan were not men to be questioned.

A FRIEND IN A STORM

A few days before Samuel and Juan left Grand Turk to salvage the marijuana, Peter and Maria sensed that a storm was going to hit. The winds began in the early afternoon, and then rain clouds filled the sky, invading the coast of northern Colombia. Soon, the wind began to blow hard, and the sporadic rains increased in intensity. The unseen air washed across the face of the earth like a sea wave. When it ran into a building, it wrapped itself around the structure, rushing with great force along its sides. The clouds moved rapidly across an obscured sky, their underside forming dark protrusions.

There was deep rumbling, then a loud bang followed by another deep rumble as if heavenly bowling balls were hitting the celestial floor and rolling down the alleyway. At the end of the roll, there were very loud crashes as the balls hit the pins and sent them flying. Peter said, "It is Jesus and his disciples bowling in the heavens."

The cosmic bowling noise increased. The clouds sunk to five hundred feet above the earth and churned as they moved across the darkening sky. The clouds lit up from the inside like old pinball machines. The interior flashes grew in intensity, then became ominous. Darts of light escaped from the clouds. The darts increased, forked, and spiked, touching buildings, palm trees, and the ground. The sky became a marvel of noise, lights, and white-spiked fire. Each time the thunder exploded, the earth and all on it shook from the percussion.

The flat streets accumulated water that rose to the ankles, then the calves. In unpaved areas, the streets turned into deep mud. Low areas flooded. Houses built of sheet metal were torn apart. Tar paper houses collapsed onto themselves or blew away and rolled across the land like malicious tumbleweeds. Loose sheet metal smashed into other houses destroying them. Low-lying houses were awash in muddy water.

The intense storm continued all night and well into the morning, but did not grow to hurricane category in Colombia. When the rain finally stopped, the sun slowly broke through, and the water began to vaporize into steam. Broken electric lines lay on the earth and in the water, electrocuting a few people in their path. The rich and poor alike dripped with sweat and moisture.

Electricity was quickly returned to the affluent. They escaped the worst of the heat and sharply increasing humidity with air-conditioning. Cars began circulating, and well-to-do people were returning to normal life.

Recovery for the very poor was another story. The little clothing and bedding they had was wet, dirty, and scattered in the mud. Their few cooking utensils were also caked with mud. The wood and charcoal they used for cooking were saturated and would not ignite.

Many were without shelter and stood or squatted on the land where their little home had previously been. Fresh water from the community source was inadequate to wash and clean everyone.

Maria's concrete house, located in a slightly elevated area on a paved street, was little affected by the storm. As the water evaporated, there was little visual remembrance of the storm. Peter, Maria, and Mariana drove through the outlying neighborhood to seek out their friends and acquaintances. They piled the neediest and their clothing into the pickup and took them back to their house where they could wash. Maria and other women prepared food for them to eat, which was paid for by Maria out of her dwindling pirate money.

Peter bought large supplies of corrugated tar paper and gave it to the men whose houses had been destroyed or needed repair. It was a time of distress for the poor, but with help from Peter and Maria, the people were encouraged. For a while, the first floor of their house and little yard were crowded with people camping—they shared a life with them.

As a girl, Maria had lived in the house with her father or at the convent when her father was away. When on board the ship, she was the captain's daughter. In Haiti, surrounded by grinding poverty, she was protected by her money, by Juan, and the pirates. At the end of the few days during which the poor lived in their yard, Maria said to Peter, "Their lives are so poor. I did not know the depth of their poverty. They have no skills, no social ability, and little grace. If you scratch the surface, everything about them is poor. Total poverty controls their lives in every way."

At the wedding, Peter's American supporters and friends saw what he was accomplishing so they increased the money they sent to him; but the amount received did not cover the expense of the ministry. The people had parasites, worms, amoebas, and tremendous other health and dental issues. They lacked a good diet. Some of the children were greatly neglected and needed shelter and love. Using her money saved during piracy, Maria helped them as best she could.

As her belly grew, Maria's main focus turned to her little house and her deep love for Peter, her daughter, and her unborn baby. Unlike her traumatic unwed pregnancy with Mariana, this baby had a father and a home. In her heart, Maria felt that this little house that once belonged to her father was now truly her home. She decorated it herself, and she and Peter had freshly painted rooms. Maria's instincts told her to pad her nest egg in preparation for the birth of the baby, but each day more of her savings were spent on the needy. For the first time in many years, she felt vulnerable. She had no gun. No pirate team to help her – just Peter.

With the ceasing of Juan's piracy operations, life had become very predictable in Haiti for Maria's friend, Isabela. She passed the time pleasantly enough with Stephen and their children, but he lacked zest and imagination, and their kids were more occupied with the little one-room school and the other children. Stephen, old, but ridiculously strong, paid Theodore to fly her to Barranquilla for a week.

After flying far to the west to avoid the bad weather, Theodore turned south then flew east along the Colombian coast. The storm had moved off the coast of Barranquilla and the weather was clear. Barranquilla approach sequenced the twin-engine Piper to land behind an Avianca jet. Ground control directed his plane to the customs area. They knew the plane and on many occasions had very thoroughly inspected it. The officials left it and Theodore alone, but they detained Isabela. She was dark, spoke rather poor Spanish, and carried a Haitian passport. They wanted to know why she was coming to Colombia and how she could afford a private charter plane.

Theodore intervened saying to the immigration official, "Leave her alone. Don't you see that she is with me?" The official figured she was one of Theodore's lovers and stamped her passport. Outside the immigration/customs area, Maria greeted Isabela with an embrace and kiss on her cheek.

Isabela responded, "You look more beautiful than ever."

"Must be the pregnancy glow!" She said pointing to her pregnant belly.

"You look happy and beautiful."

Maria said, "I miss you!"

"I miss you too! Life has been so quiet without you. I can no longer go to your house for tea or coffee and hear of your adventures! The pirates have stopped, so Stephen is bored and stays mostly at home."

The pilot, standing next to them, tried to understand what they said, but their words tumbled out of their mouths in the oddest mix of Spanish, Creole, and English. After trying to follow what they were saying, he threw up his hand and said, "You two are crazy." He got into a taxi and went to the house of his latest Colombian girlfriend.

On the way to Maria's house, Isabela said, "I can't wait to see your house. You have often told me about it."

The outside of the house, well painted, looked nice. Inside, the furniture pleased Isabela, but going into the patio area behind the house, she looked at the tiled floor and blank concrete walls. "Where is your garden? Where are your flowers? Even in Haiti, you had flowers in tin cans. Why no flowers here?"

Maria shrugged.

Patting Maria's tummy Isabela said, "Your unborn child is like a garden growing inside you. We will make a garden for your house too."

The following morning, Isabela left the house early. When Maria woke up and did not find her friend, she worried. A short time later, Isabela returned in a taxi with newly purchased gardening tools and small potted flowering plants, and lots of bougainvilleas. Upon seeing the flowers, Maria smiled ear to ear. She hugged her friend.

The women placed the soil in concrete planters and in the large pots that Isabela had purchased. They focused on their work and chattered happily in their mix of languages. They worked for a while and then went to a local café. They drank coffee and tea and ate the *oreja* pastries that Maria craved. It was still early summer, and the mornings were relatively temperate. They took a long walk.

Maria shared, "I feel vulnerable. Donations are not enough. The people we work with need so much. I spend much of my money on the poor. You know me, I have always been good about giving to those in need, even in Haiti. But now I have my own family and a baby on the way. More than ever, I want to have savings for my family."

Continuing to pour out her feelings, "What hurts most is that I disappointed myself. As a girl, I wanted to serve God. Instead, I did the opposite. I so wanted to be a good girl, but I turned out so bad. I failed in what I most wanted." Tears fell from her eyes, leaving imprints on the soil where she was planting.

After a while, she added, "I threw away my gun. I felt secure with my gun and my money. I trust Peter, and I try to trust in God, but I am afraid."

Together, they poured the soil from the burlap coffee sacks into the planters and flower pots. Isabela let Maria talk as they worked until Maria had to take a break. "My back hurts," she said.

Later walking to the nearby cafe, Isabela laughed and spoke of the pirate days. Maria joined her friend as she laughed and shared stories about Juan and the pirates. Prompted by Isabela, they both mimicked Juan's expressions and his walk. They copied the voice of some of his crew and laughed so hard their stomachs hurt.

Isabela took a scarf from Maria and put it around her shoulders. She stuck one hip out, put her hand on the other, and put a stick in the small of her back where Maria often carried a pistol. With a punk look, she said, "My name is Maria. I am bad. Don't tread on me or I will make you sorry."

Maria almost fell to the pavement, laughing at her friend's imitation of her. Completely unaware of their past, the barista smiled at them and said, "You two are silly. What language are you speaking? No one can understand." Maria just shrugged her shoulders and smiled.

Isabela made fun of Juan's macho looks and again mimicked the way he walked. She suddenly stopped and asked, "Maria, was Juan a good lover?"

"He is only a pirate. He was good for long hot sex, but was always distant. He never gave himself to me, no matter how much I tried."

"Did you love him?"

"Yes, and I tried to save him."

"You're crazy. Even I know that you can't save the devil." Isabel said as held fingers behind her head so that they looked like devil horns.

Under Isabela's care for her friend, the days and work in the garden passed quickly with happy laughter. They placed the jasmine, the wildly colored bougainvillea, and other plants into the earth. The garden was coming together as haphazardly as the structure of their speech.

Peter, the only person who managed to figure out some of what the women spoke, commented, "We will soon see a garden."

Isabela smiled at him. She noted the kindness in his eyes. In the mornings, Mariana went to school and Peter went to one of the little missions they were establishing. The bougainvillea was extravagant: red, purple, yellow, and orange. The new jasmine plants spread their scent. Loving their fragrance, Maria leaned towards the tall plants and placed her nose near the jasmine flowers each time she entered and left the walled garden.

The recently purchased flowering plants were thin but tall. The two women tied them to stakes and to the walls. Isabela bought chairs and a canopy that they positioned in the middle of the garden. After many days, filled with talk — crazy laughter — and some tears, the planting was finished. The two friends sat in the shade and perspired freely.

Isabela looked at her smiling and happy friend. She said, "Your God is the true God and is great. He has made a garden in your life and now in your home. You do not see it, my saintly friend, but I see that you are no longer hard, but soft as the new soil we just prepared for the plants. I think your God loves you very much."

"Do you really think he loves me?"

"Do you not see the garden?"

Looking around her, Maria said, "Yes."

"No, not that garden. I mean your life. You have a new heart, a new baby in your belly, a daughter who is happy, and a husband who loves you. Also, the people who come here to visit love you. Do you not see the bougainvillea all around? I know the Voodoo gods, but your God is beautiful. Open your eyes to what he has given you. And about the money? It was pirate money. Let it go. I think your God will provide for you."

Maria looked at her with grateful tears in her eyes.

The next day Isabela bought some paint for one last project. The two women decorated the walls of the garden with bright, tropical colors. When the paint was dry, Isabela began painting bright and preposterous looking animals on the back wall. Isabela passed Maria the cans of paints and she painted even brighter animals. When Mariana came home from school, she joined them and created a silly giraffe. The cheerful garden with the quirky menagerie of colorful creatures was now complete.

On their last night together, Maria, Peter, Mariana, and Isabela had dinner on the patio. Theodore joined them. Seeing Maria so happy, he asked, "Maria, what happened to you?"

She responded, "I am happy with my new life."

Peter stood up, took his wife in his arms, kissed her, and said, "It is God's gift to you."

IVAN'S STORY

The day that the storm hit the Dominican Republic, Ivan arrived at the house of Ileana's parents in the early evening. Although it was the rainy season, it had not rained for days. The dusty air was heavy with humidity and clouds were on the horizon.

The maid opened the door. Dressed in a lightweight, flowered summer dress and sandals, Ileana greeted Ivan inside the front hallway. Her dark hair rested casually on her shoulders and spilled onto her back. Her light skin contrasted perfectly with her dark hair and eyes. On a silver chain, a Catholic silver crucifix lay against her chest between the top of her full breasts.

Ivan looked at her and smiled. "Wow! You are beautiful."

She gave him a look reserved only for him and blushed. "There are unexpected guests . . . friends of my parents. They have problems."

Ileana led him into the living room. It was the second time he met the old couple—the friends of her parents, his maternal grandparents.

Ivan was cordial. A couple he had not met, about his father's age, was also there. After being seated, it became clear from the conversation that the woman was the daughter of the older couple. The sudden realization came to him that the woman in front of him was his mother, Elizabeth, and that the man was her husband.

Ivan couldn't help staring. He had only faint and mixed memories of her, remembering mostly the searing loss he felt when she left Haiti and returned to the Dominican Republic without him. This was the woman who had deserted him, completely abandoned him. She had never even looked for him. She went on to a new life and did not look back. Her new family had occupied her, and she had taken him out of her heart.

Ivan turned pale in the darkening room, and he withdrew into himself. Ileana immediately sensed something was wrong. She looked at Ivan. When Ivan looked back at her, she could see profound hurt in his eyes. He seemed lost in a tempest in an unseen sea. She wondered if he was having a heart attack.

He was, though not a physical one. The very core of the hurt in his heart—abandonment—had ripped open and the pain flowed throughout his whole being. He was the lost, motherless child again. Unknown. Unloved. Unwanted. He paled to the very core of his being as though his blood had entirely left his body.

He entered into a cold, quiet, and dead place. He struggled to remember good thoughts. He found a place of refuge and strength: Juan had helped him. He found another place to stand; the business was successful. He reflected on his past life and the one he now led. He had been a kid abandoned to the streets, and then a pirate, but now he was someone else. He reasoned that he did not have to prove himself to this woman—his mother. She was merely a person of no consequence in his new life. He forced his thoughts to tell himself that he had gone on to a new life, as she had.

The thought of his new life pushed against the lifelessness of abandonment and allowed him to settle, but after a time, anger arose at the hurt this woman had caused. The inner rage rose with a vengeance. He forced himself to think again about what he had been taught by Fernando—to forgive, as Fernando had forced himself to forgive Fidel Castro for ruining his life and country. He recalled Fernando's words: *I have learned in forgiving that forgiveness is one of the big keys to life.* Juan sent him to Fernando to learn. The thoughts came in a jumble, but from somewhere within, Ivan forced forgiveness.

He came in from the horrible storm, left it, and stepped ashore. He was again seated next to his beautiful Ileana. He noticed her very concerned look for him. He smiled at her as much as he was able. He had weathered that part of the storm.

The other people in the room had not noticed Ivan's reaction. Ileana's parents, her politician brother, and the others were all listening to the older man—Ivan's grandfather. From the conversation, Ivan understood that a medium-sized commercial hotel the older couple owned was in decline.

The aged man said, "Although our hotel is in a good location, the more modern facilities have taken away many of our clients. Our economic life is in bad shape. We spent all the money we could borrow remodeling half the floors of the hotel, and now we have that debt. The remodel did not recapture our clients, so we are worse than before. We have a heavy debt to pay. We must sell our house, and maybe with that money, we can pay the loan and survive. We will have to move into the hotel."

The old man said that his daughter Elizabeth would also have to live in the hotel. He went on to explain that her husband, a prosecutor, had been wrongfully accused of corruption and was out of work. The principal political party was trying to discredit him. His name was in the newspapers, something the old man said he understood well since he, himself, had experienced the same thing years ago. "For that reason, I took my family to Haiti for a while."

The old man was trembling. His son-in-law looked stricken in his face and posture.

Ivan felt nothing for these people. But he listened to them, just as he had to his employees when they told him of their problems. When the group moved to the dining room and a moment arrived when he had to say something, he expressed sympathy.

The dinner with Ileana's family passed in seriousness imposed by the problems of their friends. Ivan was concerned only when Ileana's brother, a friend, expressed concern that perhaps the opposing politicians would try to implicate him.

Ivan and Ileana left after dinner. Ivan made his departure as cordial as he could, but felt the need to be alone with Ileana. The rain was just beginning. They had only driven a short distance in Ivan's four-wheel drive Ford when the rain began to fall hard. The inside of the car filled with the noise of the raindrops flattening themselves against the roof of the vehicle.

Ivan struggled within himself as he maneuvered the car through the now heavy rains and the deepening water. He sought clarity as to what to tell Ileana. Her family was tied to that of his birth mother. He had a past that she did not know.

As the water deepened across the road, Ivan pulled into a park not far from Ileana's house. The park was on higher ground, and the water did not pool there. He pulled off the road, turned off the windshield wipers, but let the engine and air-conditioning run.

There in the dark, Ileana sensed something was stirring within Ivan. What she sensed was not with her eyes, but with her heart and through the connection that existed between them. She waited.

Ivan turned on the interior light. "Ileana, you have to know more about me, about my family, and where I come from. You must know where I have lived and what I have done."

His face was pale, his expression serious. Ileana loved him with all her heart and soul and had waited long to find out the mystery contained within the man she loved.

In a solemn tone, Ivan began. "I was raised in Puerto Principe, Haiti. My father made his living by taking people to Florida in boats illegally. My mother and her family were from this country. They left Santo Domingo for political reasons. We spoke Spanish, and I learned Creole in the streets. We lived near them, and they cared for and protected me some, but I was a street kid. I remember hearing them say that I was a savage.

"When I was around six, maybe seven, my mother and her family left for the Dominican Republic. I was left behind with my father. We moved to a very poor area. There was a lot of violence, and I was often beaten up. My father left me mostly on my own.

"My father soon made enough money to buy his own boat. When he made more money, we moved to a better area, although still rough. He had his own life and didn't care much about me. I went to school sometimes. Even very young, I learned to protect myself with a knife.

"After a couple of years, my father decided there was more money in smuggling marijuana into the United States. He also stole from yachts, foreign fishing boats, and small inter-island freighters. The money was easier to come by, and he worked less. He spent a little more time with me. There was a Haitian woman who lived near us. I played with her kids, and she cared for me. My father paid her.

"We eventually moved to southeast Haiti, on the coast. From there he continued smuggling and robbing yachts at sea. Business was good.

"A small school existed in the village where my father established his base. A young woman, Maria, and her friend Isabela paid for a good teacher. I was about eleven when I started to study there. The teacher was from Colombia; he spoke and taught us proper Spanish and Creole. I learned to read, write, do math, and I read many books. At my father's base, we spoke mostly Spanish, in part because it was so near the border with this country. My father speaks good English. His mother was an American and he and Stephen, who was one of his crew members, taught me English.

"I was about fourteen when my father insisted that I go on the boat with him. I learned about boats, how to navigate, and how to take a boat into Florida without being caught. I also learned how to steal from yachts. We were smugglers and pirates, and my father was the chief. He had a crew of seven or eight. I was one more.

"Life was not bad on the southeast coast. We had money. My father built a good house, and he was at home often. His brother, my uncle David, lived with us and was nice. He and Maria made sure that I studied and learned."

Ileana stared at him in silence, unable to move. Tears welled in her eyes. Her body began to tremble.

"My father had friends. One friend, a smuggler, taught me how to operate bigger boats. As I grew up, I realized that although I did not hate my life, I did not want it. I told my father, and he said maybe he would help. His friend, Fernando, whom you know from Paraiso, owed him a favor.

"Fernando's baseball manufacturing plant was financed by my father years ago. When my father asked him to teach me about business and society, Fernando agreed. I became his student. I had tutors, studied hard, and worked jobs of every kind in the baseball plant. It was difficult, but I stayed. Fernando trained me to be of his class. He came from a family of Cuban aristocrats. His parents had lost most everything during the revolution but stayed in Cuba. Years after, Fernando went to Haiti. Much of what you see me as today, he taught me."

In her innocence, Ileana struggled to understand, to find words. She had been raised in a close family. Her life had been sheltered and good. Her knowledge of drugs, thievery, violence, and family discord were known only from the newspapers and gossip.

"You are the front man for a family of pirates, smugglers, and criminals." Ileana declared, near hysteria.

Ivan's heart sank. With intense emotion, he said, "No. I am my own man. That is my family, not me. But yes, Paraiso is mostly owned by my father and his friend. When I finished with Fernando, I told him I wanted to go into business. Somehow, I convinced my father and his friend to invest. They did, reluctantly. They only did because my father said I had become so different   . . . and because of Fernando. But they invested. Paraiso was mostly my idea. Fernando directed the form, but the idea was mostly mine. We never dreamed it would become such a big company. God was with us, and we sold a part to Havana Dreaming, never imagining it would grow so fast."

Ivan paused and took a deep breath. "The rest, you know. But that is my history."

"Why do you tell me now?" demanded Ileana.

Ivan softly replied, "Because, the old couple sitting in your house right now are my grandparents. Their daughter Elizabeth is my mother. Your friend Elena is my aunt, the younger sister of my mother."

"What? No!" Ileana slumped forward and cried. She screamed, "They left you!"

"They did."

"How is that possible? They are good people. This cannot be. No. Why would your mother marry a smuggler and pirate? The story is not right."

"It is right. She was in rebellion and disillusioned because of what happened to her parents. I am telling you the truth."

Ileana was confused. "It doesn't matter—No, it does matter. But either way, you are the son of a thief and crook. You are the son of a smuggler of persons. But worse, *you* are a pirate, a thief, and smuggler. You are a criminal. Did you kill anyone?"

"No."

"That does not matter. You have done awful things. They are all wrong. Your entire life is built on stolen money!"

"No, Ileana. My life is built upon my decision to become someone different. But, yes, the money that built the business originally came from crime."

"You are the crime family front man."

"No, I am a man who grew up in a crime family. I made the change. My father did not push me to launder his money. I pushed him to invest. By some miracle, he did. I did not think he would."

"I so much respected my mother's friends, but they are awful people! They abandoned you to your pirate father. Why are they

PIRATES, SCOUNDRELS, AND SAINTS

seemingly good? Why didn't they love you? What is wrong with the world?"

"They didn't think I was worth anything."

"But how could your mother leave you? She never spoke of you. She abandoned you! And so did your grandparents. They are terrible people."

"No, they are just people. They owe me nothing."

"They are awful. They owe you everything."

"Nothing. They owe me nothing," Ivan pleaded. "You don't understand. I have a new life. *I am new.* I had a chance, I took it, and I worked hard. I will give them a chance. Besides, Fernando taught me to forgive, just as he forgave Castro."

"They are horrid. And you are a criminal. Your father and his brother are criminals. You have done wrong. How could I ever have loved you?"

Ileana crumpled forward. She felt confused. She put her face into her hands and cried with deep sobs for a long time. She so much wanted Ivan to comfort her, yet when he tried, she pulled away.

When Ileana finally stopped crying, she looked at Ivan. He was downcast and sad, but also showed concern for her. The initial shock past, she wondered about him. In her mind, she replayed all that he had said.

After a long pause, in the shock and in pain, she withdrew — she extracted her heart from inside his. She pondered whether she could ever trust and give her heart again to such a man as Ivan had revealed himself to be. Her emotions and thoughts ran through her heart and soul.

For Ivan, the internal awareness of the withdrawal of her heart from his brought back the flood of childhood abandonment. At that moment, he again became Ivan the street kid, whose mother had abandoned him. He felt utterly alone, worthless, and rejected. The feelings came back with great power. The loss, the sadness, and the deep hurt rushed in and overwhelmed him. He had released his birth mother and her family out of a heart of forgiveness; but the strength, the base that allowed him to release them, in large part, was from the love of Ileana.

There is little pain like that of a broken heart. It wrecks and affects the whole being, making a person a walking zombie—a dead person living on automatic without real emotions, lifeless. All the loss, all the hurt of his life came crashing down on Ivan, as did a stark awareness of the wrongness of his prior life—a life he had not chosen but was born into. Suddenly he was glad that he would have to return to piracy to raise money for Paraiso. He had tried to live honestly with kindness, and it had not worked.

Ivan and Ileana sat, each alone, looking at each other. With nothing left to say, Ivan began the drive back to Ileana's house. Standing water covered the streets. Some of the smaller cars had stalled. The heavier Ford easily cut through the partially flooded streets. At Ileana's house, Ivan opened her car door, walked with her onto the porch, and stayed with her until the maid opened the front door. He stayed by the doorway. At the far end of the front hallway, his maternal grandparents, his mother, and her husband could be seen gathering their things. In the hallway, Elizabeth approached, speaking to Ileana alone. In deep anguish, Ivan quietly murmured, "Here comes my mother." With the words still on his lips, he turned, opened the large front door and walked out, pulling the door closed behind him.

For the first time in a long time, Ivan was angry. Angry at the life he had been born into. Angry at his birth mother and her family for leaving him in it. Angry at Ileana for deserting him. He had worked hard to make a new life, and he did it, but the past robbed his present happiness. Theodore had warned him. He wondered what else from his past awaited to destroy his present. He considered leaving Paraiso and Fernando and returning to his past life.

Behind the closed door, Ileana stumbled backward against the wall. Her mind was desperately trying to grasp all she had heard. Ivan had been a pirate, the son of friends of her family who did not care to know him. The words *what* and *why* flooded her mind. She clutched her chest, sobbed with her whole being, convulsed, and began to slide down the wall. Before Ileana collapsed to the floor, Ivan's mother rushed and caught her. The woman looked at Ileana with great tenderness. Ileana stared back at her and thought, *Why couldn't you have loved Ivan . . . your son?* With that, she fainted.

SANTO DOMINGO AND PARAISO

Following Ivan's disclosures, Ileana remained distant from him. She knew that she loved Ivan and that he loved her. Love was not the issue; the issue was accepting him for who he had been, for his tainted past, and the roots of Paraiso. Although she wanted to love him as before, her conscience did not allow her to do so. She was a Hispanic woman raised with strict standards, and she felt she did not have permission to give herself entirely to him. She had no one to confide in and no one to grant her that permission. She placed their future on hold. There was a mostly unspoken distance between them.

After almost two weeks of partying in Santo Domingo with Carmen and Henry, Juan and Samuel decided to visit the Paraiso office. They entered the reception area as though they owned the place, which they did. Their entrance was not, however, due to their financial participation—it was just their entrance. They walked into a bar the same way.

The young receptionist asked their names, and the two men obliged. Their names meant nothing to the woman, the men's ownership buried behind a dozen trusts and companies.

"How can I help you gentlemen?" inquired the receptionist.

"We want to see Ivan," responded Juan.

"I am sorry, sir, but señor Ivan is not here. His assistant, la señorita Ileana is here, perhaps she could assist you."

Juan had never met Ileana, although he had heard much about her. He responded that yes, she could help.

Ileana was wearing a pretty, knee-length summer dress with a relatively high neck, as she approached through the glass doors. Her abundant dark hair was off her shoulders. She was both attractive and professional.

Ileana looked at the men before she opened the doors. She immediately noted there was something distinctive and commanding about them. She felt faintly fearful as she walked into the reception area.

Through a forced smile, she asked, "In what way may I serve you, señores?"

"We are here to see Ivan, but you are much prettier," responded Juan.

Ileana mildly blushed as she gave him a look that communicated that the meeting would be all business.

Juan smiled at her, then laughed. "You are professional, but also very pretty. Everything Ivan has told me about you seems to be true."

Ileana studied Juan, then Samuel. "May I ask how you know Ivan?"

"I met him when he held me up," replied Juan.

Ileana blanched. She wondered if Ivan had stolen from these men and if they were seeking payback. Telling the truth about his present business, she said, "*Señor*, Ivan never holds up anyone. He is a serious and honest businessman."

Juan and Samuel couldn't help themselves. Remembering Ivan with a pistol in his hand, they chuckled.

Ileana was taken aback, but the way Juan laughed made her take a good look at him. There was something of Ivan in the man she was speaking to—a faint resemblance and something about his air. It occurred to her that perhaps the man was Ivan's father, the real pirate. She further paled. A tremor passed through her body. Her smile froze on her face.

Juan looked at her with a questioning look and smiled a comforting smile. Ileana recovered and made polite conversation.

Ivan had lost much of the pirate inheritance of his father, so it was only in the course of further conversation that Ileana definitively concluded she was speaking to Ivan's father, the ex-husband of her family's friend. Her thoughts bounced. She fanned her face with her hand. Much to her surprise, she was not repulsed. There was nothing repulsive, neither in Juan's manner or appearance, nor in that of the other man, whom she gathered was Juan's close friend. It occurred to her that he might be the smuggler Ivan had mentioned. She thought him better looking and a well-bred man gone somewhat to seed.

Before Ivan, had she known the truth of such men, she would have excused herself as quickly and as curtly as possible without endangering herself. Under these circumstances, she did not. They continued in light conversation, as she studied them.

Seeing the thoughts cross her face, after a pause, Juan said, "Ivan is much more refined. I am his pirate father."

Samuel said, "Juan is purposely teasing you."

Juan meant the pirate comment as a joke. Everyone is a pirate in the Caribbean. He had no idea that Ileana knew the truth. Ileana did not know how to respond.

Juan rescued her. "I have heard much about you. Ivan says that you are very smart, and a good businesswoman, and very pretty."

Samuel interjected, "Ivan has told the truth. You are all those things. Only, he did not tell us you were more than pretty . . . you are beautiful!"

Responding to their flirtations, she said, "Oh, my, but you two are dangerous. What brings you to Santo Domingo?"

"We were on a salvage operation, but the storm delayed us from continuing," answered Samuel, anxious to have his chance to talk to the pretty young woman.

They asked her to lunch, which Ileana accepted after an internal debate. Her choice was sushi. Ileana had captivated them sufficiently enough that they agreed to eat raw fish. As the meal progressed, Ileana's demeanor changed from distant to friendly. She knew that Juan was a pirate and suspected that Samuel was the smuggler. How could these men be criminals? They did not seem evil. They were a bit charming. They laughed and made small jokes. Occasionally, Samuel seemed silly. Most importantly, she saw nothing of meanness in them. She enjoyed the obvious friendship between the two men.

Ileana was brought up to think that all lawbreakers were sleazy, mean, and offensive low-lifers to be feared. These men did not conform to her thinking. She reflected that they could be yacht captains or sailors of fine sailing ships, or even aging athletes of the type that had a long personal history. In her heart, it occurred to her that something was wrong with the world. Some supposedly good people were awful. These men—criminals—seemed pleasant, while her family's proper friend had abandoned her son, and her father, whom Ileana always thought so correct and admired, had abandoned his grandson.

Juan, seeing the confusion in Ileana, turned the conversation to Paraiso, upon which she quickly expounded at length. Her heart was in Paraiso. She said that Paraiso had a good and prosperous future. Her caveat, which she did not mention, was it being founded on illegal money. She wondered how long it could last.

"You know that Ivan has plans for more resorts," Ileana said. "He has been going to other islands and even to Mexico to look at locations."

The men responded that they had heard something of future development plans.

She said, "Ivan is an exceptional businessman. He has vision. Everyone in the industry respects him. Señor Fernando is ultimately in control, but people think Ivan is the driving force behind Paraiso, even though he is young. Everyone is wondering what he will do with the company."

"So are we," replied Samuel.

Ivan did not remain angry. He even managed to forgive his birth mother and her family. He had lost his mother years ago. The event was still a wound in his heart, but without the infection of non-forgiveness, it did not fester.

He reflected that when he left Haiti, it was to leave the small leagues and join the big leagues, a concept he was still learning. He had allowed Fernando to remake him, and Ivan put all of himself into the process. At first, he had learned his new role as a good actor learns his part in a play. Later, he became the part he was acting. That challenge and the success he was living would have been enough if he had not fallen in love with Ileana. His love for her had changed his view toward the world. Loving Ileana, his focus had shifted to making a place in life for both of them. Life had become plural.

With Ileana withdrawn, Ivan began to mentally reposition himself in life and reformulate his purpose. He was a new man and a serious and growing player in the resort business. He belonged to the right country club, had many of the right friends. He was sought out by investors, bankers, and politicians, as well as a host of the needy and the poor. He was respected, considered a good and fair man, and not weak. Some feared him due to the business acumen of Paraiso.

Ivan had accomplished his initial goals. Winning the rest of his goals and the game he was playing could be had by just continuing at his current skill level. Now though, it all seemed somewhat meaningless. In piracy he would be safe from love and from the opinion of others.

Ileana's withdrawal not only opened him up to questioning his goals and their meaning, it also opened him up to other women. Ivan had met Gloria at a tourism conference. She worked at a lower mid-level position in a government tourist agency. Gloria was tan-skinned, young, pretty, and available. When she found out who Ivan was and the trajectory of Paraiso, she bought a new low-cut blouse and began to spend as much time as she could at the café near the Paraiso offices. The day before Juan and Samuel went to the Paraiso office, she saw him sitting in a corner and sat at the next table. Taking the opportunity, she said to Ivan, "They call me Gloria. I am so sorry, but I have forgotten your name."

"I am Ivan. I remember . . . you work for the Secretary of Tourism."

"That is very kind of you to remember. I don't recall your work," she lied. "Do you work in the tourist industry?"

"Yes. A company named Paraiso."

"I am sorry. I am not sure I have heard of your company," she said as she leaned forward to expose her breasts.

"We have a resort in Barahona."

"Oh yes, I have heard about it. I was told it is very nice."

The waiter brought soup. Gloria took her utensils from inside the napkin and let it drop onto the floor next to Ivan.

"Let me help," said Ivan, as he leaned over to pick up the napkin. He noticed her shapely legs and thighs that were exposed under the table. She moved her legs slightly apart.

"Thank you," she said placing her hand on his thigh, giving him a pat.

Gloria was funny, vivacious, and a good listener. At length, she asked, "Would you like to join us for dinner? My friend from the Secretariat and I are meeting to discuss tourism opportunities."

Focused on tourism, Ivan willingly accepted.

"Please meet us at 7:00 in my room. Number 434." She gave him a business card from the hotel.

Ivan arrived shortly after the hour. He knocked multiple times and was just about ready to leave when Gloria opened the door. Her wet hair was wrapped in a towel, and she hid behind the door. "Oh, Ivan!

I forgot. My friend had to cancel, and I didn't remember I had invited you. Please wait just a minute."

She returned moments later wearing a hotel supplied bathrobe and opened the door.

"I am sorry to disturb you. Continue with your bath," said Ivan.

"No, no, no! I owe you a dinner for being so rude. I insist that you come in. What do you like?"

"If it is the same to you, what do you prefer?"

"There is a little Italian place. Bohemian. I can wear my jeans and a T-shirt. I have to dress up for work all the time."

Ivan nodded in agreement. She went to her suitcase and took out a pair of jeans and a black T-shirt that said Saint Tropez on it. She pulled the jeans on without underwear, underneath her robe. With her back towards Ivan, she tossed the robe onto the bed and put on the T-shirt, with no bra.

Without Ileana's emotional protection and love, Ivan didn't hide his interest in Gloria's pretty figure.

"Before we go, would you like a glass of red wine?" Gloria offered. "It will go well with Italian food." A tall, second glass followed the first.

At length, Ivan said, "OK, now I am very hungry."

She laughed, and they left together. Acting half drunk, she put her arm inside Ivan's and giggled, "I drink so little. I feel that I am very affected."

Dinner was animated. They both drank more wine, and she unleashed all her seductiveness to make sure that he spent the night with her. Ivan left her room after lunch the following day.

Juan, Samuel, and Ileana had just returned to the offices when Ivan entered the lobby fresh from his encounter with Gloria. Upon seeing his father and Samuel with Ileana, his mood darkened. He had purposely kept them from her and her from them. He quickly reasoned she now knew the truth, and it didn't matter. Ivan smiled and entered the inside reception area while within his heart, he took two more steps back from Ileana. He protected himself.

Ivan usually liked seeing Samuel and Juan. Juan was the man who believed in him enough to give him his chance in life, who happened to be his biological father. Samuel was his father's friend. But his worry about Ileana's reaction to the two men restrained his welcome. He stood with them, superficially making jokes while being sensitive to Ileana's reactions. She did not appear to be disturbed, and from her behavior, she seemed quite comfortable with both men.

In response to a question Ivan asked, they described in detail the past few days on Samuel's small ship. The storm and the events were laid out. Ileana turned toward them, her mouth open and eyes fixed. She said, "Is what you say true?"

Ivan responded for his father and Samuel, "If they say it, it is true, and probably much more dangerous than what they say."

"I didn't know that people did those things, except in the movies. Did you really pass through the hurricane?" Ileana asked again as she stared at the two men.

"Juan and I both work out of boats. Sea storms happen in our work," replied Samuel, matter-of-factly.

Ileana smiled at the word *work*. "Your work?"

Ivan remembered his time on his father's boats and also the voyages to Colombia on Samuel's boat. "I am jealous of your trip. I wish I had been there. I miss the sea and the adventure," he commented through a dreamy expression.

Ileana looked at him with an appraising look. "You want to go through a hurricane?"

Ivan nodded.

Ileana, uncharacteristically, looking overwhelmed and confused, excused herself. "I have to get back to work." She shook hands with Juan and Samuel and gave everyone a pleasant good-bye smile. The men went alone into Ivan's office.

Partly due to the change and success in Ivan's life, and partly due to the maturation of his personality and to the growing good character of his son, Juan enjoyed the meeting with Ivan. He saw some of himself in Ivan: the boldness, the man of action, the risk taker, and the ability to handle people as required. Ivan was, in fact, his heir, but was also his own man. He noted that Ivan had accomplished what he, himself at one time had briefly desired—a place in the society of men.

In the course of conversation about his life and that of Paraiso, Ivan poured out his situation with Ileana. "My mother is a friend of Ileana's family, as is her father. Ileana's friend, Elena—our friend—is my aunt. I have told Ileana of my past life and that you are a pirate. She is now distant from me."

Juan stared at Ivan. The meeting with Ileana made more sense to him now.

Samuel said, "She searched us with every look and word."

Without remorse, but with uncharacteristic sensitivity, Juan said, "I am sad for you that your mother left. She left because of my unfaithfulness and my business life. It was because of me, not you, that she left."

Ivan seemed saddened by the conversation.

Juan asked, "Do you love Ileana?"

Ivan hesitated.

"Do you love the woman you smell of?" asked Juan.

"No."

Juan said, "Without the pirate money, you would never have had success. It was that success which allowed you to meet Ileana. The work that enabled you to win her may cause you to lose her. There are many other women, as you have found out. Do not worry. You will find another."

"I work with her, and I see her. But I cannot have her heart like before."

Juan said, "You may love her still, but she is losing you in pieces."

"She is a fool," stated Samuel in a flat tone. "My young friend, you are a good man. Let's see what we can do. Soon we will have you both on board for dinner."

BACK IN THE SADDLE AGAIN

The next morning Ivan did not shave and he got his hair cut very short. He then went to the used clothing store and bought two sets of clothes and a pair of used shoes and boots. Dressed in old jeans, a stained T-shirt and run-down shoes, Ivan met with a man who sold very fast seagoing launches capable of making long passages. The meeting was at his small office located on the outskirts of town next to the ocean. Ivan wore dark sunglasses and introduced himself as "Juan".

The boat dealer shook his hand, looked at Ivan, and smiled. "I used to know a pirate named Juan. He is probably dead by now. He had a young son. You aren't related to Juan the pirate are you?" he asked giving Ivan a once-over look.

Ivan was so taken aback that it took him a moment to recover. He never wanted to be identified. After a moment, he put on a big fake smile and said, "I guess I am his namesake. Hopefully he was rich!"

There was a brief laugh, and then the boat dealer said, "Juan the pirate I knew was small time. He worked out of Haiti. No money there. What can I do for you?"

Ivan told him he was looking for a panga style launch about 45 feet long. "It has to be fast, carry a large load and lots of gasoline," said Ivan.

The boat dealer looked at him, took him into a building next to the water and showed him poor quality photos of various boats.

"I need it very soon and I do not have much money so it does not need to be pretty. It is for commercial use. Small inter island trade."

"Yeah sure. If it can be ugly and old, I have one with four kind of new outboards on the back. It carries lots of gas, it can get to Colombia – not that you would go there, of course. I fixed the transom and hull myself. It is strong enough to take a pounding."

The boat was located nearby in a small prefab steel building that desperately needed a paint job to stop the rust. Inside were half a dozen panga launches, most of them were only about 25 feet long; one was new and under construction, the 45-foot boat was against a wall. It was huge – very wide and much bigger in every way than the boats his father used. Raw new fiberglass was in obvious contrast to the original hull. From the number of patches, it was clear that the boat had been in bad condition.

With an expert eye, Ivan inspected the outside and inside of the boat. He determined that it was sound and most likely strong with all the new fiberglass work performed on it. The boat dealer reappraised

Ivan as he watched him work. He concluded that Ivan knew what he was looking at.

"Even the gas tanks were replaced or strengthened. We cut out the floor to fix the hull and tanks. The tanks won't leak. I even added two more. This boat has a very long range. The steering and controls are old, but work well. We fixed everything that needed to be fixed. This boat is a low-cost vessel perfect for contraband. I shouldn't sell it to someone who just wants a trading boat."

Ivan looked at the motors. He took off the engine covers of two of them and examined the inside. The engines had been cleaned and it was obvious that some wiring had been reworked.

"The engines are very strong. No problems with them. They are only about 10 years old."

Used to his new life of business, the beautiful Paraiso property, the country club and that circle of friends, the boat just looked old and ugly. Ivan concluded that if he had to sink it to get rid of the evidence of piracy or smuggling, that there would be little loss.

The following day, Ivan met the man on the beach in front of the man's office. Using a large forklift the man managed to maneuver the large and obviously heavy vessel into the water. The boat looked even older and uglier than when it was inside the steel building. Seeing Ivan's reaction, the man said, "I can spray paint it and make it look real nice." Ivan shrugged.

After paying the man $250 dollars for gas and for putting the boat in the water, the two men climbed aboard and the boat dealer backed it off the beach with its motors. Clear of the shore, he stood aside and gave Ivan the helm. Ivan made a series of turns to the left and right, felt the boat in his hands, then pushed the throttles forward. The engines reacted immediately, and the boat leapt forward and once on plane accelerated very rapidly. The motors pushed it through the substantial waves with no effort. The waves hardly moved the boat which felt very heavy and solid in Ivan's hands.

Standing at the controls Ivan recalled the initial excitement of boarding yachts and other vessels at sea. Piracy and smuggling with Juan had seemed very adventuresome when he was young, but he remembered that later on he had not liked it. What had never stopped was his love of being at sea. Ivan ran the boat eastward along the coast for a distance. Everything on board seemed to be in order. He was very aware that he had never expected to be involved with piracy or crime after he left it. He was not motivated by his own needs. He didn't even really care for himself, but he felt responsible to Samuel and his father for their investment in Paraiso. He also had a large number of employees for whom Paraiso was both employment and a huge part of their lives. In his heart, he couldn't abandon them and let the company be sold to a competitor who would not treat them well. They would just be part of a corporation, not part of the family that he had created at Paraiso. He felt he had to do something to increase the company's capital. Nonetheless, in his heart he felt sick. He was no longer Ivan the pirate or smuggler, he was a serious and scrupulously honest and ethical businessman with a financial problem to solve.

Returning from the sea trials, Ivan concluded that the boat would serve well either for piracy or smuggling. Nonetheless, he couldn't bring himself to close the deal at that moment. In a sense, he felt like he was betraying himself and all he and Paraiso stood for. He decided he would put off the purchase for a short time and see if he had options. He had no knowledge of the sunken drug ship, or that the additional capital did not come from the last of his father's and Samuel's savings.

SMUGGLER'S SHIP

Three days after Ileana met Juan and Samuel, they invited her and Ivan to dinner on Samuel's vessel. Ileana didn't know how to react to being invited to eat on a smuggling ship. At first she didn't want to go, but after thinking about how much she enjoyed the lunch with them, she agreed and decided to enjoy an excursion into what she considered to be the underworld. For the occasion, she dressed in a lightweight, black, well-fitted dress that exposed just the top edge of her full breasts. She wrapped her dark hair in a black scarf printed with skulls and crossbones.

When she and Ivan arrived at the dock, she wore black leather sandals and descended the ramp looking like a bad-girl movie star. She purposely walked with an attitude. Playing along, Ivan dressed like some iteration of James Bond, a role for which he was typecast when not suppressed by his new life. In truth, he had the knowledge, skill, and personality to be the piracy and smuggling kingpin – and he knew it.

Carmen, waiting for them in the Zodiac, which she had moored to the side of the lower dock, laughed at the sight of the two of them. She said, "Oh my God. Hollywood and piracy meet."

Ileana needed help climbing into the boat. Ivan boarded as though he had been at sea much of his life, which was the case. Carmen spun the boat around, pushed the throttle to the stop, and ran it hard out to sea.

When Ileana saw the smuggler's ship, she said, "It is a ship . . . but small. It is a handsome boat."

Alongside the little ship, the waves bounced the Zodiac against its side making the boarding difficult. Juan and Samuel helped the newcomers climb over the ship's side onto the large aft deck. A flood of memories poured into Ivan. He knew Samuel's vessel well. Standing on the deck, he also felt the emotions he had felt before when he stood in the same place looking and wondering about the future. He also simply enjoyed being on a boat and it occurred to him that perhaps he should complete the purchase of the panga.

Ileana looked around the boat with a smile on her face. She had never been on such a boat and her expression betrayed her enjoyment of the experience – about which she knew she should feel guilty. When Samuel asked if she would like a tour of the boat, she immediately agreed. Samuel showed her the boat from the engine room to the pilothouse. She asked questions and secretly thought that perhaps the life of pirates and smugglers at sea was exciting and even fun — although very wrong. She surprised herself when it occurred to her that an adventurous sea life in the Caribbean, well-financed and comfortable through smuggling, could be a good life for many. It certainly was much better than the miserable godless life of poverty, despair, and hopelessness that many people live in Haiti, Cuba, and much of Central and South America. She was too inexperienced to know that at sea there is escape into the sea itself and that life at sea is an alternative for many who do not fit in the life of human society or who are just fed up with it.

While Ileana toured the vessel and listened to Samuel tell her about life aboard, Carmen, with Henry's help, prepared a special dish of *mahi-mahi a la veracruzana* and Mexican style tortillas.

After much wine, everyone, including Ileana, spoke boisterously in a loud voice. Speaking over other voices, Henry related the horrors of the storm.

Juan said, "They already know of the storm."

"They can't know. No one could know unless they were there. But I will tell it so they can see how it was."

Henry would not be quieted. With his Bahamian accent and with animated gestures, he said, "The boat rolled from side to side and galloped head to foot. The waves came over the bow and smashed into the windows of the pilothouse. The wind tore at it and howled like a fury. The waves, wind, and liquid air joined in the roar. At night, the sky and seas were dark except when the lightning showed the insane waves. I was afraid and so sick. I preferred to die. I vomited until there was blood in my mouth. I hoped that the sure death that awaited us would be easy. Never have I been so afraid."

Only Samuel had previously experienced a hurricane while at sea, though, Juan had fought many hard seas in his much smaller and open boats. Due to the wine, the reliving of the storm was thick with emotion and chills of fear. The sensations, the danger, and the threat of death—Latinos are seemingly quick to discuss death—were examined, the mood and impressions intensified with the increasing consumption of alcohol.

Ileana asked Juan, "Did you think you were going to die?"

"I thought that it was possible. The waves were very large, and when one came from the side, the ship rolled over . . . very far."

Ileana asked, "Were you afraid?"

"No," responded Juan truthfully.

Having drunk enough to speak honestly, Samuel said, "There was a lot of excitement, but also a lot of danger."

Her sense of being proper having diminished, Ileana asked Samuel, "Do you live for adventure?"

"No. For escape."

Ileana said with a twinkle in her eye, "Is Carmen part of the escape?"

"This is my boat, and she comes with the boat."

Carmen laughed and said, "He pays well. I live with a man in Nassau."

"Does he know?" asked Ileana seriously.

"I do not tell him about all my duties."

Everyone at the table laughed. The slight cloud of re-lived fear dissipated.

Henry said, "You can live with me. I have money." Carmen gave him an inquiring look.

At length, conversation turned to the salvage operation. Because of Ileana, the nature of the cargo was avoided.

Samuel said to Ivan, "Your father almost died. A cargo hatch of a ship we tried to salvage swung open with great force and hit him very hard. He was thrown over the edge of the deck of the sunken ship. He floated over the edge head down. I thought he was dead. I grabbed him and held the mouthpiece in his mouth. He responded very little but kept breathing. It was very dangerous. I had to carry him to the surface."

Ivan paled and felt cold. He was immediately surprised at his reaction. For the first time, he felt protective of Juan. He took a good look at his father. Juan was obviously enjoying himself and felt very much alive. Ivan noted that his father's dyed hair was mildly thinning. There was also a bit of a difference in his facial structure. Juan was aging. For the first time, it struck Ivan that Juan the Pirate was mortal.

The awareness of Juan's mortality brought the loss of his mother and her family, and the partial loss of Ileana, upon him. Sadness washed over his face. It also reaffirmed his responsibility to his father and Samuel to make sure that Paraiso prospered.

Ileana asked Ivan, "What is wrong?"

"Only that nothing is lasting," he said with a touch of sadness.

Ileana looked at him questioningly.

"When I was Ivan, the son of Juan the Pirate, I had been uncaring about myself and invulnerable. If I had known the cost of being Ivan the Respectable, I might not have changed."

"Do you regret the change?"

"Not now, but perhaps in the future."

Ileana looked at him without fully understanding.

Juan chose some old Cuban music to play on the stereo. Samuel danced with Carmen. Juan danced with Ileana, Ileana was smiling and laughing as she danced.

After more wine and the passing hours, caution lessened, and the men and Carmen talked of smuggling and other adventures. Juan mentioned a catch of fish that he had "liberated" from the hold of a foreign fishing vessel and sold for good money to a Dominican fishing company. Ileana paled slightly at the completed realization that they were, in fact, pirates, smugglers, and thieves, but not without charm and an intriguing odd mix of class signals. They were neither like the Latin underclass nor like the rich. They carried an indefinable attitude in every action and obviously did not submit to the rules. Although their attitudes and lawlessness did not earn them membership in the social clubs, it made a place for them. Their only semi-hidden, don't-tread-on-me attitude warned that they were not people to offend.

Intoxicated for the first time in her life, her defenses down, Ileana saw that she had erected barriers between herself and Ivan. As she danced with the son of the pirate in the salon of the smuggler's ship, and with the smuggler and pirate, she laughed. She, Ileana, was with such people and they were fun. She could not help but compare the current party with some of the uninteresting parties she had attended. The polite people who attended those parties were always so careful not to offend and injure their social standing; these people didn't seem to care who they offended.

Taking a pause from the dancing for another sip of wine, Ileana sat down and looked at Ivan. She wondered, at what cost did he accept his mother's family—those people who abandoned him? People who did not recognize their own flesh and blood? He had done so without apologies from them. Not compromising herself, and without approving of their professions, she partially accepted Juan and his friends. Juan was Ivan's father, and in a sense, they all were Ivan's family. Still, her family and friends would never give her permission to be with Ivan if they knew of his past.

The merengue was Ileana's favorite dance, even though it was not modest. Next to Carmen, she joined Juan, Samuel, and Ivan in the dance with wine-induced abandonment. She laughed as she allowed the men to twirl her. Henry, not knowing the dance, remained seated.

Finally, sweaty and tired, Ileana whispered to Ivan, "Take me home."

Ivan embraced the men, patted their backs, and gave Carmen a chaste kiss. Ileana air-kissed each person's ear and said, "*Mil gracias,* I enjoyed myself very much." As she breathed those words, she reflected again that no one in her family would ever allow her to be with Ivan if they knew the truth about him and Paraiso.

The wind had calmed, and her entrance into the now stable small boat was with grace. Carmen piloted it along the shore in front of the city to the harbor. The city lights made Santo Domingo look like a jewel set on the coast. At the dock, the guard took Ileana's hand and helped her out of the boat. She blew Carmen a kiss as the boat backed away. Ivan left her at the top of the dock ramp with the guard and retrieved his Ford. As the guard opened the car door, Ivan handed him a tip, shut the door, and drove Ileana home.

YΛCHTSMEN

N either Carmen nor Henry knew anything of Juan's and Samuel's ownership of Paraiso. In fact, they did not know much about any of Juan's business. Juan had been presented to Henry as an adventuresome friend who was willing to help them with the salvage operation. So, when Samuel and Juan decided to take the relatively short trip to the Paraiso resort, they sent Carmen and Henry back to Nassau.

The weather was still hot, and there were occasional rains and humidity, but it was late enough in the year that the hurricane season was close to ending. In spite of the season, the popularity of the Paraiso resort, both with Havana's clients and those of Paraiso, resulted in a good occupancy rate. The docks, too, had a substantial number of boats tied to them. Some of the boats were left by their owners for use in the winter season, and some of the boats belonged to people who spent the entire year cruising or living aboard. The big dock had a large yacht tied to it, so Samuel did not take his small ship inside the breakwater that sheltered the Paraiso marina. Instead, he tethered it to a mooring buoy.

Samuel and Juan lowered the ship's Zodiac into the sea. The two aging men, well-shaven, dressed in Hawaiian shirts, wearing sunglasses and baseball caps with the ship's name embroidered across the front, steered the boat through the small waves toward the shore.

The trade winds moderated the afternoon heat. Occasional light spray, caught by the wind, sprinkled the men. Samuel took a detour to the dock, steering the little boat among the other vessels, both power and sail, which were tied to mooring buoys or swung on their anchors. He always enjoyed looking at boats. With the hope of Paraiso profits and the windfall profits expected from the sale of the marijuana yet to be salvaged, Juan was mildly considering buying a true yacht.

When Samuel saw Juan evaluating a yacht, he said, "Don't even think about it."

"I am trying to figure out my new life, now that I am no longer a pirate."

"I have seen that look. You are still a pirate; you are just not pirating."

"Maybe I want a yacht of my own."

"You . . . in a yacht?" asked Samuel.

"And wearing a blue blazer," Juan said with a straight face.

Samuel scoffed and then laughed. "The day I see you piloting a yacht dressed in a blue blazer, I will know that one of us is crazy."

As the little boat approached the dock, Juan jumped onto it and tied the boat's line to a cleat before Samuel stopped the motor. Samuel stepped onto the dock with the air of an aging playboy—almost.

Juan's brother David ran the marina. As he walked down the dock to greet them, he did a double take. The men sort of looked like Juan and Samuel. No . . . they *were* Juan and Samuel—sort of. David had never seen either one attired in resort clothing. They even wore yachting deck shoes. He was smiling broadly when he greeted them.

"Shut up," said Samuel.

After registering Samuel's vessel, still working to contain the smile and chuckle, David invited the men up to the marina restaurant for a beer. As they entered, the resort yachtsmen, seated at a large back table, studied the two men. Seeing David, their stares turned into greetings.

"Bring the newcomers and join us," yelled one of the men.

David led his brother and Samuel to the group and introduced them, saying, "This is my brother Juan and our friend Samuel."

One of the women said, "I didn't know you had a brother."

"It is a secret."

"Really?"

"They are arriving from Grand Turk."

Addressing Juan and Samuel, a large man at the head of the table said, "It is lucky you did not get here earlier. Last week there was a hurricane."

"We came through it. We spent a few days in Santo Domingo recovering," said Samuel.

The men and women laughed at the joke. David said, "It is not a joke."

A man asked, "What was it like passing through a hurricane?"

Samuel recounted the passage. The yachtsmen and women listened with amazement. Every face wore an astonished look.

Seated with a mixed crowd of his age or older, dressed in resort attire and making small talk, tweaked Juan's mind. He most often met this type of person with a gun in his hand. He felt disconnected and looked out the window. After a couple of beers and cheered by the crowd's friendliness, he partially settled into the civilized group.

Pointing at Samuel, someone asked Juan, "Is he telling the truth?"

"Everything he says is true, only it was much worse."

A woman said, "Are you guys for real? You are like characters out of a sea novel."

Samuel said, "We play those parts."

The crowd at the table laughed. After a time of banter, one of the yachtsmen asked Juan, "Where did you learn English?"

"From our mother," answered Juan. "She was American."

"You speak good English, but with a Caribbean accent," observed one of the women.

"I was in pirate movies," said Juan, in a deadpan voice.

"I have seen movies," responded the woman.

David laughed so hard he had to drink a glass of water. He composed himself and said, "I hope you haven't seen his movies."

The woman looked confused. Trying to redeem the moment, Samuel said, "He is only typecast in bad-guy parts. That is how he makes a living."

"Wow, he's in the movies!" she said with excitement.

Juan remained silent, but his eyes sparkled.

David's friendship and ease with the group made it easy for him to extract Juan, Samuel, and himself from them before happy hour ended. After they left, one of the men said, "I think those guys are full of shit."

"I am not so sure," commented another as he watched them walk away.

David led Juan and Samuel to his sailboat, where he introduced Samuel to Juanita for the first time. After pleasantries, David took the men on a tour of the latest property upgrades.

The tour started with a walk through the hotel, continued along the road paralleling the shore, and ended at the security gate. On the return, they stopped briefly at each of the condominium towers and walked to the other end of the property, past the new Havana resort tower to the second security gate. They turned landward and walked the mostly unlit golf course. The clubhouse was open; the last of the golfers drank at the 19th Hole, the predictably named bar.

Samuel said, "Never did I think the resort would be so nice. The buildings are beautiful. The design of the property is pure class."

Juan commented, "We own this place, but the life of it belongs to Ivan, and even to David. It will never be my life." After a pause, he added, "I am surprised you are here, David. Don't you ever worry that a yachtsman might recognize you?"

"We wore masks," responded David, dismissing the question.

In a philosophical tone, Samuel said, "Who knows what the future will bring. For now, this business life belongs to Ivan, Ileana, Juanita, Fernando, and Luis, and all these people here."

After a pause, Juan said, "I have been an outlaw. I desired nothing else."

After the tour, they returned to the marina restaurant. David told the staff to put all their meals, needs, and anything else on the Paraiso tab. The following day, David arranged for Juan and Samuel to go fishing on one of the resort's charter boats. The boat was ready at dawn. Coffee and pastries were awaiting the pirate and smuggler.

Seeing the white-skinned Samuel, the charter boat captain addressed him in English.

"We speak Spanish," replied Samuel to the man's poor English.

"So I see," responded the captain.

Before the boat left, in a serious voice, David said, "Captain, make sure you provide the best service and do not offend them."

David's tone caused the captain to look at Juan and Samuel. Spurred by the warning and the appearance of the two men, his very tan face looked respectful. He and his mate did provide excellent service and Juan and Samuel each caught a large dorado that day. It was the first of many fishing trips the men enjoyed during their stay.

That night, David invited the men to the marina bar. A band played a mix of music styles. There were two attractive unmarried thirty-year-old saleswomen, dressed in lightweight business suits, who were seated at the timeshare promotion table near the entrance. David greeted them after he found his brother and Samuel.

He said to the two young women, "These are guests of mine."

The women noticed the preferential treatment David gave Juan and Samuel. They responded with a polite hello, a handshake, and an open smile. An hour later, David invited them to join the men at their table.

"No, señor David. Although this is not our scheduled night to work, for some reason the sales director placed us here. We must do our job."

"It is best you come and sit with these men. I will take care of everything. Do not worry."

Not long after they joined Juan and Samuel at their table. When the sales manager entered the room to check on them, the women stood up to leave. Still across the room, their manager held up his hand and motioned for them to sit down. Walking over to the table, he asked Juan and Samuel, "Are you well taken care of?"

"Yes, these pretty women came to sit with us," responded Samuel.

Addressing the women, their supervisor said with a big smile, "Take good care of them. David told me they are very wealthy and influential yachting guests."

The following evening, the women arrived perfumed and provocatively dressed. They danced until late and spent the night on board the ship. The following day, the sales director freed them from their sales duties so they could spend most days and nights with Juan and Samuel.

After a few days, Juan said, "I like resort life. Maybe this will be my new life."

Two weeks later, the men returned to Santo Domingo. They moored the vessel securely to a private dock. Samuel flew to Colombia. Juan remained on board.

A PURCHASE

For a few days, Ivan was unable to sleep well. He lay in his bed in the beautiful Paraiso apartment in Santo Domingo. He worried greatly for his employees who had joined him to make the Paraiso dream a reality, he worried for Samuel and his father. He hated the thought of having to go back to being an outlaw and decided that he could not be a pirate again. He knew too many yachtsmen through Paraiso and some of them were his friends. They were no longer undefined and unknown; they were people of the class he had entered and lived in. He decided, however, that he could smuggle marijuana from Colombia to the Bahamas or other islands for later transport to the United States. His mind made up, Ivan met again with the boat dealer and struck a deal for the purchase of the boat on the condition that it be cleaned up, sanded, painted gray and that a Loran be installed along with some lights. He discovered that the boat had been used for inter-island cargo, but had been taken from the boat registry and was no longer on any official records. The boat could stay in the boat dealer's building. Except to him and the boat dealer, it no longer existed. That pleased Ivan.

Five years had passed since Ivan was involved in piracy or smuggling. When a pirate, he had been young and was only a crew member — not the person who made the decisions or deals. Nonetheless, and in spite of his position, he had met some marijuana growers and a few American smugglers and buyers. He also knew Jose, the man his father used to bring the Colombian boat to Haiti 5 years prior, who had connections with marijuana growers. If he needed to go anywhere, and especially Colombia, Theodore could pick him up in the Dominican Republic and drop him off at a clandestine airstrip before the plane made official entry into whatever country he needed to visit. No record would exist that he had left the Dominican Republic.

Feeling certain that he had contacts in Colombia, Ivan focused on buyers. He recalled two different dealers who sold very large quantities of marijuana and had each bought a couple of small Florida motel chains. He wondered if they were still in business. Ivan acquired an anonymous cell phone by someone he knew through Samuel. He also secured a computer connection and email that could not be traced to the Dominican Republic, let alone to him. He researched the two motel chains and found that in the last five years the ownership had been transferred a couple of times to various island companies. At the end of his research, he discovered that the motel owners were still most likely the same smuggler dealers he had met years before. He reasoned that even if they had left the marijuana business, if presented with really good marijuana at a discount price, they might still be interested or have friends who would buy marijuana shipments.

After a week of calls and leaving messages, he was finally able to connect with one of the smugglers. Jimmy, the smuggler, finally took his call after leaving him a message that he was only to contact him on a certain telephone. When the call went through, Ivan introduced himself as Juanito which for some reason was the name that the smuggler had insisted on calling him years before. He always wondered why the smuggler called him Juanito since he didn't meet him through his father, but through Samuel when he worked as an occasional crew member on smuggling trips. It took a few minutes of conversing before the smuggler connected all the dots and realized who he was talking to. Finally, he said, "I remember you. Other than Samuel you were the only one who spoke English. You were very good on his small ship. You had talent. How are you?"

Ivan responded, "I am very well. Life is good. I have some good businesses and I can get some product that you might like. It is very good."

The buyer was silent for a while, then said, "I am in the motel business. You have motels for sale?"

"Yes, like the ones you used to seek. And the price is very reasonable. They are properties that you could acquire, then sell with no effort and make a very good profit."

"I am not in that business anymore. Now I just buy older motels that I can fix up and keep and rent. I am no longer in the purchase and sell business."

"I understand, no problem, I know other people. I just thought that the quality was exceptional, the price low, and you would be interested in making a large and quick profit by selling exceptionally good properties that you bought at a low price."

Jimmy, the man on the line, hesitated. "I really am not doing that kind of business, but if the opportunity is exceptional, we should meet. Do you want to come to Miami?"

No date or time was set, but Ivan knew he had a buyer if he got the marijuana to either the Bahamas or the USA.

AN ENCOUNTER

After returning to Santo Domingo, Samuel flew to the Bahamas, while Juan remained on board. The morning sky was clear, the air warm, but not very humid. Juan stood on the foredeck of Samuel's vessel and watched the activity of the harbor. In his few days in the Santo Domingo harbor, he had met the port side wastrels and scoundrels and had enjoyed many hours of talking about fishing and port life. He also enjoyed the crowd that met at a nearby bar. The clientele were not yachtsmen, and he did not have to watch every word he said, although the *aguardiente* they served bothered his stomach.

In addition to the alcohol bothering his stomach, he was aware that his body was changing in other ways—he was aging. He also noticed there were changes in his thoughts and emotions—things that previously were not important to him now had some importance. He found that he cared that Ivan was happy and enjoyed his success. He wanted Ileana to love Ivan. He cared that David and Juanita were happy together. Surprisingly, aside from the money, it was important to him that Paraiso be a success. It was clear that the company would prosper as long as it could complete the last key elements of the resort. He was counting on salvaging the rest of the marijuana to provide the necessary capital. Nonetheless, he felt more emotionally vulnerable than at any time since childhood. He didn't know if the things he was experiencing were tied to his age, or the work, or something else.

After a cup of coffee and riding the lift the caffeine gave, he went to his cabin and shaved. His beard was turning grey, and his thinning hair was about half grey. Rather than applying hair dye, he cut the hair on his head to a very short length, cutting off the black dyed hair. He shaved his face closely, leaving only his trimmed, greying mustache. Wearing sunglasses and dressed in khaki pants and a polo shirt, he left the boat. The shortness of his hair gave him a different image, almost military. The men on the dock moved aside for him, like enlisted men before a colonel.

Contrary to his usual pace, Juan walked slowly along the port side road, then turned and walked toward the colonial district. After a while, he was surprised to find himself in an area of the city that he had not visited in many years, the area where his ex-father-in-law's hotel was located. He stood in front of the old hotel. It seemed a bit abandoned, as though commercial life had passed it by. He did not go in, but rather turned and walked toward the center of the colonial district. Finding a restaurant that looked pleasing, he stopped and went inside.

The restaurant was large, the ceilings high. Windows faced the street. Waiters circulated with pots of coffee and metal pitchers containing hot milk. There was a container of granulated sugar on every table. The clients drank coffee and ate pastries or ordered a full breakfast. Most of the customers appeared to be workers or local businessmen. There were some retired men and a small number of bohemian types.

Contrary to custom, Juan bought two newspapers, one in Spanish and one in English. He didn't read them often and did not care much to know the news. Choosing a seat not far from the windows and underneath a large ceiling fan, he gladly accepted the coffee and hot milk that an aging waiter poured into his cup. Fortified with the first cup of coffee, he signaled for a second cup and began, in a somewhat distracted way, to read the Miami Herald. He focused on the news related to drugs and criminal activity; perhaps he knew someone who had been busted. He went on to the sports page and read the articles about soccer.

There was an older man at the next table reading the local paper. He sat with it in front of him in a way which mostly hid him from view. Juan did not notice him when he entered, and the man had not looked up when Juan sat down. Juan sat sideways to the man. When the old man did look up, he didn't take particular note of Juan. He signaled for more coffee and went back to his paper.

After a while, as though something triggered within him, the man set the paper aside and studied Juan. Although his appearance reminded him a little of the man his rebellious young daughter had married, he did not recognize him. No thought of Juan had passed through his mind for a decade. He assumed that the pirate was long dead.

The older man went back to reading his paper, then looked up again. The man sitting with his profile to him did look a bit like Juan, although he was older, slightly heavier, and with shorter hair than Juan wore.

After a while, he looked once more. He set his paper down and stared. Juan, feeling the stare, looked back. The two men locked eyes.

Juan instantly recognized his old father-in-law. He spoke first. "Aren't you dead yet, old man?"

"I am alive, and I am well! Speaking of death, I am surprised no one has killed you."

"My saints take care of me," Juan said as he returned to his newspaper.

"The devil takes care of you. What brings the likes of you to a beautiful city like Santo Domingo?" the old man asked.

Distracted by the soccer news, Juan continued to look at the newspaper and, without thinking and without looking at the man, replied, "Go to hell. I am visiting my son."

No sooner had the words left Juan's mouth, he regretted it. He noted the old man's face, his puzzlement, and then recognition. He guessed right that the old man had forgotten about his grandson who his daughter had named Robert, and he had renamed Ivan. There was no more conversation. There had never been anything good between them. His ex-father-in-law had never accepted him and wrote him off as a low life from the day he met him. He had hated his daughter's involvement with him and had taken her away.

Juan turned his back on the man and went back to reading his newspapers. He signaled for another cup of coffee. The proud old man, reminding himself he was from a good family, even if one in danger of financial ruin, called for his check and left.

For a moment, Juan considered it ironic that the old man's forgotten grandson had an office not far from the restaurant.

A FAVOR

After work one day, Ileana's parents insisted that Ivan join them for dinner. Ivan arrived at Ileana's parents' house after dark. It was early winter, and no longer hot at night. Although he found them pleasant enough, he only came to fulfill his obligations to his still emotionally distant semi-fiancée. Even though Ileana softened after meeting Juan and Samuel, she continued to be afraid of the reaction of her family and friends if they knew the truth about Ivan.

There was brief, polite conversation before Ileana's mother expressed great concern for her friend—Ivan's mother and her family. "I am worried about them. They are incredibly stressed. Oh, to God I wish that I could help them."

Ileana stared at Ivan to discern his reaction. Her mother had no idea of Ivan's blood relationship with that family. Ivan appeared to be politely paying attention and seemed emotionally untouched. He was okay.

After a ten-minute monologue about the family's needs, her mother came to the point of the dinner. "Is there anything you can do for them? They are such nice people, and they are in great trouble."

Ivan did not respond. Ileana quickly turned the conversation to another topic. Her mother stared at her, puzzled. She did not let her mother make another comment.

After a period, Ivan said, "About your friend . . . perhaps we can use a portion of their hotel to house guests on the way to the resort. We use another hotel now. Our guests and clients stay only one night in Santo Domingo, but the number of guests is large and growing."

Ileana's mother clapped her hands and stood up. "Oh Ivan, that would be wonderful. They are in so much need. I fear they will lose the hotel without help." With the last words, she broke down and gently cried. "I have been so worried about my friends. They really are such nice people."

Ileana went pale. She didn't say what she was thinking—that they were not so nice. They had abandoned Ivan when he was a young child.

Ivan said, "Ileana will do what is necessary. There will be contracts, and we will have to make changes to the hotel."

Ileana stared at him.

"Oh, anything you can do. And thank you," exclaimed her mother.

In a strained tone, Ileana blurted out, "He will help, but nothing is as it seems. He should not do anything for them."

Her mother glared at her normally polite daughter. Ileana glared back and barely resisted the urge to leave the room.

Ivan took her hand and said, "Remember Cuba."

Ileana's mother asked, "I don't understand. What about Cuba?"

Ileana paused and said, "It is an island."

Ileana inspected, and for the most part liked, the architectural changes that had been made to the hotel during the partial remodel. She looked at the rooms on the renovated floors of the hotel and found them acceptable. She concluded that those rooms were sufficient to fulfill the need for transient lodging. She found the lobby, restaurant, and bar to be so outdated as to be almost ghastly. The service and menu were also unacceptable.

With mixed emotions, Ileana took control of the hotel. She loved the owner and his wife as though they were family, but she was very angry with them for deserting Ivan. She entered with a heavy hand, in part, because it was necessary to make fundamental changes to use the facility, but also she wanted to punish the family.

Ileana had the lobby, restaurant, bar furnishings, and lighting torn out. She chose new colors and had the walls repainted. She replaced the furnishings with very modern Latin-flavored international boutique hotel furniture and decorations of her choosing. She billed everything to Paraiso, but kept careful records so she could later deduct the bills from what Paraiso would owe for lodging.

Next, she sent Paraiso's human resources and restaurant teams into the hotel. Based upon their appraisal, she summarily dismissed half the staff.

When the old man protested, Ileana replied, "They won't do. They're too old-fashioned and set in their ways—and lazy. Service must be of very high quality. The staff must be good, polite, smart, hardworking, and well groomed. Anyone who wants to work here must comply, or Paraiso will not send guests."

The Paraiso teams held intensive training sessions for the remaining and new staff. The food selection and menus were changed. Ileana personally selected the new uniforms. She also installed Paraiso sales personnel at a newly created guest services center. The old man and his family were more than exasperated by the changes in the hotel. They were angry. It had been comfortable for them—an old-style Santo Domingo hotel of traditional flavor. The old flavor and tradition had been removed—eradicated is perhaps the correct word. Old and trusted staff members were retired or fired. Only because of absolute financial necessity and family ties to Ileana did they tolerate—just barely—her invasion of the hotel.

It took a while for the staff members to learn to work together and figure out how the systems were to coordinate. In the beginning, they were like a group of actors learning their parts, scripts in hand. Even the directors, the hotel manager, and the restaurant manager were still learning the show.

Finally, Ileana asked Morales, the Paraiso resort manager, to help prepare for the opening. Morales gathered the managers and staff in the unopened hotel restaurant. A caterer served everyone a café latte and selection of French pastries.

A big man of Italian and Puerto Rican heritage, Morales said with a warm smile, "Do not worry, everything will be wonderful. You are all to be friends and will help each other. We will have monthly staff parties at the Paraiso resort; you are all invited along with your spouses. We are a family, and our mission is to love, help, and serve every guest. You must care for them, take time with them, and make sure they are pleased with the hotel. They are always right! You are their first taste of Paraiso. There will always be extra staff to make sure you can do your job without a rush. You must not, however, overstep.

You are staff, and they are royal-like customers. Defer to them, be respectful and all will go well. Your goal is service and pleasing them. That is first. There will be plenty of you to get the work done."

During the first few weeks after the remodel, Ileana sent only a limited number of guests to the hotel. Meeting with the department heads at the end of the first week, the restaurant manager said to Ileana and Morales, "Thank God that there were not many guests. There were problems with training, new equipment did not work, and supplies arrived late. There was small disaster after small disaster!"

The housekeeper added, "The colors in many of the sheets ran when washed and colored the towels yellow."

Morales responded calmly. "Do not worry. Explain the problems to the guests. Tell them we are working on making everything perfect. Laugh with them, spend time making everything right. Give them passes for free desserts and drinks whenever necessary."

The most difficult thing for the staff to practice was the right measure of deference. Morales insisted that they defer to the client, but not patronize them. In a hallway, they were to step aside and let the guest pass by out of respect. When guests wanted something, they were to have it, and without waiting. When guests spoke, they were to be heard.

By the third week, the number of Paraiso guests arriving increased significantly. The staff, even though performing better in their roles, handled the increased traffic with difficulty. Under Morales' direction, the managers spent long hours training the staff and perfecting the hotel systems. They worked to perfect everything from the cleaning and preparation of the rooms to the spicing of the soup. Even more time was spent teaching the staff to offer first class service with deference, but not subservience. Ileana was in the middle of everything.

The remodeled floors of the hotel were soon filled with transient guests going to, or coming from, the Paraiso resort. Some of the guests extended their stay a day or two. The lobby, restaurant, and bar were busy. The physical location was good, and the hotel had just the right mix of new with a touch of high-class, classic Latin America.

The excellent service of the Paraiso-trained staff and the sophisticated and hip decor pleased the guests and facilitated the marketing of the Paraiso resort and timeshare sales. With new life flowing in the hotel, some of the old commercial guests and traveling families returned and occupied the un-remodeled rooms. In less than three months after the makeover, the downtown Lion's Club returned to the hotel for its morning meetings. City residents took note and began to frequent the marvelous restaurant.

Shortly thereafter, the local, older, chic crowd discovered the dance floor in the new, trendy lounge. Dance instructors gave merengue and other lessons every afternoon and evening. They held dance contests. The house band, personally selected by Ileana, was excellent and professional in every aspect. The accomplished musicians played a wide variety of Latin, rock and roll, and swing music to perfection.

Money flowed. The old man and his wife and their family began the work of paying off their debts. Money was also available to fight the politically motivated accusations that threatened Elizabeth's husband. The family forgave Ileana for roughly commandeering their hotel. Due to his age, and awareness that the hotel industry had changed, the old man gave up every pretense of management.

Ivan was not directly involved in the project. He followed the developments and noted Ileana's attitude towards the old man and his family. Early on, he realized that it was only a matter of time before the old man and his family lost the hotel. He knew he could just wait until the old man lost it, then pay very little for the property. The old man would have been reduced to virtual poverty, and his mother to hardship. If the hotel had been lost, perhaps in scandal due to the unpaid debts, his mother's beleaguered husband would have been even more vulnerable.

At the end of the project, over lunch in the hotel's dining room, Ivan said to Ileana, "You are angry with the owners of this hotel."

"They abandoned you," she replied.

"They owe me nothing. Besides, the business with them is good. Everyone is happy. For us, our guests like the hotel experience so much that they are buying our timeshare at the hotel before they take their flights home."

"You should have bought the hotel," stated Ileana.

"I helped them, but not because they are blood-related. I am not trying to win them back. I did it because Juan, Samuel, and Fernando helped me. I had very little help before that. I mostly raised myself. When they helped me, I learned how good it is when someone helps. I changed, and it was good, so I am passing the good on. The fact that they do not merit the help makes it all the more valuable," said the pirate's son.

"If they had taken you with them, you wouldn't have been a pirate," Ileana responded.

"If I had not been a pirate, I would not have met Fernando and Paraiso would not exist," replied Ivan.

MORE SALVAGE WORK

C armen returned to Santo Domingo. She had Samuel's ship fueled and bought the ship's supplies for the galley. Dirty from sitting in the small harbor, she spent a couple of days cleaning the vessel inside and out. Samuel and Henry arrived shortly afterwards by plane. Although Juan had been on board for a fairly long time, he had returned back to Haiti and arrived by truck.

The following morning, not early, Samuel motored his vessel out of the moorings and into the Caribbean waters. The waves were four feet high and short coupled. The little ship rode them smoothly as they proceeded on course to the sunken ship.

Juan manned the helm inside the pilothouse. Carmen prepared the late breakfast with the willing help of Henry, who liked looking at the edges of her baggy, low-cut, underwear-free, cutoff jeans and loose-fitting bikini top.

The door and windows of the pilothouse were open. It was filled with light and warm humid air, fine sea mist, and the smell of the ocean. The sunglassed men, wearing resort-style shorts and new Hawaiian shirts that David had given them with the Paraiso logo, stood at the forward window near the ship's wheel. On autopilot, the vessel kept on course towards the first coordinates. The electronically monitored engines required no attention. The men were unneeded, except to avoid a collision with one of the many coastal fishing boats in sight.

Carmen came up the stairs with plates topped with eggs, ham, and toast. Henry followed her with a wine carafe filled with thick, black coffee.

"The coffee tastes good," said Samuel after his first sip.

More time had elapsed than they had intended since they found the ship, the hurricane, and sold the first load of marijuana. Henry paced inside the pilothouse. After a while, he said, "I put my money in an anonymous Cayman Island bank account. It is growing. Already, I have $680,000. If we are successful and salvage and sell the rest of the marijuana, I will have over a million dollars. I am the first man ever whose ship came in underwater!"

"You are just another Caribbean treasure hunter," commented Carmen with a wink.

"I also bought a twenty-five-foot launch with a four-stroke outboard. It has a nice Bimini top."

"Be careful you do not show too much money," warned Samuel.

After a pause, Henry responded, "I am declaring some income so I don't have tax problems, but what happens if we are caught with the marijuana on board?"

"There is not much risk of randomly being caught at sea. Remember the helicopter that circled us? The planes and helicopters report the position of the suspects, and the coast guard purposely intercepts them."

"If we are caught, what happens?" asked Henry.

"Why are you worried?" queried Juan, with a harsh look.

"Now I have money. I have something to lose."

"That is part of the life of a smuggler."

"But you all are not nervous."

"If you want the money, you must take the risk," responded an irritated Juan.

With more civility, Samuel added, "It will be okay."

Privately to Juan, Samuel said, "The Americans know of us from our prior trips. We must be extra careful."

Carmen prepared fish in the evening. She spiced it with salty capers and fresh limes. Samuel brought out a bottle of rum. He drank moderately. Juan, Henry, and Carmen drank until sleepy. The men went to their berths; Carmen slept on the pilothouse settee. Samuel hand-steered the vessel. There were no other boats in sight. He looked at the moon, stars, and sea. He looked at Carmen. Turning on the autopilot, he went over to her and placed his hands on her body. She responded by moving her hips up and down. He pulled her shorts off, took off his shorts and had sex with the half-sleeping woman. When finished, he dressed and went below for leftover coffee, which he warmed in the microwave. The rest of the night he was at the helm. The sea was not rough, the stars brilliant, the moon three-fourths full. The coffee kept him company and kept him awake. At dawn, he awakened Carmen, who drank a cup of coffee and relieved him at the helm. Samuel fell asleep on the settee.

The vessel arrived at the coordinates of the scuttled drug ship midday. The ship was a hundred yards from their descent point. Juan assisted Samuel as he opened the ship's hatches and released the remaining bales of marijuana, and they shot toward the surface.

Carmen gathered them into the Zodiac. When the men surfaced, she was still in the little boat, hauling the bales out of the water and placing them inside. The bales already retrieved lay in a jumbled pile on the back deck of the ship.

Carmen yelled to them, "I am fishing."

Samuel took the regulator hose out of his mouth and said, "You have a good catch."

"It is a special catch of square grouper for the very special cookies I will bake tonight," replied Carmen. "Now get your butt out of the water and help me land all of these fish or you will not have any of the cookies."

Juan and Henry opened the aft hatches and Henry began storing the bales under the deck After all the bales were out of sight, Samuel closed the hatches. Using the crane, Juan lifted and secured the Zodiac.

A short time later, a Coast Guard helicopter passed over the little ship at an altitude of about 500 feet. It made a lazy 180-degree turn and, descending to less than 100 feet, it made a slow pass off their starboard side.

"What shit," uttered Juan. "The bastard Americans are everywhere."

"It is the curse!" exclaimed Carmen.

"Don't be a foolish woman. There is no curse. If there were a curse, the American helicopter would have arrived when the bales were on the deck."

"It is still the curse."

"Just wave at the helicopter and smile."

The men and Carmen waved at the aircraft. The pilot dipped the helicopter as though in a salute, continued the turn, and passed off the port side of Samuel's vessel in a westerly direction.

"What do you think?" asked Juan.

"They saw nothing of the cargo, though they could know of the sunken ship. The Americans may return or try to intercept us and board us. Unlock the hatches in case we need to throw the bales into the sea," replied Samuel.

"Yes, yes, it is better to throw the marijuana into the ocean. Better not to have money than go to prison," interjected Henry in a nervous voice.

When the helicopter was out of sight, Samuel started the engines. Juan went forward and winched the anchor against the ship's hull. Samuel turned the vessel to the northeast.

"The Coast Guard patrols west of Haiti and north by the Caicos Islands. The helicopter may belong to the Caicos ship," said Samuel in a tight voice.

Samuel pushed the throttles almost to maximum power. The vessel leaped forward, struggled partially out of the water, and moved quickly through and then over the sea. The quartering waves twisted the forward motion of the ship.

"Do you think the helicopter will return, *jefe*?" asked Carmen, her face pale.

"Perhaps. Make sure that the bales of marijuana did not open. If we have to throw them overboard, I do not want any of the product left in the hold."

Holding on to the handrail, Carmen descended into the salon then into the hold through its interior door. Juan accompanied her. Together, they squeezed between the bales to see if any bale had ripped open.

Returning to the pilothouse, Carmen reported, "There is no spill. If we throw the bales into the sea and are later boarded, they will find nothing."

Samuel hand-steered the vessel and checked his radar often. He saw occasional small blips indicating only yachts or fishing boats. There was no fast approaching large blips which could be a Coast Guard or a navy ship.

Henry nervously walked the decks looking into the air and across the sea.

Samuel pushed his ship hard. At dusk, they were more than 200 miles from where the helicopter had circled them.

When Henry came into the pilothouse to tell Samuel that he didn't see any aircraft or ships, Samuel sighed. "I think we are OK. We are running fast to the northeast. They will not expect us to be so far east. If they are waiting at the logical intercept point, they will not find us."

At midnight, they were east-northeast of Grand Turk. At two o'clock, Samuel relaxed some and decided to take a risk and run fast to the northwest and into the Bahamas. Juan stood by his side. Carmen was asleep on the settee. Henry continued to walk the decks to see if he could see or hear any aircraft or ship. Just before dawn, they unloaded the cargo into the safe house on Long Island, Bahamas.

A MEETING IN NASSAU AND PLANS

It was well after lunch and the café was empty. Juan and Samuel sat under the shade of some palm trees at the far end of the outside dining area. They ate fried conch and drank the good local beer.

"I learned from Ivan's associate Luis that the resort construction is mostly completed and that the income from timeshare sales and the resort and marina operation cover the operating expenses. However, the construction is almost at a standstill and there are questions concerning whether Paraiso is financially stable. The reduced construction is beginning to affect the timeshare sales. Luis says Ivan is concerned that if sales drop that the income will not be sufficient to keep the resort operating. Right now, the resort income pays all the bills, except for the cost of construction. Luis says that Ivan is beginning to feel desperate," observed Juan.

Samuel sat back, drank the rest of his beer, and signaled the dark-skinned young waitress to bring another. When she served the beer, he took the opportunity to look down her blouse. She noticed and smiled at him, then bent over to place a napkin under his glass.

She turned sideways and looked back as she walked away.

"They are nice," said Samuel to Juan, referring to her breasts.

Juan smiled, "Luis told me that Paraiso only needed a couple of million dollars to finish all the construction and to firmly establish the resort. We will have that much when we sell all the marijuana."

Samuel sat back in his chair, "You got me into this investment. If you were not such a good friend I would consider pushing you off my boat in the middle of the Caribbean."

"It will make more money than anything we have done. We just need to complete it. How do you want to handle the sale of the marijuana?"

Samuel responded, "We have some options. The one that will make the most money is we transport it to Florida and wholesale it there to a dealer. We could also just sell the whole shipment to Florida 'importers' who move it from the Bahamas to Florida — but we will only make about half of what we make if we take it to Florida ourselves. We can hire people to take it to Florida like we did with some of the first load, but the cost is high and that cuts a lot into profits. Another option is we sell it off my boat to Florida dealers. We can prearrange the sale and stay off shore and let them pick it up in their boats. We are the 'mother ship.' Taking it close to Florida allows us to get a better price for the marijuana. That operation though is becoming more and more risky, the Americans are aware of the mother ships and look for them. If discovered, we will be intercepted."

Juan and Samuel ordered another round of beer. There were no other customers sitting outside and only a few sitting inside the restaurant. When the waitress returned with the beers she resumed flirting with them. Juan invited her to sit down.

"I can't sit with you. My manager prohibits it."

The men joked with her. She joked back, perhaps hoping for a big tip or perhaps hoping it would go somewhere. The two men appealed to her. After a while though, she had to excuse herself to attend to the customers inside the restaurant.

"She deserves a big tip," said Samuel with a smile.

"I'd like to take her home," responded Juan.

Ignoring the comment, Samuel responded, "I think we should get a fast and big launch that can carry lots of product so we can take the pot to Florida. That will make the most money. If the launch is, say 45 or 50 feet long and wide, maybe we can transport all of the pot to Florida in one trip. It is risky and we must move fast, there are Marine Corp airplanes that fly over the Bahamas and waters between the islands and Florida to spot smugglers. The police and Coast Guard intercept them."

The men finished their beer as they talked of their favorite soccer teams, discussed American and Cuban baseball, and then signaled the waitress to pay their bill. She bent over as Samuel handed her the money. They left her a big tip for which she thanked them with one last view of her breasts. She had pegged them correctly as older men with money who would tip her if she flirted with them, but still had hoped they would ask for her phone number.

After spending a couple of days with Samuel looking at boats, they did not find a boat with the load capacity that they wanted. Finally, Juan told Samuel he remembered a boat dealer in Santo Domingo who sold new and used open sea launches that could make fast trips from Colombia to Florida if the weather was good.

Returning to Santo Domingo, Juan made contact with the boat seller and met him at his "office" outside of town. He had no knowledge that Ivan had bought a boat. The dealer vaguely remembered Juan, but much time had passed and he was not sure if he was the pirate that used to work out of Haiti. Juan was older and had a new appearance. To avoid giving offense, the boat dealer made no inquiries regarding piracy. He simply explained that he had no used boats, the last one he had was sold to a younger man who he suspected was a smuggler. When Juan pointed at the boat that Ivan bought, the dealer showed it to him. It was long and large and had a large cargo area. It had obviously been repaired and recently equipped with a Loran, lights, more fuel and high-speed bilge pumps in case it took on water. It was also freshly painted a medium gray and looked almost like a government patrol boat.

"I would buy it if it were for sale. It would be perfect," observed Juan.

"It is not for sale, but I will look for another one," stated the dealer.

"Tell the owner that I would like to buy it. I have work to do in the Bahamas."

It occurred to Juan that perhaps the buyer, a presumed smuggler, was not experienced and would accept a low price to take the marijuana to Florida.

Juan said, "If he doesn't want to sell it, tell him that at the right price, I may have work for him. I have some merchandise to take to Florida."

The boat dealer looked at Juan carefully and concluded that he was the pirate he had met years ago, but said nothing. Being too observant could cost him his life or at a minimum damage his business.

A week later, Ivan came to inspect his boat. He checked out the installation of the additional fuel tanks, the high-volume bilge pumps, and the fiberglass work and paint. He smiled broadly after looking it over.

In the time between the purchase and the time of the inspection, Ivan had thought a lot about smuggling. He liked the idea of being at sea and making a mad dash run from Colombia to the Bahamas. He even liked the idea of making the run into Florida to deliver the merchandise. What he did not like, was that the merchandise was illegal and he was returning to crime. He had so thoroughly left piracy and crime behind that he felt very uncomfortable returning to it. His only motivation was to provide the relatively small amount of capital required to complete Paraiso, protect his father's and Samuel's investment, and to provide a continual job for his very faithful employees that he considered family. He felt responsible for them. In spite of his concerns and what he considered his obligations to everyone, his heart was far from piracy and smuggling, and when the boat dealer mentioned he knew someone who would buy his boat, Ivan told him that perhaps he would sell it. The boat dealer added that the same buyer might have work for him.

Taking off his used clothing and old shoes, Ivan shaved and put on his executive clothing before going to the office. After talking with Ileana and Luis, he sat down with the income and expense reports of Paraiso. Timeshare sales had diminished some; but the hotel and marina guest numbers had increased. It worried him that sales were not higher, nonetheless all operation expenses and bills were paid and the little progress on construction was funded from cash flow. After Ivan spent the better part of the day examining the books and resort status, Luis asked to meet with him. Small talk completed, Luis unburdened himself.

"Ivan," he said, "some of the timeshare salespeople say that some potential buyers are questioning why the resort construction is so slow. That is why timeshare sales have slowed down. When are the investors going to complete the resort?"

Ivan told him that he would look into it. It was clear that something had to be done quickly. Ivan made arrangements to leave the office under Luis' supervision so he could drive to Haiti and meet with his father. It was time to get a final answer on the question of additional investment. That evening he drove the three hours to Barahona, checked into the resort, walked around and inspected the property thoroughly. He spoke with Morales who told him what needed to be completed and urged him to get the resort work completed as soon as possible.

The following morning he made the trip to his father's house in Haiti. Stephen and Isabela and their family still lived next door and greeted him warmly. Besides Stephen he saw no other of his old pirate ship mates. Juan was no longer an active pirate. He found his father standing by the water in front of his house. He was fishing.

After some small talk, they took a seat on the porch of the house. His father's younger Haitian girlfriend came out and served them coffee. Ivan came right to the point. He explained the income and sales report to his father, and also the immediate need to complete the limited work that needed to be done in order to assure everyone that Paraiso was the first-class property that it appeared to be and that it was prosperous and successful.

Juan sat back, smiled and said, "Samuel and I figured that was the case which was why we provided the last capital infusion. We still have some money, but not the couple million Paraiso requires. Nonetheless, we will have it." He then began to tell Ivan of the salvage operation and explained that it was the source of the last capital increase. He also told him that he and Samuel had enough marijuana in the Bahamas safe house that, when sold in Florida, would provide all the necessary capital. Juan explained that they were looking for a boat.

It was Ivan's turn to sit back and stretch. He smiled to himself as he figured that the buyer the boat dealer mentioned was his father.

"I already have the boat for the job. I think you have seen it. The boat dealer mentioned there was a prospective buyer."

"So you were going to begin smuggling marijuana from Colombia to Florida to provide the missing capital," Juan said without surprise.

Ivan nodded. "I knew that through Jose, I could buy first class marijuana."

"We have 6,000 pounds of Santa Marta Gold sitting in the Bahamas. Take your boat to Long Island. We still have the same safe house from years ago. Paraiso belongs to Samuel and me, it is a great resort already successful. It is our responsibility to provide the final capital."

Ivan left shortly after. He was glad that more money was coming, but worried for his father's safety.

When Ivan returned to the Santo Domingo office, Ileana mentioned in passing that there were rumors that Paraiso was in financial trouble. Ivan shrugged and said, "I have spoken with the owners and they will increase the capital soon and the resort construction will then continue at high speed. Tell everyone that we are soon to complete the resort."

Ileana smiled and went out of her way to mention the renewed construction plan to Morales and other key resort personnel. The mild worry that had touched the employees was eased and the salespeople were able to increase timeshare sales.

Out of the office, Ivan worked with the boat dealer to ready the boat for the trip to the Bahamas. All the fuel tanks were filled and a canvas cover built and installed. An opening in the cover allowed the helmsman to sit or stand before the steering station when the rest of the boat was covered. The new higher capacity bilge pumps could keep the boat dry if it did take on water. With the additional fuel, the boat had the range to easily travel to Long Island, Bahamas without refueling. He had the engines checked and tested and after inspecting the canvas cover and examining the boat carefully, he concluded that the boat could make the trip without incident. He chose Isabela's husband Stephen, the old but still very strong American who had been a member of his father's pirate crew and his uncle David, to be crew on the trip of over 800 miles. He didn't want to involve his uncle who had left pirating behind, but he needed a crew of two in case of bad weather. If the weather was good and he could run the boat at 30 mph, it would take about 24 hours to get to the island. If the sea was rough and he had to run the boat at low speed, the trip could last many days and be very hard and dangerous.

Taking David from the resort marina, Ivan moved him into Paraiso's office apartment. David worked on getting supplies for the boat trip. He bought enough food and water for four days in case they encountered bad weather. He then went and picked up Stephen. Ivan put them up in a small commercial hotel near the boat. Working together, David and Stephen installed fastenings at various places inside the panga launch in order to secure the food and water and other supplies. It would be dangerous to have them sliding around the boat on the long trip They bought three sleeping mats and blankets which they positioned and secured on platforms inside the boat almost a foot off the floor so they would not get wet. They also constructed side boards along each side of the sleeping mats so that in rough weather, the person in the bed would not roll around or be bounced out of it. After a week of preparations, the boat was ready for the trip. Ivan arranged for Luis to be at the helm of the Paraiso office and informed Ileana that he would be out of the office for perhaps a week on Paraiso business. Not being as close to Ivan as before, she did not have the freedom to ask him what he was doing. In her heart, though, it occurred to her that perhaps he was returning to piracy. Then again, arguing with herself, she told herself that piracy was no longer in Ivan's heart, nonetheless, she discerned that Ivan was up to something. She wondered if they had a future together.

AT SEA

Ivan, David and Stephen left the boat dealer's beach at dawn. Good weather was forecast from the Dominican Republic to the Bahamas. Winds were moderate, the seas about 4 feet, and visibility unlimited. The forward two thirds of the big launch was covered with canvas, the helm station and the aft 15 feet were open. Ivan sat at the helm while his uncle and Stephen were sleeping on the mats under the canvas. Running to the east, the heavy boat cut so sharply through the waves that there was no jarring and the big launch hardly pitched fore and aft as it passed over the oncoming waves. The engines ran quietly at the reduced speed of 30 mph, the loudest noise was the parting of the water and the sound it made as it ran along the side of the boat.

Alone at the helm as the sun rose above the ocean in front of him, Ivan was mentally and emotionally captured by memories of his father's boats. They had been similar in design, but not as long or nearly as wide and had been more affected by the waves. An hour into the trip he began to feel the life of the boat. It became less a separate entity and felt like he was a part of it, a part of the sea, and connected with the voyage. He took off his light jacket and stood up. By the time David and Stephen woke up and began to prepare cereal, he was standing rather than sitting at the helm and wearing only a tee shirt. The sensation of being on the open sea – like being in a desert that stretched in all directions – and the freedom of running across it without set limits allowed him to relax. By the time the boat reached Punta Cana 4 hours and 120 miles later, he was meditating on his life in Santo Domingo. With the unlimited open space around him, his businessman life seemed surrounded with parameters of economics, customer relations, employees, and responsibility everywhere.

At Punta Cana, David took the helm. He steered a northwesterly course towards the Turk and Caicos Islands. For a while, to the left of the vessel, the distant highland above the coast of the Dominican Republic was faintly visible.

Ivan sliced open a bread roll and filled it with sliced meat from a package. He then cut a piece of cheese and placed it on top of the meat. He spread mayonnaise on the other half of the roll and added two slices of jalapeno chilies and folded the two halves together. Taking a bite, he recalled that it was the same sandwich he used to eat when he was at sea many years before as a pirate or part of Samuel's smuggler crew. Memories of being an outlaw pleasurably flooded his soul, he looked around, smiled, and pushed his shoulders back.

An hour later, the wind picked up and the seas from the east grew in size. The growing seas were quartering on the aft starboard side. Although the ride in the big launch was still comfortable, David slowed the vessel to better match the speed of the waves and reduce movement. The sky still looked clear and there was no indication that the weather would change drastically, nonetheless Stephen and Ivan better positioned the steel arches that supported the canvas cover and double tied the cover over the front of the boat. Only the helm and a smaller aft portion of the boat were left uncovered. When spray or a wave did bring water aboard, it ran to a low point where a bilge pump returned it to the sea.

At the reduced speed they were still 60 miles from Grand Turk at nightfall. After midnight they passed Grand Turk. Providenciales was ahead. In the partial lee of the Turk and Caicos Islands, Stephen took the helm and increased the speed. David opened the canvas that covered his and Ivan's sleeping mats. Ivan, in bed, opened his eyes. The moon was almost full with no clouds. The men could see the water ahead and the shadow of the islands off the right-hand side of the fast boat. Stephen was the only one awake when the boat passed Providenciales. West Caicos could be seen on the left. At Abraham Bay on the right side of the vessel, Ivan took the helm again and chose to run westward with the increasing waves behind him. After circling around Acklins, he steered a direct course towards Long Island. The unprotected passage to Long Island was rough, and Ivan slowed the boat.

Finally, in the lee of Long Island, Ivan increased the speed and the boat ran fast over the smooth water. The change in the feel of the boat awakened both David and Stephen who ate some cheese and bread. Knowing the trip was nearing an end, they freely drank aguardiente.

Late morning, and slightly intoxicated, they motored the big launch into the Stella Maris marina.

THE SAFE HOUSE AND THE RUN

The safe house was only about 3 miles from the marina. The air was warm, the terrain flat and the walk delightful after being at sea for a day and a half. Drinking more aguardiente, their spirits were high.

The front door of the house was locked so Ivan led David and Stephen to the beach side of the house. Samuel and Juan, laying in the sun, stood up when they heard the newcomers.

Samuel was the first to speak, "You made a very fast trip. We didn't expect you to arrive until tomorrow. The weather must have been good."

Ivan smiled, "The seas weren't too high."

"Only 4 or 5 feet for the most part. Some were higher around Grand Turk. It was fun," added Juan's brother David.

"Spoken like a true harbor master," laughed Samuel.

Conversation was light, and about 4 p.m. Samuel went inside and returned with thin sliced meat seasoned with lime to prepare Carne Asada.

"Is the boat ready?" asked Juan.

Ivan nodded yes. "It ran great all the way from Santo Domingo to Stella Maris. We had it fueled at the marina and it is ready to go."

Samuel took Stephen, David, and Ivan into the house. Made mostly of wood, the house was constructed on a high concrete perimeter foundation with a basement. The basement floor was dirt. Kneeling on the dirt floor, Samuel dug into it until he uncovered, then opened, a door to a hidden storage room. The bales of marijuana were stacked inside the large and deep hidden chamber. Well wrapped, they gave off no odor.

"Impressive," said Stephen, "when do we take it to Florida?"

Samuel replied, "The buyers have a house on Vaca Key not far north of Key West. We will take the weed to them tonight. Thunderstorms are going to hit the Florida coast after midnight. We leave right after dark and travel fast. The seas and weather are good now, before the storm hits we should be able to run at about 50 mph. We will get as close to the coast as possible. When the storm comes, the waves may grow to six or more feet. The big launch, heavy with marijuana will still ride well, but we will have to travel at a much slower speed. We must not be far away from the Keys at that time or we will not arrive before dawn. The storm will keep the surveillance aircraft out of the sky and the smaller patrol and police boats at their docks."

After dark, the five men removed the marijuana from the storage room and loaded it onto the launch which Ivan had motored onto the beach behind the safe house. Once loaded, overheated and sweating, the men pushed the launch into the sea, then leaned against the boat as it floated next to the shore. With a bag over his shoulder, Juan climbed aboard the boat.

As Ivan watched his father, many thoughts demanded his attention. He remembered the pleasures of being an outlaw and that because he was the son of an outlaw, and a onetime outlaw himself, there was money to start Paraiso. It was the very success of Paraiso that increased the consequences of his past being discovered. He had many employees who were part of Paraiso, and he had a full social life and respect among business people. If Paraiso failed, he and his employees would suffer a great loss. Nonetheless, in spite of the exhilarating trip from Santo Domingo and the joy of being at sea and the freedom of it, Ivan did not want to return to being an outlaw — even though he considered marijuana a relatively benign drug.

Juan started the motors, Samuel, David, Stephen, and Ivan pushed the bow of the boat free of the sand. Samuel was the first to climb aboard. Stephen followed. Juan said, "Push the boat a little further out."

As soon as the boat was away from the beach, Juan put it into gear and motored away leaving his brother David and Ivan on the beach. Juan said, "Take care of business. You both have a new business. This marijuana business is ours. If we are not successful, do what is necessary to keep the company prosperous. Go slow. Theodore will pick you up at noon at the Stella Maris airport."

With those words still hanging in the humid air, Juan pushed the throttles forward. The boat rapidly accelerated toward Florida.

At the helm of the speeding boat, knees bent, Juan braced himself against the steering station. Looking ahead, he stared into the warm and moist night as he thought about the Americans who were at that moment searching for him and other smugglers like him. The Marine planes would soon be in the sky, the Coast Guard and even a few Bahamian boats would be between him and Florida. Once near the coast, there would be sheriffs' boats. If the aircraft detected him, the authorities would be trying to intercept him. On a good weather day, it would be a crapshoot whether or not they were detected; and if detected, whether he or some other smuggler would be chosen to be intercepted rather than them.

The very heavy boat, pushed by its big outboard motors, was still fast. The waves were not yet large, and the loaded boat ran across the sea with ease. The immediate course was south of Andros Island.

Stephen retrieved the water and other supplies from the locker underneath the helm station. He passed everyone the bottle of aguardiente and made sandwiches with the rolls that were still soft due to the humidity. He and Samuel put on the dark clothing that Juan gave them.

The outboards roared and at the high speed they were traveling the water ripped at the hull. Only in a loud voice could the men speak to each other. There was little conversation. However, the wonder of running across the sea at night under an almost full moon captured them. Stephen was happy to be back at sea. It had been a long time since he had been on a pirate or smuggling trip. Samuel was always glad to be at sea but didn't like the risk of smuggling into the US – it was too dangerous. Juan was completely lost to the moment. He felt like his old self again, Juan the pirate; even though he was just on a smuggling trip. He thought there was less risk being a smuggler than a pirate. He would not encounter an armed yacht crew who could shoot at him.

The weather, as predicted and hoped for, began to turn foul after midnight. Before the moon and stars were totally obscured by thick clouds, Stephen and Samuel put a thick net over the cargo so it would not be thrown out of the boat. Not long afterwards the moon was hidden completely and they could not see the water ahead of them, except for the part lit by the phosphorescent spray. Even over the sound of the engines and the noise from increasingly rough water, the men could hear the distant rumblings of the approaching storm. Quickly the waves grew in size. The launch plowed through them at an angle and due to its weight the ride was relatively easy. However, the impact of the waves forced Juan to reduce speed. They were still 40 miles from Vaca Key and now running at only about 20 miles per hour. Juan estimated they would arrive at about 3AM.

At 2AM the storm unleashed its maximum power – the sky filled with sheet lightning and jagged bolts of electricity struck the water not far from them. The waves grew, but Juan did not decrease speed. As the boat hit the waves heavily, Juan held onto the boat's wheel as he stood before the helm station – both bracing himself and riding the movement with his fluid body. The other two men held on tightly to keep from being bounced into the sea.

When the dim lights of the keys became visible through the rain, steering a course with his Loran, Juan pushed the boat faster as he steered a direct course towards the general location of the buyer's dock. In the intense rain, his Loran guided him. On the VHF, he radioed the buyers. "We are waiting," was the response.

The rain lessened as he got near the island and he could faintly make out the landing place. He slowed down and took the boat into the little cove hiding the buyer's dock. The marijuana purchasers were waiting with a medium sized cargo van next to the landing place. The three buyers and the boat crew worked together to unload the bales of marijuana and get them into the van and close its doors. The buyers, well known to Samuel, handed him a suitcase filled with 1.5 million dollars, half the agreed upon price. The balance to be paid after the marijuana sold.

Backing the boat away from the dock, Juan steered the vessel through the still intense blanket of rain and aimed it back towards Stella Maris on Long Island. Worried that perhaps there were police or coast guard boats that could intercept them . . . and their money, he ran the boat fast through the diminishing storm. When the waves shrunk as the storm dissipated, he ran the boat even faster. Far from the Florida coast, he gave the helm to Samuel and unrolled one of the sleeping mats, reclined on it and immediately fell into a deep sleep. He awoke as they approached Long Island. It was late morning. He checked the boat for residual marijuana. There was none. Samuel took the boat to the beach behind the safe house. Juan waded through the knee-deep water with the suitcase of money. Ivan and David were leaving for the airport when he handed the suitcase to them. Both Ivan and David were amazed that they had returned so quickly. Ivan smiled broadly when he realized that he had a million and a half dollars with which to reignite construction at the resort. That much money would accomplish a lot in the Dominican Republic.

COLOMBIA

S everal months later, the Paraiso Resort construction was almost completed. With the renewed work on the resort, any doubts about the solvency of the company were removed and there was a strong resurgence in timeshare sales. Life returned to normal rhythm.

Theodore picked Juan up in Haiti. They departed Puerto Principe, the miserable Haitian capital, early one morning. The spring day was unusually cloudy. The plane broke out of the clouds at just over 6,000 feet. Juan climbed over the seat and lay down in the second row. Soon, he was fast asleep with a baseball cap blocking the sun from his face.

Theodore looked at the few high-altitude contrails of the commercial airplanes. They were 25,000 feet above the small twin-engine Aztec. The sun was warm, the air cooled at 10,000 feet. Theodore was not in a reflective mood when they took off, but when Juan went to sleep, he began to think about what a long, strange trip he was living and seeing his friends live.

Just over five years ago, Juan, Maria, David, and Ivan worked together as pirates. Ivan left and, through the help of Juan, Samuel, and Fernando had become someone else. In the process all the fairness in him had blossomed, and his quick mind and abilities had come alive.

Theodore reflected that he never, even in a dream, could have imagined such a change in a person. When desire, vision, and the time arrived for Ivan to choose a life he wanted rather than the one he had been born into, he chose well and with great success. When able he had given his uncle David a chance to leave Haiti and have a new life—one that he desired. To the best of his knowledge other than taking the boat to the Bahamas to transport the marijuana, Ivan had lived a completely straight and exemplary life. Theodore knew that Ivan had only been involved in the Bahamas out of duty to his father, Samuel, and the resort team. Ivan had returned to his businessman's self immediately.

Then there was Maria, the pirate and whore. Everyone knew she was tormented over her life as a pirate, but she was the best pirate— great at stealing and great in bed. He remembered her sexual prowess well and missed it; but when she almost died, she met Peter, the defrocked and disgraced priest. She fell in love with Peter and, as she often said, with Jesus. She left piracy behind. Theodore smiled and wondered how the ex-priest could handle her in bed.

Next his thoughts turned to Juan, the true pirate, asleep in the backseat of his plane. Theodore puzzled over him. He never thought he would soften, but he had . . . somewhat. He didn't think that Juan gave a damn for Ivan, yet he had helped him and now seemed to care about what happened to him, especially with Ileana and Paraiso.

Theodore's face appeared both reflective and puzzled as he re-thought the reason for the current trip. Although Maria did not know, Juan was going to Colombia to pick up the boat he left with Jose and give it to her as a wedding present. Enjoying the beauty of the open sky, he laughed at the memory of Maria's efforts to convince him to find a fulfilling life in God. He told Maria, "I don't know if God exists, but I doubt it. And if he does exist, I don't think I want to know him. This world is screwed up. The standard of right and wrong floats on opinion and opinions change. The US is going the way of Mexico. Soon, there will be rampant lawlessness, more corruption, and maybe even a revolution, although no one sees it. And then there is the question of the earth—populated by over 7 billion people, all clamoring for needs."

When Theodore started the descent, Juan woke up. He cleared the pressure from his ears by holding his nose and blowing, then climbed over and sat in the copilot's seat just before they landed.

Maria and Jose, the keeper of Juan's Colombian boat, met them at the airport. Maria looked beautiful, very happy, and full. She welcomed Juan with a warm hug. She embraced Theodore.

Leaving Theodore and Maria, Juan got into Jose's old car with him. The two of them drove eastward toward Santa Marta. Theodore took Maria's arm and led her into the airport lounge. He ordered a double Scotch, looked at Maria and said, "Don't say anything."

"Drink what you want, problem child."

Later, when arriving at the front door of Maria's home, Peter welcomed Theodore. As they embraced, Peter smelled the whiskey, and said, "I love you, Theodore. You are a sensitive man who knows how fallen mankind is!"

Theodore stood apart from Peter and looked at him with respect, as though in the presence of a great man, not a disgraced one.

The following day, Theodore woke up around mid-morning. Mariana had already left for school. He found Peter and Maria sitting under the canvas-roofed pergola in the walled backyard. "Oh my God," he said upon seeing the colorful, outrageous menagerie of animals painted on the back wall. The pilot walked by Peter and Maria and pushed the lush, extravagant flowers aside to peer at the paintings.

"Maria, are you taking drugs?" asked the pilot with mock seriousness.

Peter responded, "No, she's just charmingly nuts. Isabela was her accomplice."

"That explains it all," exclaimed Theodore with a laugh.

Theodore sat down. He noticed that Peter looked very tired. The men's eyes met.

"We have more work than we can get done. But it is good work. It is just that the people have so many needs. Their needs weigh greatly on my heart," explained Peter. Shortly thereafter, he left to go to work. Maria and Theodore went to a nearby café.

It was not long before the conversation drifted into their shared past. They spoke of Juan, of piracy, and her "sex toy"—that is what Theodore called her pistol that she used to carry on her thigh or, when at sea, under her belt at the small of her back.

"Do you remember the time you flew to Mexico with me? That was when the landing crew did not light up the field and we were unable to land."

Maria laughed and said, "Yes, we landed on the road at night. You parked the plane in a driveway! We walked for a while and then hitched a ride. Downtown, you called the federal police who you had paid off. The police chief pilot took the plane to the airport and the next night the army came with a truck and loaded the plane with marijuana! I couldn't believe it."

Later in the afternoon, Maria took Theodore to see some of the churches they had started. The outside of the churches, houses and old buildings converted into meeting places, did not impress the pilot. Paint was peeling, concrete crumbled from the walls, sewage seeped from the ground. A pathetic hand-painted sign mounted on an outside crumbling wall read, *Iglesia Pentecostes.*

Theodore said, "I hope you know what you are doing."

"Live in your disillusionment, my old friend. There is goodness here," stated Maria with sarcasm.

The next day, Peter asked Theodore to accompany him to the airport to pick up a few Americans who sent money to support the mission.

Arriving early, Peter chose to sit in the corner of the least occupied airport restaurant. His well-proportioned face was lined with vertical creases, and his hair was substantially gray. He sat there with an untouched cup of hot tea before him.

"You are tired," said the pilot.

"More than tired. We work hard, there are always problems, and often God only gives us money at the last minute."

"Why do you do it?"

"There is nothing else that counts."

"Is there anything that counts?"

It was not until he heard English-speaking voices at the counter that Peter shed his exhaustion and remembered he had to go to the international gate. He then noticed the large group of men and women gathered at the entrance of the restaurant. He expected only three visitors so it did not occur to him that they were the people he was expecting until one of the men called his name. The man who called to him brought the crowd to where he was sitting with Theodore and introduced everyone—pastors of churches and leaders of various Christian organizations.

Peter looked confused.

A woman in the group said, "We have come to see if we can help."

When Peter heard the word *help*, his face softened, and his eyes watered.

In the overloaded mission van, Peter drove the visitors to an obviously poor section of town where he parked in front of a building that was shedding paint and plaster. Exiting the air-conditioned van, the Americans blinked in the bright, sunlit, dusty air. Not used to the humidity, greater than normal so late in winter, almost immediately their clothes stuck to their skin. Peter turned their attention inside the open front doors.

Children and youth were bringing tables from the rear of the building and placing them in the shaded areas of the center courtyard. A bell rang, and more kids exited partitioned areas where classes had just ended.

The Americans were warmly greeted by the kids and adults who spoke to them in rapid, excited Spanish. The visitors nodded and smiled. The Americans who studied Spanish in high school or college tried to understand and respond in the few words they could bring to mind.

In the kitchen at the back of the building, a dozen women were preparing and beginning to serve food. Peter sat with Theodore and the Americans at a side table reserved for staff and volunteers. Immediately, students brought plates full of meat, rice, and beans.

The inside of the building was brightly painted concrete. The roof was corrugated sheet metal with an open space in the middle through which brilliant sunlight flooded. The tables, chairs, and benches were painted pink, red, and pastel blue and green. Many of the children conversed in happy, loud voices. Although uncomfortable in the damp heat, dust, and intense light, the Americans were caught up in the mood of the group and began to talk freely among themselves about what they were seeing.

Peter said, "This is the family resource center. There is a school, free meals, a medical and dental clinic. We give away free clothing and offer other services to the best of our ability."

In the next few days, Peter took the visitors to all the churches. The American pastor in charge of the visitor group said, "I can hardly believe what I am seeing. You have quite a few little churches and now this community center. All this, and in such a short time. I am very impressed." The pastor smiled at Peter.

Peter looked at him and wondered what he was hearing. In his exhaustion and stress, he had no awareness that he was no longer Peter, the shamed, defrocked priest. He was now the leader of a successful ministry comprised of new churches and a community center to serve the poor. He also was unaware that what he had suffered through his alcoholism had given him a heart of compassion and hope for the poor and the needy. His own experience also had given him the faith to know that God could transform people.

The group leader said, "We will help with additional money and people." Peter was so tired he could not respond. The man patted him on the back.

The day after the Americans returned to the United States, Juan departed Santa Marta in the launch he kept in Colombia. The sea ran out of the East and his trip to Barranquilla took only two hours.

As arranged, Maria, Peter, and Theodore were waiting for him on the wharf and watched the boat approaching. Juan ran it hard and spray flew wildly from its bow. Circling birds raced to keep up with it. Like Juan's Haitian boat, this one was industrial looking, a variation on a type of craft used for fishing. Juan wore sunglasses and a bandana tied around his head.

After he tied his boat to the wharf, the two saints and the scoundrel, Theodore, climbed into it with the pirate. Juan pushed the throttles forward and took the vessel out to sea. The salty ocean spray charged from the sides. Caught by the wind, it soaked everyone.

Maria stood up and asked, "May I steer?" Juan moved aside. With one hand, Maria supported her watermelon-sized belly. With the other, she pushed the throttles to their stop and recklessly ran the boat at full speed. Peter came and stood next to her with a big smile on his face.

To the pirate and renegade pilot, God's priest said, "I have found the woman to run with me in this new life."

No one said a word.

A couple of hours later, after Maria had driven the boat along the coast enough to satisfy herself with being at sea, she steered it back to the wharf from which they left. Juan took the helm and moored the boat in a slip at a nearby private dock. With a bit of bluster — but no ceremony, he said to Maria, "I no longer need this boat. It is yours.

You can keep it at this dock. The gas and maintenance are paid. Soon, the boat will be repainted white, changed inside and all but one of the big outboards removed. If anyone comes looking for the pirate vessel, no one will recognize it."

Maria looked hard at him, took the keys, and smiled with gratitude. Theodore could see the tears forming in her eyes. Maria kissed Juan on the cheek.

Dinner was in an old restaurant near the ocean. The humid sea breeze swept through the open interior. Geckos stared from the walls. The four friends ate fried grouper, rice, and beans. Theodore and Juan each drank whiskey.

At the end of the long dinner, Maria said, "When I was a pirate, I loved the days and nights on the ocean."

Juan replied, "I know."

"Now I can be on a boat again."

"You were one of the best pirates."

Juan and Theodore stood up, shook hands with Peter and gave Maria a chaste hug. By the street, Juan motioned for a taxi.

Inside the taxi, the pilot said to Juan, "The gift of the boat was the most penitent act I have ever seen."

"Shit to penitent acts. I didn't need it anymore. It was in the way and I got rid of it," replied Juan.

Theodore knew that Jose had asked Juan to sell him the boat.

THE ARISTOCRAT AND ILEANA

The old man, Ivan's maternal grandfather, coffee in hand, sat in the same café where he and Juan had encountered each other. The waiters moved among the customers with trays of coffee and milk. Some of the customers, mostly men, ate breakfast. The day was very hot and humid.

The old man had learned much. From Ileana's mother, he had found out Ivan was raised in Haiti. His investigations had shown that Fernando was a successful manufacturer of baseballs that he exported to several American companies. He had learned that despite all the apparent social likeness and family-like closeness, Fernando was not Ivan's father and that Ivan was not a blood relative.

Although he had determined who Ivan was not, as much as he tried, he could not discover Ivan's past. He found that Ivan had not attended any of the international Haitian schools which would have taught classes in English and Spanish, as well as Creole. The old man reflected that perhaps he had gone to school in America, though doubted it. Although Ivan spoke English well, it was not 'schooled' English, nor did Ivan exhibit the usual American customs.

There was more which confused the old man about Ivan. In the various encounters he had with him, encounters he engineered after Ivan's help in saving his hotel from his creditors, he was unable to place him in life. Ivan's soul was certainly not Haitian, although there was Haitian influence. Nor was Ivan completely Hispanic, although there was more Latin in him than anything else. In Ivan's looks, there was something American. But most importantly, there was a quality in Ivan that the old man could not identify.

Recognizing Ivan's qualities of generosity and civility, there was something in Ivan that was independent and maverick—he was not just a typical businessman. As much as the old man tried, he could not fit Ivan into any mold. It seemed as though Ivan had simply appeared out of nowhere just as Paraiso had seemingly sprung from nowhere.

Then there was Juan, whom the old man had seen just weeks ago in the very same café in which he was now sitting. The aging pirate had looked good in spite of his pirate life. He had noted the pain on Juan's face after he mentioned his son. That comment is what stuck with the old man. The look on Juan's face, almost protective, is what set the old man to investigate Ivan. Was the son that Juan mentioned the son of his daughter or the son of some other woman? The old man had completely forgotten about Juan and his son, but after the chance meeting with Juan, he could not help but remember the boy, and now thought of him often. He had not seen the savage kid since he was five, or maybe six years old—and only then had suffered to have him around. He was the uncouth offspring of his daughter's rebellion.

The old man was mostly lost in his thoughts, but not so lost that he did not notice Ileana enter the café with Ivan. He stared as Ivan entered with the boldness and strength of a successful outlaw, but with refinement. At that moment, the puzzle became clear. The maverick he saw in Ivan was that of Juan. He also saw the inheritance from Juan's American mother and the influence of his own family, and he saw something else. He saw a man who had overcome disadvantages and abandonment, became successful, and had not become angry or bitter.

He sat quietly for a moment, and then the inevitable question arose in his heart and mind as to whether Ivan knew who he was. For the first time in a long time, the old man reflected on his departure from Haiti, his refusal to take Juan seriously, and his rejection and abandonment of his grandson. He had failed to take care of his own family and failed to believe in the boy. What he thought was impossible, that the boy could become someone good, had been accomplished without him, his daughter, or his family. Somehow, a pirate and a pirate's son, in the inexplicable course of the events of this life and of the God he believed in, made something of Ivan that he had thought unimaginable.

The old man stood up and collected his paper and coffee, then walked over to the table Ileana and Ivan occupied. The couple stood up and greeted him. Ileana welcomed him, with the usual respect. Ivan, without any trace of resentment, invited him to sit. As the conversation progressed, Ileana looked closely at the old man, and then at Ivan. There was a slight family resemblance. She felt uncomfortable all of a sudden. Why hadn't they taken Ivan with them to Santo Domingo?

Ivan was at ease. He needed nothing from him and had decided the old man and his family owed him nothing. There was no debt or credit to make him feel uncomfortable.

The old man was less composed. His face showed the agony in his heart: the agony of wanting to know if Ivan knew who he was. The feelings consumed him. For a moment, Ivan's eyes met the old man's eyes—and the old man knew that he did. Ileana caught sight of the eyes of both men. The old man perceived that she knew, also. Not a word of the discovery was spoken. The conversation drifted to the upcoming baseball season.

In the course of the conversation, the old man noticed what his daughter had told him, that there was an invisible division between Ileana and Ivan. He pondered the matter inwardly and after a while correctly guessed that it was Ivan's background that had separated the two.

Finished with his coffee, the old man stood up and thanked Ivan. On the surface, the 'thank you' was for the place at their table, but all understood that it was for something deeper. To Ileana he turned, and with a look that touched her in her innermost being, he told her, "Ivan is a good man."

With all her heart, Ileana asked quietly, "May I love him?"

The old man answered. "There is not one better. Hold on to him."

The distinguished old man who knew the full story endorsed Ivan. As a respectable Latin woman, the permission Ileana could not give herself had been granted.

Ileana trembled and stumbled.

Ivan caught her. He put his arms around her and held her. Ileana folded into the embrace of the saintly aristocrat who had been born a pirate.

Ivan's grandfather smiled at the young couple before him and walked away. He had done the only good thing he could do for the pirate's son and was happy.

The End

ACKNOWLEDGMENTS

Thanks to the many people who helped me through the years to get this book finished and published: Susane Plaza, Cheryl Feeney, Michele Trapp, Michael Reisig, Lizzy and Nicki Mostofi. All of them tolerated me writing the book and getting their comments.

Susane and Cheryl not only tolerated me, but they also helped me with countless edits and rewrites.

And thanks to my son Mike Acker for helping me get this published.

BOOK TWO: VENGEANCE

BARRANQUILLA, COLOMBIA

Maria placed the remaining items from the trip into the sea bag as she cleaned the boat. Her young son slept in the baby carrier strapped to her back.

The two men descending the dock ramp caught her attention. Their T-shirts were taut against their muscled chests. They approached with closed fists and cold stares. Not intimidated, Maria paused only briefly, then continued with her tasks. She listened for the sound of their soft shoes rasp against the bottom of the rough metal ramp before looking up again.

The tall, more muscular man spoke first. His voice hard, he asked in a rude tone, "Woman, how are you?"

"I am well," answered Maria.

Noticing the lettering on the side of the boat, his voice changed to a more respectful tone. "We do not want to bother you, señora."

He pointed to the words "Jesus Saves" on the side of the boat. "The lettering on the boat... do you work with the nuns?"

"I do not work with them, although I respect them," Maria answered. "I studied in a convent when I was a young girl." She gave no explanation for the name of the boat.

After a pause, the man said, "We are looking for someone."

"Who are you looking for?"

The two men scanned the boat as much as they could from their position on the dock.

"We are looking for the owner of a boat about the size of this one. It is black in color and has outboards across the back."

"Why are you looking for the owner?" Maria asked. She remained calm.

"Señora, he is a pirate. He and his crew robbed our employers—Argentine gentlemen who were on a ship," he said with rancor.

Maria suppressed her wish for the pistol that she used to always carry strapped to her leg.

"I know of no such boat or Argentine gentlemen," she said, deadpan.

Her young son stirred as he slept on the floor of the boat.

"You are often on the docks?" the man asked.

"You should search for someone else," she replied. She shifted her young son.

"Do you have information for us, señora?"

Maria pointed to the lettering on the side of the boat. "Look for *him*."

The men looked at each other and smirked.

"Yes, señora. Everyone should look for him," the larger man said. The other nodded in agreement. As with most Hispanics, they feared the wrath of God.

"By your accent, I can tell that you are from Argentina," Maria said. "You have been taught about Him. *He* should be the one you seek."

"We are good Catholics," responded the shorter man. "We go to confession and mass, but we are not here for religion. We are here to search for pirates."

"Everyone is a pirate—a renegade from God," Maria said.

She returned to scrubbing the boat.

"Thank you, señora." The two men backed away. At a respectful distance, they turned and walked up the dock. They looked at each and shook their heads.

The larger man said, "That woman is crazy. Too bad she's a religious nut with a kid. She is very pretty. We could have fun."

REVIEW AND NEW RELEASES

Thank you for reading my book!

Would you take a quick moment to help me out by leaving a review on Amazon? Reviews are the best way to help others discover this book so that they can join in the adventure.

Please type in "Timothy Grant Acker" in Amazon to find this book and leave a review!

Book Two and Three are in the works as well. Sign up here to stay connected and be among the first to find out about updates and releases!

https://tinyurl.com/psssubscribe

Made in the USA
Columbia, SC
01 February 2022

55192876R00207